www.haseleyhinton.com

HASELEY HINTON

Shadow of the Seacrow

SECOND BORN BOOKS
Edinburgh

Published in 2009
by Second Born Books
an imprint of Starbit Media

42/4 Morningside Road,
Edinburgh. EH10 4BZ.

ISBN 978-0-9561135-0-4

Environmental print managed by Big Sky, Findhorn.

Contents printed on 100% recycled paper. Cover printed on
80% recycled card. Vegetable-based inks used throughout.

Cover design and typesetting: www.starbit.co.uk

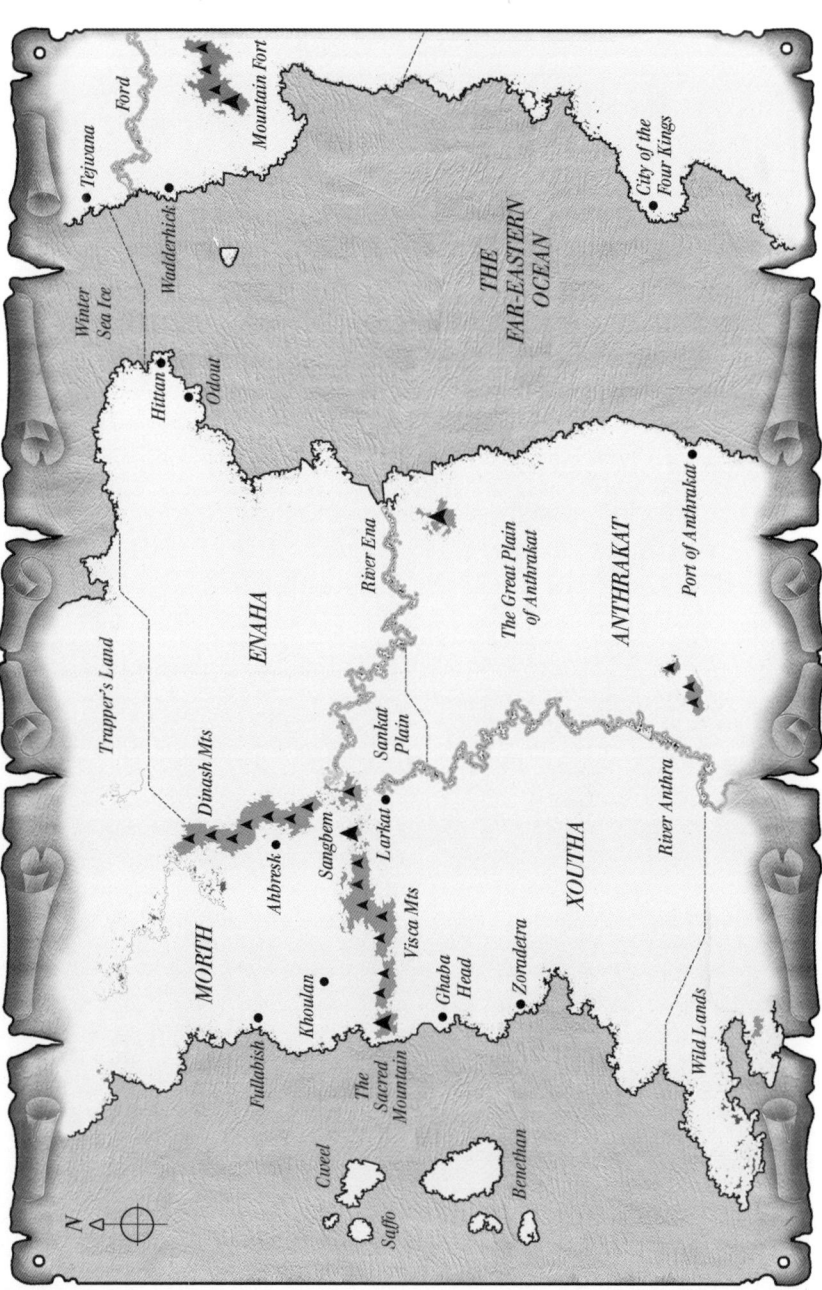

PROLOGUE

A pale human heaved open the door of the flooded airlock and struggled out into the watery darkness. It was impossible to tell if he was floating towards the surface or even which way was up. A patch of ghostly green light seemed to be spreading slowly across his field of vision. He tried to swim towards it but, as he fought against the urge to inhale, he began to feel sickeningly dizzy. His mind started to play tricks on him. The emerald glow was the canopy of the big beech tree in his grandparents' garden, half a universe away. Ship was a small boy again, being pushed on the old rope swing, lifting high into the graceful branches then swooping down to the ground before hurtling into the sky once more. The sunlight was glimmering through tiny gaps between the leaves, every shade of green and gold, and in that moment he knew he was about to die.

The swinging stopped and he found himself lying outstretched in a comfortingly familiar shingle cove. It looked exactly like the one he had been taken to on summer holidays long ago, except that, just a few metres away from him, there stood a strange black-feathered creature with a bright red beak. It was turning over pebbles industriously as if looking for something important. It picked up an object and began dashing it against a rocky outcrop with sharp swings of its head, but then tossed it disdainfully into the air when its efforts had no effect. Ship reached out his hand and caught it just before it hit the ground. It was knobbly and hard but seemed almost weightless. Mimicking the bird's actions Ship smashed the shell hard against a large stone and it sprang open. Inside was an amorphous mass, pinkish-brown and slimy. He sniffed at it cautiously, wondering if it was edible, but it smelt disgusting. He put it down in view of the bird which hopped forwards and ate with relish. The creature quickly found more shells and dropped them near Ship's hand. It stood just out of reach, head on one side, eyes fixed steadily on him.

As Ship obediently opened the shells one by one, his attention turned to his surroundings. He realised that he was hemmed in by a foreboding semi-circle of sheer cliffs. At the end of the cove there was a great mountain of rock with an archway at its base that seemed to be inviting him to explore it.

"That's the only way out of this cove, isn't it?" Ship asked the creature as he hauled himself to his feet.

The bird did not answer but stood watching him intently, its scaly legs a little flexed as if waiting for the stranger to lead the way. Ship hobbled towards the dark, moss-covered opening. He ducked under the low arch and distinctly heard the sound of splashing water. As his eyes adjusted to the gloom, he saw a shimmering waterfall cascading down into a deep pool at his feet. Above the cascade he thought he could detect a hint of misty daylight.

The rock-face behind the waterfall looked treacherously slippery but there were pits and crags that seemed to promise a possible climbing route. While Ship was concentrating on moving each limb carefully from one slimy hold to the next there was a rush of air against his ear. As if to show him how it should be done, the feathered creature from the beach flapped past him and flew up to the light. Ship almost lost his footing as a startled cry, like that of a young woman, suddenly rang out from above. There was someone up there.

CHAPTER ONE

It was early autumn in the round of the Great Alignment, the long awaited lining up of the moon, the sun and the largest wandering star. A black seacrow with a bright red beak was flying over the Khoulan monastery, set on a small rise in the undulating pastures of the fertile land of Morth. The monastery stood out golden against the green of the grass, its ancient rough-hewn masonry augmenting the colours of the autumn sunlight. As the seacrow looked below him he saw his shadow flicker over a young monk mounting an unusually fine looking cam-horse. The monk was wearing a light blue robe, pale as the sky at the horizon and billowing in the breeze. His head and face were clean-shaven, as were those of all the monks, but the fur on his neck formed a dark velvety covering, leading into a mane of short hair which followed the line of his spine down into the folds of his robe.

The mattouk, their leader, was marked out by his robe of a rich deep blue. Raising his voice a little he spoke in an authoritative tone to the mounted man.

"Fare you well, Kesh. The journey ahead may be tiring, but soon you will stand face to face with the Prophet of the Burning Ship himself. Remember that you go to represent the Khoulan Community at the witnessing of the Great Alignment but, more importantly for me, you go to acquire your belt of pilgrimage so that when you return you will officially become the mattouk designate, ready to take my place as soon as the need arises."

"Dear Mattouk Calim, I hope that 'need' will not arise for many more rounds yet. Peace and long life to you, my Lord."

"Peace and long life, Kesh."

The men around the mattouk echoed this farewell as Kesh set off down the track from the monastery. He was closely followed by his servant who was also dressed in a Khoulan monk's robes. He sat astride a slightly less shapely cam-horse. The servant led a third horse laden with provisions and gifts for the Prophet of the Burning Ship. At the end of the monastery track they both turned left and followed the road which ran parallel to the coast, heading south towards a distant belt of mountains.

The seacrow followed them for a while looking for tit-bits drummed up from the earth by the horses' hooves or dropped from their luggage. Then Kesh heard his servant suck the air in sharply between his teeth.

"Whatever is the matter?" he asked.

"That crow only just missed being trodden under your horse's feet. He must be desperate for worms to eat."

"Perhaps he is just showing off. I am sure he knows what he is doing."

After a while the crow grew bored with the monks' slow pace and climbed up into the blue of the sky. His small black shadow passed once again over the monks as he sailed along the coast, heading directly for the mountains.

The Sacred Mountain was a tall mass of grey rock, the first in a long line of mountains that stretched far inland to the east. One face of it formed a cliff that dropped almost vertically into the sea and at the top were the buildings that housed the Prophet of the Burning Ship and his community of followers. The buildings were of different ages but all built of the same dark stone as the mountain and were barely distinguishable from it, except for one tower on the north side, which formed a rather unnatural looking peak. The oldest part of the community was seated on a flattened area near the top of the mountain, with everything else built up around it so that the most recent building was perched right on the edge.

Just beyond the base of the cliff there was a little cove. As the mountain spanned the border between Morth and its neighbour, Xoutha, this cove was the first landing point on the coastline of a different country. The seacrow flew on to explore the coast a little further. He passed over several more beaches that made pale golden lines between the smoky blue of the sea and the yellow green of the land. Spaced out along the string of beaches were mossy headlands reaching green fingers into the churning ocean.

Soon the seacrow came to the coastal city of Zoradetra, where lay the palace of the Xouthan emperor. Unlike the Khoulan monastery, this palace was made of finished stone, darker in colour and cut into elaborate decorative pinnacles. The seacrow alighted on the ledge of one of the high westward facing windows of the palace stateroom. Some of these windows had been flung open to let in the dying rays of the autumn sun. They also served to let out some of the wood smoke that curled up from a great log fire in the opposite wall and escaped the draw of the chimney stacks now and again.

From his vantage point the seacrow witnessed a momentous event taking place in the stateroom on that day.

A middle-aged man dressed in richly coloured robes sat on a throne set on a raised dais at one end of the stateroom. There was a young woman standing to his right, behind the empty chair that had been her mother's. Both their necks were covered in a generous coating of short sleek fur. The young woman had long hair that hung from her head all down her back, joining with the hair of her mane. The older man's hair was shorter and darker in colour, except on his temples, where there were streaks of grey.

The stateroom's ceiling was so high that the elaborate carvings on the joints between its beams were barely visible from below. Its double doors had dimensions that would not have constricted the movements of a giant three times the height of a man. Its windows, each the width of a man's shoulders, were so high that they looked like rows of vertical stripes of light set in opposing ranks on the eastern and western walls. Those on the western wall were currently letting in long shafts of golden light from the sinking sun. The room had a wide flag-stoned central aisle, while the generous spaces behind the fluted pillars on either side were filled with noblemen and women dressed in long colourful robes and adorned with flamboyant jewellery.

Trumpets sounded and a man in uniform announced the arrival of Thrull, Prince of the Benethan Islands. A man strode in through the grand doors at the far end of the aisle. He had broad shoulders and long unruly hair that covered most of his head and face. He was followed by six guards carrying spears and shields with long swords hanging conspicuously from their belts. They were all wearing cloaks of animal

14

skins but Thrull had folds of purple cloth showing from underneath his spotted bearskin cloak.

Bradmutt, the emperor's military chief, rose from his seat to the left of the dais and, in the Xouthan language, formally invited Thrull to step forward and state his business.

"I have come to ask for the hand in marriage of the Emperor's daughter," he said loudly in perfect Xouthan.

Bradmutt took three paces forward so that he was face to face with Thrull.

"The Emperor has no sons. Along with his daughter goes the expectation of inheritance of the Empire of Xoutha and all its subjects, until a son is born to her and comes of age. Do you accept this responsibility?"

"I do."

"And what gift can you bring in return?"

"I bring all the Southern Islands of Benethan and also Cweel and Saffo of the Northern Islands."

Bradmutt turned to his Emperor, who nodded gravely.

"These gifts would be acceptable."

The Emperor now drew himself upright in his seat. He cleared his throat deliberately and turned to his right. "Daughter, do you consent to a betrothal to this man?"

The young lady, who was seeing her prospective fiancé for

the first time, looked at her father with frantic eyes, shaking her head almost imperceptibly from side to side. Her father raised one eyebrow.

"Father …" she whispered.

"Last night you agreed …" he whispered back in perplexed anguish. "For the sake of your country, for the sake of your ageing father …"

There was the briefest pause before she yielded and said aloud, "I consent."

At this point the seacrow, smelling no food as yet, got restless and stretched and flapped his wings. The emperor caught the movement of the long shadow of its wing tip as it seemed to brush across his daughter's face. He frowned and pointed a finger at the nearest courtier and then at the window. The casement was quickly shut. The presence of a seacrow was regarded as a bad omen in Xouthan lore.

The seacrow hopped off at the approach of the courtier and flew down to the cliffs below to investigate a collection of bones that had been thrown out during previous feasts.

Meanwhile the emperor got to his feet, drew himself up to his full height and addressed the company.

"I hereby announce the betrothal of my daughter, Maina, to Thrull, Prince of the Benethan Islands, the wedding to take place one round of the seasons and one turn of the moon from this day." He turned to Thrull and said, "May your union be blessed with joy and prosperity. Thrull, I invite you to sit at my daughter's side this evening. We shall feast

16

in celebration." The emperor sat and added quietly to his daughter, "And you two can get to know one another."

The seacrow eventually caught the scent of cooking and followed it to the yard behind the kitchens. He pulled one or two tasty scraps from a bin, but when the cooks saw him they ran into the yard banging pan lids together and making such an intolerable din that the seacrow left. Despite carrying a full stomach he made his way back along the coast and found the travelling monks now a little nearer to the Sacred Mountain.

CHAPTER TWO

"The sun is sinking, Ahbrem," said Kesh. "It will shortly be time for meditation. We must make a camp."

"Very well," said the servant.

"This flat ground seems as good a place as any. We don't want to go too far away from the road."

The two monks dismounted and Kesh made a fire while his servant laid out sleeping rolls and unpacked food and pans from the luggage.

After their meditation, for which they sat on the ground and stared into the flames of the young fire, they settled down to eat and noticed a black bird pecking at the earth around their horses' feet.

"Ha!" exclaimed Ahbrem, "There is that seacrow again. He is following us."

"How do you know it is the same one?" challenged Kesh.

Ahbrem frowned but didn't answer.

"Did you know that the Enahets call seacrows 'khul sahuk'?" Kesh asked him. "It translates as 'spirit eater'. They leave their dead out to be eaten and they believe it is the function of the seacrows to pick out the eyes and carry the soul aloft to heaven."

"Come closer, khul sakuk," Ahbrem said to the seacrow.

"Sahuk," corrected Kesh.

"Sah..huk," Ahbrem tried carefully and then shrugged. "Come here, Sakki." He held out a crust and the seacrow hopped a little closer.

"I have thought of a way to tell if the same crow comes to us again,' Ahbrem said as he watched his new friend eat. 'We could feed him jultie berries. They will stain his beak for days. We have some amongst those berries we have wrapped in parchment."

"Why don't you try it, then? We should eat the berries up tonight, anyhow. They will not keep."

Ahbrem pulled a parchment package out of one of the bags of luggage and they shared their berries with the seacrow. All ended with stained fingers or stained beaks.

Later, when they were lying on their mats next to the dying embers of the fire trying to sleep, Ahbrem broke the silence.

"I am sure rats would do the job just as well."

"What job?"

"Setting the spirit free."

"Oh," replied Kesh. He chuckled. "You have no poetry in your soul, Ahbrem."

"It is my most valued attribute," Ahbrem told him.

"Mattouk Calim took me aside before we left and said to me: 'Ahbrem, you are the best man I could have chosen to look after Kesh. You alone can keep his mind on Heaven and his feet upon the ground.'"

"Did he indeed!" said Kesh. He turned over, trying to make himself more comfortable. "We must try to sleep now, my dear friend. Goodnight."

"Goodnight, My Lord Mattouk Designate."

"Not yet," Kesh muttered to himself. "Ahbrem, we have been friends for years. I cannot have you addressing me as Lord."

"Once you reach the Sacred Mountain that will be your official title. You will have to grow accustomed to being addressed as Lord."

"Humph! Not by you, I hope, unless we are in the company of others."

***

The seacrow was not at breakfast and did not follow the monks as they made their way to the Sacred Mountain. They thought they had lost him. They were welcomed at the Morthern gate of the Community of the Sacred Mountain by five monks who had been sent ahead some weeks before. Their horses were led away to the stables. However, before they could meet the Prophet of the Burning Ship, they had to follow tradition and climb the mountain waterfall to be cleansed of the outside world. They were led down a flight of stone steps that were tunnelled into the south side of the mountain. There was a door at the base of the steps with a satin cord slung across it to bar the way. That was, they were told, the disrobing chamber for the trainee Xouthan priestesses. To the right another, thicker door with a large rusty bolt led to the cove and jetty where the maidens' boat was due to land. This was the first time in history that, in order to view the Great Alignment in the presence of the Prophet of the Burning Ship, the Xouthan priestesses were to arrive at the mountain on the same day as the principal Morthern pilgrims.

Their guide turned and went back up the steps. Ahbrem unwrapped the cloth sack that was to hold their old robes and started to undress. Kesh was curious, however, and tried the bolt on the heavy door.

"What are you doing?" Ahbrem asked, alarmed.

"I … I" faultered Kesh. "I just want to step on Xouthan land. We are so close. Only this trusty bolt holds us back."

The bolt yielded and the door swung open. Seeing the cove empty, Kesh stepped into the daylight.

"Xoutha!" Kesh exclaimed. "Why, it is just like Morth."

Ahbrem smiled at him indulgently from the doorway, like a tutor allowing his student a respite from his studies. Kesh took a few breaths of the Xouthan air and then he called his friend.

"Ahbrem, come and look. There is a seacrow pecking amongst the pebbles. It has a purple beak."

21

"He has followed us all this way," Ahbrem exclaimed as he stepped out into the light.

"He can not have followed us through the mountain. How did he know?"

"He is waiting for the Xouthan maidens, perhaps."

"Of course!" laughed Kesh. "Clever bird."

"Hurry now! Our friends will be thinking we have drowned in the waterfall."

They both turned back and went through the door to disrobe.

The waterfall was slippery and steep but there were ropes to guide the climber and strange flameless torches on the walls that shone through the water droplets, making them yellow like the setting sun. Ahbrem went up first and shouted back advice to Kesh as to how to negotiate the more difficult parts. Kesh was relieved to reach the platform at the top and he glanced back down the waterfall in order to savour the moment. Through a narrow door at the top was a cosy little room with piles of bright white towels and here they unwrapped their bundles of fresh robes.

Before they were quite dressed a voice echoed in the cavern behind the door.

"What was that?" Kesh asked.

"I don't know," said Ahbrem, frowning.

Then the cry of a woman came distinctly through the splashing of the water. Kesh put his hand on the door to go back into the cavern.

"My friend, you must not," said Ahbrem, stepping between Kesh and the door.

"But that may be a maiden slipped on the rocks."

Ahbrem took Kesh by the shoulders.

"Kesh, she will be naked," he said. "If she slips, no harm will come to her. There is a deep pool to break her fall."

"Then I hope she can swim," said Kesh, reluctantly stepping away.

Ahbrem hurried his friend out of the robe room.

CHAPTER THREE

From her window Maina could see the town decked out in celebratory pennants, the colours blowing joyously in the breeze. The road they decorated led from the castle, curved down into the town, threaded between the pretty stone cottages and ended at the harbour. That was where Maina would walk at the rear of the procession the next day. As a trainee at the Temple of Tarn, she was due to leave for her year at the Sacred Mountain. As daughter of a High Priestess she would be first in line to become the next High Priestess once her training was complete. She would also hold the position of Most Honoured Maiden in the procession and be the last one to step onto the boat that was to carry them along the coast to the mountain. Most of the town would be there to see their daughters, granddaughters and nieces leave. They would all be witness to her anxiety. One slip of the foot on the gangplank would change her honoured position into a meeting with the chilly water and, if she was lucky, a clumsy rescue by someone foolish enough to follow her in.

Maina's broodings were interrupted by a tap on the door.

"Can I come in?" said Wyn, her nurse-sister, captain of the Temple Maidens.

"Of course. Come in, come in most welcome sister."

"Have you packed your chosen items?" Wyn asked.

"I have, but it's been so difficult to choose just three."

"So what are you taking?"

"My mother's amulet must go. When I was having doubts about training for a priestess I prayed to Tarn for guidance. The next morning, quite unexpectedly, your mother brought me the High Priestess's amulet that she had been keeping since my mother's death. I knew it was the gods' sign to me that I, too, should take that path." She drew in a long breath. "It is very precious to me. Of course, the purse my father gave me must also go, although I am sure I will have no need of its contents, and finally the book of sacred texts your father gave me when I began my training. That too is very precious to me but not just because it was given to me by your father. Some anonymous trainee must have spent a very long time copying it out onto that flimsy paper, which is as thin as silk, and then carefully stitching it all together. Your father honoured both me and our profession by choosing such a gift."

"He wanted to mark the occasion, I remember. Of course, your own father provided your trainee priestess's gown, as did mine for me."

"So that makes up my three chosen items."

"You're not including your betrothal gift from the prince?"

"I don't wish to be reminded of the betrothal."

"To such a handsome man! You are indeed a most honoured maiden," said Wyn, not afraid to tease the woman who had been brought up as her sister, nursed by her own mother since the day the emperor's wife had died giving birth to her.

"I wish that honour was not mine," Maina said. "He looks brutish. There is no emotion in his eyes, except perhaps greed. He is probably fighting over another island at this very moment, looking to expand his princedom. I fear he thirsts only for the power he will achieve by providing an heir for Xoutha." Maina sighed. "I think my father would rather I had been a son to battle for the empire. Then I might at this very moment be reclaiming the Sacred Mountain for Xoutha's exclusive use."

"I'm sure that's not true. Your father loves you deeply."

"And I love him, and it is for that love that I consented to the betrothal. My father fears old age. He wants a son-in-law to share his burdens and a grandson to hand the empire to. No doubt Thrull will win more land for Xoutha but I doubt he will show much respect to me once we are married."

"Does he respect the gods?" Wyn asked anxiously. "Will he accept a priestess's judgments? You could become High Priestess before long. It is very important that the husband of the High Priestess understands the importance of her position. You know the astronomers are predicting an alignment of the sun with the moon and with Tinus just before the sun sets tomorrow evening. The coincidence of your arrival at the Sacred Mountain with this alignment is very fortuitous. I believe it portends your progression to High Priestess."

"I must learn to meet the challenge of whatever the gods have laid out for me. I know the islanders' beliefs deviate from Xouthan religious principles a little. I think perhaps Thrull looks too stupid to fully respect the power of the gods."

"Too stupid to see the error of his ways," said Wyn. "But

perhaps too clever to be easily thwarted. You may have to tread carefully, Maina, if your will does not match his."

"I have been thinking the same," said Maina. "But enough of this gloomy talk. I don't have to marry the man for another round of the seasons yet. Let's concentrate on what is to come tomorrow and forget the problems that lie so far ahead. We are to visit the Sacred Mountain and meet the wise Ship Prophet and I have many questions for him."

The day of leaving dawned dry but breezy. The pennants flapped and Maina's cloak billowed from time to time as the procession passed through the town. Eager faces lined the streets and children threw down petals at the feet of the Temple Maidens as they had done every round of seasons on this occasion. Maina thought wistfully back to the carefree days when she and Wyn had seen the maidens off with baskets of petals gathered from the palace gardens.

The harbour was calm but the boat rose and fell gently as it nudged the wall. The four oarswomen stepped aboard and took their places, two on either side, and Wyn, the captain of the crew, sat between them to take charge of the little sail. There was a maiden sitting on a tiny seat at the rear by the rudder arm and between that and the sail there was a raised seat with a canopy on a little platform. This was the place set for the Most Honoured Maiden.

On the lowest exposed harbour step, damp and slippery from the previous tide, Maina glanced down and saw deep into the cold green waters. Pale shapes seemed to be moving far below her as the light distorted the images coming from the harbour bed. She hesitated. She anxiously watched the gangplank moving up and down above the water as it balanced between steps and boat. Then she felt a warm hand grasp her own. Bradmutt, her father's Chief of Warriors, had come down the steps to steady her. Husband to Maina's wet nurse and father to Wyn, he had welcomed Maina into his family from the first. Bradmutt had been like a second father, in many ways more approachable and more supportive than her own had been. Comforted by his steadying arm, Maina successfully stepped across to the boat and took her seat of honour in the stern. She rested her feet on the chest of gifts that her father was sending to the Ship Prophet.

Trumpets sounded and the boat was cast off and pushed out into the harbour. The maidens, like those who had gone before them, had practiced hard for this journey. They began to row out of the harbour in perfect time. Maina looked towards her father, and Bradmutt, who was back at her father's side. She bowed her head to take her leave and then raised her chin proudly and stared ahead as the boat glided through the harbour gates and out to sea.

Krista was at the rudder. She was the slightest of the maidens and the least powerful rower but she was an expert navigator. The little boat turned northwards and began to follow the coast.

The sun passed its zenith and the voyage was going well. Maina was confident that they would reach the Sacred Mountain well before evening. But then the breeze began to strengthen and blew in a heavy bank of cloud. Maina shifted uneasily in her seat as the awnings began to flap around her. The breeze gave way to lively gusts of wind that whipped up substantial waves. The boat rocked and Krista had to tug with all her might to stop the wind blowing them too close to the cliffs of the shore.

Suddenly an almighty crack told them the boat had struck a rock. Krista gave an agonised cry and the rudder arm swung wildly around. Krista was cradling one arm with the other, her face contorted with pain. The other maidens were all struggling to help Wyn to lower the sail and Maina was the only one free to catch the rudder. She began to wonder if her fear of water was about to be justified. She climbed down from her seat of honour and signalled to Krista to yield the rudder seat.

"You can't," protested Krista.

"I must," said Maina. "You will have to tell me what to do."

Maina sat and Krista crouched in the bottom of the boat near to her feet.

"Turn the boat to face the waves. Pull the arm towards you, hard!"

"Gorlan, great God of the sea, protect these, thy maidens!" Maina shouted into the wind as she wrestled with the flailing length of wood.

The boat rocked violently as a wave hit them broadside. Women were thrown from one side of the boat to the other and Wyn, captain of the crew, was thrown against Maina.

"Perhaps your prayers are not yet strong enough," she said. "You must try again. For all our sakes pray harder, or we will all be lost."

"No, it cannot end like this," Maina cried, seeing fear in her

29

sister's eyes. "My mother died to give me life. It cannot have been for naught! Gorlan, great God of the sea, these maidens wish to live. Save them, save them, please. Almighty Tarn, God of the sky, keep these, thy maidens, from the sea and they will serve you all their days."

She pulled harder on the rudder and the boat turned sluggishly towards the foaming crests.

"Rocks to port!" went up the shout.

"Ease up!" shouted Krista, then "Pull hard again. Pull hard!"

The boat was facing the waves but the waves seemed to be taking them closer to the rocky shore and now on their right there loomed a mighty cliff face. On the top of this headland was the most northerly Xouthan fort of Ghaba Head which they should have passed far out to sea. Instead, they were so close that the women could pick out the individual stones in the fortress's walls. Maina hung on to the rudder arm, pulling and pushing with all her might, following Krista's commands. Her arms began to ache and she could barely catch her breath. Waves splashed over the bows, soaking her cloak and gown. All the maidens had wet hair and clothes and all the dignity they had shown when gliding out of the harbour was forgotten.

Then an undercurrent took hold of the boat and sent it spinning slowly round, despite all Maina's efforts. Luckily the current proved to be a friend to the maidens and the boat was carried further out to sea. The cliffs fell away and they were carried northwards around the headland. Though drifting out to sea, they could now see the Sacred Mountain, and the little beach and jetty where they were due to land.

"Maidens take oars!" shouted Wyn.

With an almighty effort they pulled out of the current and past the headland. Suddenly they were out of the wind and able to row for the shore.

Wet and dishevelled, the maidens clambered onto the jetty and tied up the boat.

"Our thanks, High Priestess," Wyn said to Maina as she joined her on dry land. "Your prayers were answered after all."

"I am not High Priestess yet," Maina told her. "And it was your skill and the fortitude of all these maidens that saved us and brought us here, I think."

"Surely it was Gorlan who sent us the current of water which washed us off the rocks," said Wyn.

"Indeed," said Maina, not wanting to imply a lack of gratitude to the gods. Then she raised her voice and addressed the group. "Praise Gorlan for our safe delivery. I thank you all for your bravery and hard work. Now let us prepare to meet the great Ship Prophet."

The Sacred Mountain towered above them and at the end of the little beach there was a door set into the rock at its foot. It was the door that gave access to the waterfall through which they must pass to reach the prophet's sanctum.

CHAPTER FOUR

The maidens straightened their clothing as best they could and then lined up two by two behind Maina, except for Krista. She was supposed to take up the rear of the procession but Maina kept her by her side, careful not to jostle her injured arm. Maina pulled on the weather beaten bell rope. No sound could be heard. Maina waited, then pulled again. Still no bell could be heard but after a few moments footsteps were heard coming down stone steps and the rusted bolt on the inside reluctantly shifted.

The door opened to reveal a young woman in the white gown of the student priestesses of the Sacred Mountain. She bowed to Maina and then embraced her warmly. Maina and her crew were the first fresh faces she had seen from her homeland for nearly a year and the boat they had brought would carry her back to her home in just a few more days.

She led them into the robe room, carved into the rock, gloomy and damp. Here they saw by candlelight seven bundles wrapped in a strangely shiny cloth. They contained the white robes that the maidens would all wear once they had passed through the waterfall of the Sacred Mountain, leaving behind their old clothing and their old lives, climbing up to the sanctum where the Ship Prophet lived.

Maina was first to go. She undressed behind a curtain and tied the robe bundle around her middle. Then she took the deep red velvet cloak off the peg next to her and slipped it around her shoulders. Although the robe room was smaller and dingier than she had imagined, the instructions for the procedure she and the other maidens had to follow had been learned by heart. The robe bundle and velvet cloak had been described so often they seemed comfortingly familiar.

She stepped out from behind the curtain and was led onto the damp platform at the base of the waterfall. The water splashed loudly in the echoing cavern and the spray felt cool against her face. She looked upwards to the point high above her head where the water first emerged from the rock face and cascaded down towards her. It was dark in the cavern but strange flameless lights on the cavern walls picked out the waterfall's foamy whiteness and glinted off the smooth wet rocks.

"Step carefully. The rocks may be slippery but there is a rope to steady you. May Tarn be with you." The student bowed and turned back into the robe room.

For a woman who feared heights as well as water, the task ahead was a daunting one. Maina took hold of the wet rope and put one foot tentatively on the first foot-hold in the rock. As she pulled herself forwards she looked up again and saw another figure above her in the waterfall. Slender and graceful but definitely male, the figure stepped across to a platform at the top of the fall. The dark hair on his back glistened as another figure in a pale blue robe stepped out and placed a cloak around his shoulders. He turned his eyes and looked down the way he had just come. Maina caught her breath and quickly stepped back onto the bottom platform out of sight.

'These must be Morthern monks,' Maina thought.

She knew that the mountain was sacred to them also.

Following the last war for the Sacred Mountain in her grandfather's day, the Morthern monks had been granted rights to visit the Ship Prophet's sanctum but followers of the two religions were usually kept apart. Maina's father had long nursed a wish to drive the Mortherners off the mountain altogether and Maina knew that he secretly hoped that the Prince of Benethan would be the man to help him to do it. Until then the two parties had to be content to share. But sharing the ritual of the Cleansing of the Waterfall had never been part of any bargain that Maina knew about.

She listened and heard a door close, echoing around the cavern above the rush of water. She waited a while. She knew she could not go back to the robe room. She would have failed her training before it even started. She listened again but heard only water cascading over rocks. Suddenly a loud voice filled the cavern.

"Fear not, priestess. Ascend the steps."

Maina gasped. Her heart pounded. Was Tarn speaking to her? Was she so important that a god would bid her onwards?

Again she caught hold of the wet rope and put her foot on the first step.

"If a heathen Mortherner can do this, so can I," she told herself determinedly.

She slowly felt her way up the slippery rocks. She was three quarters of the way up when her foot slipped. She let out a cry but steadied herself with the rope. She could not help but let out another shout as she lost her footing completely and found herself swinging in the air and bumping against the rock face. She was holding on desperately as the wet stones bruised her. Her arms were wrenched by the fall but her grip held firm. She scrabbled against the slime-covered rock face with her feet, stifling the instinct to call out for help. The monks might still be close enough to hear her and the shame of having Mortherners come to her rescue was too horrible to contemplate.

Eventually one foot found a toe-hold and she hauled herself back onto the steps. Now streaked with slime, she welcomed the stream of water through which she had to pass but she was more cautious than ever.

Maina jumped as the loud voice suddenly boomed out again.

"Fear not, priestess. Ascend the steps."

"I am ascending as swiftly as I am able, my Lord Tarn," Maina replied and pulled herself onto the upper platform just as the monk had done.

The door opened and Maina half expected to see the Morthern monk but a white robed Xouthan trainee stepped forward, holding out a large white towel. It felt warm and comforting on her shoulders. She entered the robe room and dressed in the white clothes from her bundle. She had passed the first test. She had become a Sacred Mountain student priestess. She was now just one year away from the right to claim the title of priestess of the Temple of Tarn.

CHAPTER FIVE

The maidens were all through the Ceremony of the Waterfall, except for Krista, who was in the sick room with her arm heavily bandaged. They had all been shown their new quarters. They would be sharing them with the outgoing students for the first week while they learned skills necessary to take over the students' duties for the coming year.

Now they were standing in a line outside the doors of the Great Hall of the Sacred Mountain waiting to meet the Ship Prophet. Maina spent this period of silent suspense in contemplation of the legend of the Ship Prophet. It told of how he had arrived at the Sacred Mountain many rounds ago in a ship that had sunk in the cove. He had climbed the waterfall to the top of the mountain and had lived there ever since. Protected by the gods, he had survived many generations and had been visited by many Xouthan priestesses. After the last Morthern war, when the Xouthan empire had suffered heavy losses, an agreement had been made to allow Morthern monks access to the Sacred Mountain. As men were not normally allowed inside Xouthan sacred buildings, the monks had to be accorded the status of 'honorary women' but the priestesses tolerated their intrusion with much resentment. Maina knew little about Morthern monks, except that they had strange beliefs and that they were able to take the role of priestesses because, unlike other men, they lacked the drive for killing. As they served the same purpose as priestesses, it was assumed by Xouthans that they were more like women than men. Nevertheless, Maina was not keen on sharing her experience of the Sacred Mountain with them and hoped she would not be expected to speak to any of them.

It was therefore with a sinking heart that she saw that a group of Morthern monks had entered the vestibule and were now lining up opposite to the student priestesses ready to make their way into the Great Hall.

She spoke to a graduand priestess who was standing nearby.

"Surely these monks are not going to be allowed into the sacred Great Hall?"

"It is the Ship Prophet's hall, not ours," she replied. "Usually we visit separately but this evening we are to witness the Great Alignment, which is sacred to the Mortherners as well as to us."

Maina frowned as her expectations for the ceremony rapidly crumbled. Throughout her years of training, Maina had looked forward to the moment of coming face to face with the Ship Prophet. Now, although she had not yet seen him, she was already disappointed.

Once they were all seated inside, the graduating priestesses sang a beautiful anthem glorifying the Ship Prophet as the messenger of the gods. They were the first to be honoured. They each walked up the aisle to receive their amulets of office from the prophet. Next it was the turn of the trainee priestesses. Maina headed the line of maidens who walked forwards to receive a badge of welcome from the prophet. He looked old and wise, much as Maina had expected. She was curious to see for herself the long flowing white hair on his head and chin which she had been told about and she was even more fascinated by his hairless neck.

Following the Xouthan ceremony the Morthern monks set up a chant, beautiful yet eerie, with extraordinary harmonies echoing around the hall. It made Maina feel uncomfortable. She suspected that she was hearing the corrupting chaos of the heathen mind made into music. The priestesses then had to wait while the monks lined up to be given dark blue belts of pilgrimage from the Ship Prophet.

Afterwards all of the participants in the hall filed out onto the balcony in order to witness the Great Alignment. The balcony ran all along the west side of the hall and overlooked the sea. The Sacred Mountain dropped steeply below the hall, giving the impression that the balcony was suspended over a void and that the ornate balustrade was all that kept the occupant from plunging down the cliff face into the sea. At one end of the balustrade, up against the rock of the mountain, sat a black seacrow. Its bright red beak was stained and blotchy and the crow appeared to be trying to clean it on the stonework. It was hopping around, facing first one way then the other but every now and again it seemed to look up at the western sky as if it, too, was waiting for the Great Alignment.

It was a perfect evening for the event. There was plenty of clear sky and it was not long before the moon and the brilliant crescent of the wandering star could be seen converging on the setting sun. The wanderer was so large that its now dark disc could be seen passing the edge of the sun. Then the moon passed in front of both the other bodies, eclipsing the reddened sun and making the world go dark with a powerful suddenness that filled every soul with awe. Afterwards, some light returned and the gods filled the sky with a celebration of clouds glowing in a riot of pinks and golds, as the moon, star and the sun sank from the sky. Maina would have liked to have lingered there on the balcony, watching the fading light but she obediently followed the other maidens back into the hall and from there to their quarters.

The day after the ceremony Maina was due for her first personal meeting with the Ship Prophet. She grew suspicious that her meeting with him was not going to be a private one when she found herself waiting outside the Ship Prophet's study at the same time as two Morthern monks.

A Xouthan graduate came out of the door with an empty cup on a tray. She indicated that Maina should go in. Her worst fears were realised when one of the monks followed her into the Ship Prophet's study.

The room was lined with shelves of books and scrolls. Tables in the room were covered with open books, charts and maps. A small window opposite the door looked out seawards. The Ship Prophet sat in a large comfortable chair with his back to this window.

"Hello, my children," he greeted them in the language of the Sacred Mountain.

They both bowed.

"You are Maina, yes? And you must be Kesh. Please sit down." The Ship Prophet indicated two chairs in front of him.

"Now, I've heard a little about you both from your teachers but you must tell me more."

There followed a silence. Neither wanted to be the first to speak, nor were they sure how to address this legendary being.

"Maina, perhaps you could start by outlining the beliefs of your people to Kesh."

"Um," Maina began but the Ship Prophet must have seen the look of startled horror on her face.

"Very well, perhaps you could prepare a piece about them for tomorrow," he told her and tried a fresh tack. "Now, I'm told you have many questions to ask me. Perhaps we should begin with one of those."

Maina thought for a moment and then took a deep breath.

"Ship Prophet, I would respectfully like to ask you why there is a Morthern monk here with us."

The Ship Prophet laughed.

"Xouthan students usually ask me why I look so different, where I came from, or how I got here. It is refreshing that you do not find me so curious." He paused. "Why is there a Morthern monk here? That is actually a very important question. There is more than one answer. Firstly, you and your fellow students were due to arrive just at the same time as these Morthern monks. They were coming to witness the Alignment from the Sacred Mountain, as is traditional. The two events just happened to coincide so it made sense for me to welcome you together. Secondly, I wanted you two young people to meet one another. You are representatives of two very fine cultures but you Mortherners and Xouthans only seem to speak to one another when there is some dispute over this mountain or, worse still, over me. What I would like more than anything is that you two get to know one another and, moreover, that you come to understand one another. I want your peoples to stop fighting over this mountain and to stop squabbling for my attention." He paused again. "And please don't call me 'Ship Prophet'. Simple 'Ship' will do. That goes for you too, Kesh." He paused again. "Perhaps, Kesh, you could try explaining your beliefs to Maina."

Kesh sat upright and began as though reciting.

"We believe in the only true God, Harg, creator of all things, first among the Blessed Spirits, Protector of Believers, who will bring, in the fullness of time, complete triumph over Denharg and lead all true believers to everlasting happiness and joy."

"So is there anything there which you didn't already know about the Morthern religion, Maina? Are there any questions you would like to put to Kesh?"

"You say you believe in the only true God, and then you mention Denharg," Maina challenged with a criticism often discussed by her teachers. "Is he not one of your gods?"

"He is not a god," answered Kesh. "He is the Spirit of Darkness, whom we shall eventually defeat with the help of Harg."

"And what about your other gods? Do you not pray to many and various spirits?"

"We pray to the spirits only as intermediaries. They are not gods either," Kesh told her.

"Thank you, Kesh," the Ship Prophet said. "Now, Maina, I want you to come back here tomorrow to outline your beliefs to Kesh and I want you, Kesh, to have some questions for Maina. I know there is a great deal of common ground between you, not least the Sacred Mountain." He chuckled to himself at his little pun. "It is really just a matter of finding the ideas you share and bringing them out. I want to congratulate you both on your fluency in what you call your sacred language. I am forever grateful that your ancestral religious leaders, who came to meet me in ancient times, chose to adopt my language. It makes it so much easier for us all to communicate with one another." He thought for a moment, "You see, there's more common ground. It makes no sense for your two religions to be in conflict with one another. However, I think we have done enough for today. Come here after breakfast and we will talk some more and I will tell you about the task I have chosen for you."

CHAPTER SIX

Each year the Ship Maidens were set a special task in addition to their daily duties of studying and of maintaining the Sacred Mountain community. The Task was usually something quite simple. The outgoing Maidens' Task had been the making of decorative hangings for the newly built Great Hall of the Sacred Mountain, where the graduation ceremony had taken place. The most dangerous part of this Task, Maina had been told, was buying in the materials. For this the Most Honoured Maiden and her captain were sent to the nearest Xouthan settlement, together with a small bag of coin and a packhorse to carry their purchases back. So Maina felt no great excitement at the prospect of being told what this year's Task was to be.

She did, however, feel a little apprehensive at having to explain her beliefs to a Morthern monk. She knew that the Xouthan religion was superior. She could never respect a religion that allowed men into temples. Nevertheless, she wanted to make sure she did credit to the gods when explaining them to a non-believer, especially in the presence of the Ship Prophet himself. She sat up well into the night writing down what she would say.

She decided she would start with the part of the Legend of Origin that dealt with the separation of the tasks for the different sexes. So the next day, when Ship asked her to outline her beliefs, she began by addressing Kesh directly.

"We used to be like you. In ancient times there were male priests and they ran the temples but, even then, the duty of attending temple and paying respect to the gods was undertaken by women much more often than by their husbands or sons. Men usually only attended temple to ask some favour of the Gods – success in love, say, or safety in battle. Women folk were always more conscientious in keeping the rituals of the gods from day to day."

Then Maina began to recite from the Legend of Origin.

"In the days before the coming of the Prophet of the Sunken Ship to the Sacred Mountain, many generations ago, the mighty gods descended to the Temple of Tarn to give the Four Laws of Living to their servant Sandbert, priest to the first king of Xoutha. Sandbert scribed the laws as spoken by the gods and passed them on to the king and to all his people. At first all the laws were obeyed by all the people but, as the children of Tarn prospered and multiplied, the king sought to expand the country of Xoutha into an empire to make room for the many children the gods had sent to them. He began to enlarge his armies in order to battle for land to add to Xoutha. Sandbert was concerned that the struggle that this would entail would violate the Fourth Law of Living."

She broke off to explain. "The Fourth Law commands:

Slaughter not except for meat.
The flesh of man thou must not eat."

Then she continued with the Legend of Origin.

"Ere long commenced the Great War for the Xouthan Empire. The warriors of the king violated the Fourth Law. The king had held discourse on the Fourth Law with his priest and Sandbert had been persuaded that the two lines of the law

44

should be taken to mean merely that, if a man is slaughtered, he should not be eaten. But one day when he was alone in the Temple of Tarn, the gods spoke to Sandbert and told him that both lines of the Fourth Law should apply to men. In other words, that man should not kill man. Sandbert was very troubled by this, as he had served in the king's army as spiritual adviser and had killed enemy combatants on several occasions. He decided to resign his position and he handed over his keys of office to his wife. From that time on, warriors were banned from entering temples and, since most men served time in the armies of the king, the priesthood was given over to women. Sandbert's wife became the first High Priestess and wives and mothers were given the task of looking after the spiritual welfare of each household and of attending temple as required."

Ship saw Kesh's frown and asked, "You find this difficult to accept, Kesh?"

"This principle makes saints of all women," Kesh said, not without the hint of a sneer. "Women are the source of much evil. They are temptresses and utterers of many falsehoods. Do you have no women who commit murder? Do no women ever commit a crime in Xoutha?"

"Those who commit crimes are banished from the temples and punished by imprisonment," Maina told him.

"And what of women warriors? If your womenfolk are given so much power, there must be some who want to become warriors. Or is that not allowed?"

"There is a division of responsibilities in Xoutha," Maina told Kesh. "Men lead the military and political councils and

45

courts of law. No woman can become a king. It is not usual for a woman to wish to become a warrior. If a woman were to take up such duties she would not be allowed to enter a temple thereafter." Then she challenged Kesh by asking, "So, in Morth, if men are responsible for maintaining religious rituals do men attend temple more regularly than women?"

"They do not attend more than women, no, but they do take responsibility for the spiritual and moral leadership of the household."

"We were told by our teachers that, in fact, Morthern men also actually attend temple less often than their women."

"That …" Kesh hesitated, "Is probably true ... in many families."

"So should not these women be given the responsibility for the family's spiritual welfare?"

"They take some responsibility but the man is head of the household so in the event of any disagreement or where there is doubt …"

"His decision would take precedence," Maina finished for him.

Fearing that hostility was building up between them Ship interrupted.

"Well, I think this might be a good time for me to tell you about your Task."

Maina and Kesh both turned respectfully towards him.

Ship began. "I have recently heard tales from distant lands about a group of unusual people who are similar to me in certain ways and this has made me curious. You both know I arrived here many years ago. My ship sank but I managed to swim to dry land and crawl out just below your Sacred Mountain."

"The gods were most generous to us. They gave us a wise Ship Prophet to advise and guide us," said Maina.

"We praise Harg for the gift of the Prophet of the Burning Ship," said Kesh.

"I am eternally grateful to both your peoples for allowing me to remain on the Sacred Mountain and for supplying all my needs. However, you may have noticed that I am a little different from either Xouthan or Morthern kind and I have always longed to hear news about people of my own kind."

"There are others like you?" asked Maina, wide eyed.

"There may be. You see, there was an escape pod, I mean, a smaller ship, which left the mother ship when it got into difficulty. Five of the crew were on it."

"Crew?" repeated Kesh.

"Yes," said the Ship Prophet. "My ship had a crew. People like me, hairless and long-lived, given the right circumstances.

"There are other prophets?"

"We are not prophets. I only accepted the title of prophet, because your ancestors thought I was a god and I couldn't let them go on thinking that."

"But you must be a prophet. You foretold the destruction of the fort at Ghaba Head," said Maina. "It is written in all our historical texts. It was the reason we had to agree to compromise at the end of the Second War of the Sacred Mountain."

"I merely told the Xouthan emperor that, if he attacked the Morthern capital city, he could expect some kind of retaliation. I suggested Ghaba Head might be attacked only because it was the most northerly fort and therefore closest to Morth. It was just a guess."

Kesh and Maina were both staring at him as if in disbelief.

"I am sorry to disappoint you. I am not really a prophet. I can only tell you what may happen, if you take this or that course of action, because I am old and I have seen many things. My crew, if they are still alive, are probably not calling themselves prophets, although they may be calling themselves gods, or wizards, or angels, for all I know. The unusual people in these distant lands that I have heard described seem to have a great deal of power, though, so I will call them kings. I have heard nothing of my crew for a very long time. I assumed at first that their landing craft had been destroyed and that they had all been killed, but …"

"Killed? Surely prophets - I mean, your kind - are immortal," Maina interrupted him, a little shocked.

"I am old," said Ship. "If I was immortal I would surely not age. I would still be young and fit and I could go myself to see if these strange kings are some of my own kind. As it is,

I am growing tired and my joints are stiff. That is why I am asking you two to travel on my behalf."

"Travel where, master?" Kesh asked.

"Many miles, I am afraid, across the sea. But not the sea that laps at the feet of your Sacred Mountain. There is another sea, I hear, on the other side of the plains of Anthrakat and on the other side of that sea there is another land where these kings rule, or so I have heard, with terrible magical powers."

He looked at the two faces now turned to his in rapt attention.

"Half my heart hopes that these are not my people. It would be a criminal misuse of their powers to rule a land by fear. And yet, I would truly love to see the face of one of my own kind again before I die so I would really like to know one way or the other."

"Die?" exclaimed Maina.

"Eventually, yes," said Ship. "Will you go for me? I just need you to see if these kings actually look like me and, if they do, I would like you to ask one of them to come and visit me. Will you accept this as your Task?"

CHAPTER SEVEN

Maina and her maidens had been down to the little jetty at the base of the Sacred Mountain to say goodbye to the graduates who had been mere Temple Maidens themselves just one round of the seasons before. Wyn had thrown a little garland of flowers onto the water as an offering for their safe passage. Then Maina and her crew had watched the boat disappear around the headland at the end of the little cove. In less than a round it would be back and then they too could return to Xoutha but to the new trainees that voyage seemed a long way off.

Maina did not follow the other maidens back up the steps to the Sacred Mountain straight away. She told Wyn that she would join them in a while, and she turned instead and walked along the little beach. A pale sun had risen from the morning mist but was now past its zenith and doing little to lift her heart. The waves broke gently but regularly on the shore. Gorlan was at peace. The graduates would have a safe journey home. Each spent wave rolled the pebbles noisily downhill as if it was trying to suck them into the sea. This little cove was a haven of solitude and a last link with the world outside the community of the Sacred Mountain and Maina paced up and down the beach thinking over what she had learned in the few days since her arrival.

The Ship Prophet, or Ship as he wanted to be called, was not at all as she had expected. He claimed not to be immortal, despite having arrived on the mountain many generations of High Priestesses before. Also, there were perhaps others like him, albeit far away. But the most difficult aspect of the experience so far had been sharing the Ship Prophet with the Mortherners. Their beliefs were so different to the Xouthan's. Although Maina had known well that the mountain was also sacred to them, she had not expected to have to share her first meeting with the Ship Prophet with a Morthern monk. She did not understand how the Ship Prophet could also be a part of a religion that did not recognise Tarn or Gorlan or any of the gods of nature.

Distressed by the presence of Kesh at her first meeting, Maina had requested a private consultation with the Ship Prophet. This would give her a first chance to speak to him alone. She had many things to ask him. She uttered a prayer to Tarn to guide her through the meeting and through the coming year. She bent to pick a late flower from the grass topped rocks at the end of the beach and threw it into the surf as an extra offering to Gorlan. She thanked him for the calm of the sea and asked him to protect the graduates on their return and also to protect her on the voyage it seemed she must make as part of her Task. Then she turned around and headed for the little door in the cliff face.

At the time when her private meeting with Ship was due, she went to knock on the door of his study. A voice bade her enter. There was a fire burning in a small fireplace adjacent to the seaward-looking window. The little room seemed cosy and comfortable. Ship asked her to sit down.

"Have you thought any more about the Task I asked you to undertake?" he asked her. "Would you be willing to help me in this way?"

"Of course I will help you," she said. "But I don't understand why I must go with a Mortherner. He does not pray to Tarn.

He will not receive Tarn's protection. And how can I cross the sea with someone who will not give gifts to Gorlan? I may even be punished for keeping company with a non-believer. How can I hope to survive the journey?"

"Maina, you must pray for Kesh's protection. Surely you can pray for two? And Kesh must likewise pray to his god on your behalf. Think of it as receiving not half but double the protection, from both your gods."

"You sound as if you believe in his gods. I don't understand. Ours are the only true gods and you are their prophet. You are our prophet. How can you believe in the heathen gods?"

"What I believe is not the question here. I did not choose to be your prophet. I did not choose to come to your Sacred Mountain or to meet your High Priestess. It just happened. Neither did I choose for the mattouk at the Khoulan monastery to see my stricken ship. I did not summon him to me. Mattouk Sahlt declared the mountain to be sacred to the Mortherners, not I."

"But this mountain was sacred to us first. We already had a temple to Tarn here."

"I know. And I remember well that the first Mountain War started because the Mortherners wanted to build a House of Harg here. I eventually managed to persuade your great, great, great grandfather to allow a gate to be built in the northern wall so that Mortherners could have access to the Sacred Mountain and a small House of Harg was built at the base of the mountain on the Morthern side. It was a compromise that enabled me to keep visitors from the two countries separate. Even so, it wasn't long before there was another war and the Mortherners were driven off. Much though I regret the killing at Ghaba Head, it was that fierce attack which led to the concessions that allowed Morthern monks to visit me once again. It marked the beginning of this current period of peace and tolerance of each other's presence on the mountain. It has lasted for many rounds and I sincerely hope it will continue. I was hoping that, with the Great Alignment and with your arrival for your final round of training coinciding with Kesh's arrival to celebrate the eclipse, we would be able to strengthen the commitment to peace on both sides."

"I am afraid I have no influence over territorial disputes," Maina told him, knowing she would never be able to persuade her father to give up his life-long ambition of driving the Mortherners off the mountain completely.

"But you are the king's daughter, are you not?"

"The emperor's daughter, yes," Maina corrected him, "but, as I say, I have no influence."

"A pity," said Ship. "Anyway, I would like you to give serious consideration to the possibility of accompanying Kesh on the Task. I think he is an honest man at heart. After all, it is not what we believe that makes us good or bad. It is what we do that matters."

Ship waited for a response but Maina only gazed at the floor. He went on, "He has already accepted the Task. He does not object to taking a Xouthan as his travelling companion. I think you could travel safely by pretending to be brother and sister. Strangers find a woman's presence comforting so they are less suspicious. Your presence would protect Kesh from antagonism and he would be there to look after you. You would make a perfect team."

Ship paused again and saw that she was still troubled. "On the other hand, we must all do what we feel is right. If you feel it is wrong to keep company with Kesh then I will not insist. I will not ask you do anything you do not want to do. You must choose to accept the Task of your own free will. You could request a completely different task for your graduation, one that you know you cannot fail, and I will find someone else to accompany Kesh. But don't give me your final answer now. Take a while to think it over."

Maina went back to her quarters. She hoped that reading the book of sacred texts which Wyn's father, Bradmutt, had given her, might offer some guidance but she could not concentrate on the page. So she went out of her room and walked the corridors of the Sacred Mountain buildings, trying to decide whether it was right to accept such an unexpected Task. Preistess Hannala, the principal educator on the Sacred Mountain, seemed to accept everything the Ship Prophet said but what would High Priestess Sketta advise? She had been their teacher for the past round of the seasons in Xoutha and Maina felt great respect for her. She would probably say that Maina should not allow any man to accompany her on a sacred task. On the other hand, as she had often said that Morthern monks were honorary women and were the Morthern equivalent of priestesses, it followed that Morthern monks were not like ordinary men. One only had to see the way Kesh's friend Ahbrem followed him around to know that Morthern monks had more than the usual affinity for one another. A Morthern monk was unlikely to pose any threat to a maiden. She had, indeed, seen some of the other maidens swooning in a giggling huddle after Ahbrem had walked past, saying what a shame it was that a man with his good looks should be wasted on the preisthood.

Still, sharing a sacred task with a heathen was another matter. What would Priestess Sketta have to say about that? The Mortherners worshipped false gods or, as they claimed, one god, who must be false as Harg was not mentioned in any of the Xouthan texts. That would mean that the Ship Prophet was wrong about their combined prayers giving double protection. But how could the venerated Ship Prophet be wrong? Was she, Maina, now learning truths beyond the knowledge of Priestess Sketta and all who had gone before her? Was she really so honoured that the Ship Prophet would reveal secrets to her which had been kept from her predecessors? Could it really be that the Mortherners beliefs had some truth in them? Surely she had to believe what the Ship Prophet told her. After all, the High Priestesses all came to the Sacred Mountain for their final round of training. The utterances of the Ship Prophet were the final words in their preparation for the spiritual leadership of all Xouthans. She must conclude, therefore, that the Ship Prophet's trust in the Morthern god was genuine and, furthermore, that his request for her to undertake a sacred task alongside a Mortherner was justified.

She took a gulp of air, surprised at this possibility of a reversal of her previous beliefs. She found herself at the door of the Great Hall of the Sacred Mountain. It was empty now but the huge doors stood wide open and she felt herself drawn inside. Her footsteps echoed in the hollow space as she walked up the aisle. She began to walk on tip-toe, not wanting to draw attention to her visit and cause anyone to come along and investigate and so spoil the solitude. At the head of the aisle, in front of the dais on which the Ship Prophet had greeted the new trainees, there stood two lecterns. The one on the right held a large copy of the Xouthan Complete Book of Sacred Texts. It was open and Maina stepped up to read the words on the page. Her eyes were drawn to a verse that told her:

"Fear not if life's travails seem hard
For obedience has its own reward.
The road to joy may pass through sorrow,
The path to truth may lead through shadow."

This seemed to be a message directed at her personally. She thought it must surely be Tarn's way of telling her to accept the task. In that moment, washed with a wave of fervent emotion, Maina decided.

She looked across at the other lectern and curiosity got the better of her. She did not read Morth well so she was glad to see that their texts, too, were written in the sacred language. She read:

"A man went to sow a field of turnip-chard to keep his cows fed in the winter months. He was met by a shepherd who was bringing his sheep down from the hills. The shepherd told him that, as the berry bushes were unusually heavy with blossom that summer, the winter ahead would be too severe for turnip-chard to survive. He told the farmer to plant kale-chard instead. But the farmer had never planted kale-chard before and didn't believe it would grow fast enough. That winter the winds blew and the snow fell and the turnip-chard was blackened by the frost. The farmer's cows went hungry and grew perilously thin. The shepherds flock was hungry too but they survived on thin shoots of kale-chard which pushed up through the snow and not one sheep was lost."

Maina frowned. These Morthern parables were not meant for Xouthan eyes but no doubt this story held meaning enough for Kesh.

Maina turned, walked out of the hall and went back to her quarters.

CHAPTER EIGHT

"You can not go on your own," Ahbrem said emphatically to Kesh.

"I will not be on my own," Kesh replied.

They were standing in the gloomy corridor outside Ship's study. The Xouthan trainee had already gone inside.

"You cannot go off on a sacred Task without me," Ahbrem told him. "You know Mattouk Calim specifically charged me with your protection. I cannot possibly let you go away from this place without my supervision."

"Your supervision?" Kesh repeated. "Who is master and who is servant here, Ahbrem? Do I not make my own choices?"

Ahbrem had no answer to this challenge so he was reduced to appealing to Kesh's better nature.

"I would be breaking my promise," he pleaded with emotion.

Seeing his genuine concern, Kesh softened a little.

"Very well, I will ask Ship if you can go as well," he told Ahbrem. "Wait for me here."

Kesh indicated the chair where Ahbrem had already waited for his friend on several occasions. Kesh tapped on the door.

Once inside the study, Kesh saw that Ship had laid an ancient map across the table and Maina was leaning over to look at it. Kesh apologised for his tardiness and joined them at the table. The map showed Xoutha and Morth and the great sea to the west that was common to both countries. It showed the country east of Xoutha, Anthrakat, and the country north of Anthrakat and east of Morth across the Dinash mountains, which was called Enaha. Kesh knew of this country through the many tales of Mattouk Calim, who had travelled there as a young man. To the east of Enaha and Anthrakat the map showed another enormous expanse of water which Kesh's tutors had never spoken of.

"I know you do not enjoy travelling by sea, Maina," Ship was saying. "So I suggest you take the shortest possible crossing, from Odout, in the north-east of Enaha. You could start your journey by aiming for this inn here at Larkat."

Ship pointed to a hostel marked on the military road which passed to the south of the Visca mountains, the mountains which ran east-west between the Dinash mountains and the Sacred Mountain by the sea and so divided Morth from Xoutha. The road was the supply route for the Xouthan watchtowers that sat along the border.

"And if you start out early enough, you should arrive by noon. Would it be acceptable for Maina to ride Ahbrem's cam-horse, Kesh? We have no mounts here suitable for such a long journey."

Kesh's heart sank as he realised that Ahbrem would have to ride the pack-horse if Maina borrowed his good horse. Nevertheless, he answered:

"I am certain Ahbrem would be honoured to lend his cam-horse to the trainee priestess."

"Ah, he need only lend his horse for a few days," said Ship. "I am told they have horses for sale at the inn. I will give you gold and silver sufficient to buy a horse for Maina and a fresh horse for yourself, if you like. Ahbrem can ride to the inn more slowly on one of our ponies and fetch your horses back."

Kesh opened his mouth to ask if Ahbrem could accompany them on the task but Ship was already saying: "On fresh mounts you should arrive at this inn here on the border before nightfall. The next day you could cross the border and join this drover's road down from the mountains. It leads across the plain and then follows the river to this little town where you should be able to find lodgings. On the next day you should be able to reach the port of Odout. Three days to Odout. I'm sure it could be done." Ship looked up at them and beamed before going on. "From there, I am told, you can buy passage across the sea ... "

Maina felt a shiver of dread as Ship traced a line across the decorated parchment, where the repeated pattern of scrolls denoted empty sea. He stabbed his finger at a point on the distant coastline.

"... to Wadderhick. Once there you can buy cam-horses to take you south, asking all the while for news of the strange kings. I am sure you will be directed. If the kings are of my kind, they will speak my language, which both Morthern monks and Xouthan priestesses have kindly adopted as the 'sacred language'. I am hoping the peoples across the sea have also learned a little of the language too so that you will both be able to communicate. If not, they will perhaps speak a little Enahet. There has been trading between them across the sea for a good while, I believe. You speak Enahet, don't you Kesh?"

"I have studied the language, yes," said Kesh.

"Perfect!" exclaimed the Ship Prophet. "I think you should start packing. I have some light-weight rain cloaks that the maidens stitched for me one round and I also have a torch which might be useful, although it won't hold its charge for long." Ship looked at their puzzled expressions as he picked up the torch and tried the switch. He sighed. "Just think of it as a magic torch but it won't work for long. You must keep it for use only in emergencies. I will write a letter for you to give the kings but you must only hand it over if they are my kind. I mean, if they are hairless and look like me."

Ship paused and then went on again excitedly. "You could leave tomorrow. No, maybe that is too soon. Leave the morning after, very early. You will need some travelling clothes that will help you blend in with other travellers. You can't travel in those robes. You will have to wear a hat, Kesh, to hide your shaven head. You must take some food, of course, and blankets perhaps, but the most important thing is to take plenty of gold and silver. Then you can buy food and lodgings on the way, fresh horses and your passage across the sea. Yes, you will need plenty of coin. Every round I receive gifts of gold and silver from both Xoutha and Morth, and I rarely have any use for it. Tomorrow I will show you my treasury. You will see it is dusty and full of cobwebs but I knew I would find a good use for the money eventually."

"I am sorry," said Kesh to Ahbrem, as he left Ship's study

after the meeting. "I am afraid Ship wants to borrow your cam-horse for the Xouthan priestess. He suggests you fetch it back by riding to the first inn on the road on one of the Community's ponies. I don't think it is going to be possible for you to come with us. I suggested you could ride the pack horse but, when I asked Ship if you could do that, he pointed out that, if he allowed you to go, then the Xouthans would want another priestess to go also and there are not enough horses for a fourth. Anyway, he has asked to speak to you."

"To me?" Ahbrem questioned.

"Yes," said Kesh. He tapped once more on the study door and when he heard Ship's voice he nudged Ahbrem forward. "My turn to wait for you," he whispered encouragingly.

"Ah, Ahbrem, come in, come in," said the Ship Prophet as the second monk stepped nervously through the door. "Now, Ahbrem, I have a favour to ask. As you know, I have asked Kesh to accompany Maina, the Most Honoured Xouthan trainee priestess, on a journey. They may be away a whole moon or perhaps two. Meanwhile, I will have all the other Xouthan maidens here continuing with their training and carrying out their own tasks. They will be without their leader. I would very much appreciate your staying with the community to help me to to look after them. I always appreciate having a visiting Morthern monk in the community to be ready to fetch help if there is an emergency and so on. Would you be willing to assist me in his way?"

Ahbrem knew he was being offered a fob for not accompanying Kesh, as Mattouk Calim would have commanded. There was only one being who could over-ride the mattouk's instructions and that being was the Prophet of

62

the Burning Ship. Despite feeling deep unease about letting Kesh go away without his protection, Ahbrem was obliged to accept the duty that Ship was allocating to him.

CHAPTER NINE

They left soon after midnight on the appointed day after resting only a few hours. Each of the horses was led down the steep track on the Xouthan side of the mountain. Wyn led Maina on Ahbrem's horse, holding her lantern out in front of her and picking her way carefully down the stony path, while Ahbrem led Kesh. The riders were wearing travelling clothes and Kesh was wearing a felt hat. The place where the path met the military road was the planned parting point and there they had to say goodbye.

"Perhaps Sakki the seacrow will follow you and give you protection," Ahbrem said to Kesh as he dismounted.

Kesh laughed unconvincingly. "Sakki knows well the hand that throws the crumbs. He will stay with you, Ahbrem. But you can tell him, if anything happens to me, to fetch my soul with haste back to Khoulan. I would like to see Morth again before I move on to the next life." He then saw the look of alarm on Ahbrem's face and said, "I was joking. Nothing is going to happen to me. We are merely going on a simple journey to seek out Ship's people. We will be back in a couple of moons before the winter cold sets in."

"May Tarn protect you," said Wyn to Maina. "And may the great gods bring you safe back to the mountain at the end of your task."

"May the gods protect you and all the maidens," said Maina. "Look after them, Wyn. They are all good women. And look after yourself too. Now, go back and get some sleep."

The women embraced and, taking his lead from them, Ahbrem embraced his friend. Kesh was a little surprised but returned the embrace.

Wyn saw this and turned to Maina with a knowing smile and a little skip of her brows. Maina nodded and returned the smile.

"Don't worry," Kesh told Ahbrem. "I'll be back before you remember that I'm gone."

Kesh and Maina mounted the horses and started off along the road. Maina looked back after a little while and saw tiny lights dancing against the great black shape of the Sacred Mountain as the other two young people carried the lanterns back up the path.

They rode for a good while in near darkness, with only half a moon to show the horses where the road lay. Then it began to rain. Kesh showed Maina the Enahet cloak that Mattouk Calim had lent him for his travels. It was made of embroidered animal skins, which were normally folded and worn on the back, the weight resting on the horse's rump, but flaps opened out at the sides to wrap around the rider, and then further flaps opened downwards to cover the rider's legs. Maina pulled out the thin cloak that the Ship Prophet had promised would keep out wind and rain. She had little faith that something so light could protect her. Nevertheless, as they rode, most of the water did indeed seem to roll off the cloak and drip to the ground while her clothes stayed almost dry.

The first promise of dawn began to fade the inky sky and Kesh shouted back to her that he would look out for a place to stop. They were passing through woodland and soon they found a clearing by the side of the road where they could tie up the horses.

Maina made to dismount and let out a groan.

"I thought you said you could ride," Kesh taunted her gently.

"I can," she replied. "I often ride round the palace grounds and sometimes all around the boundary. But I'm not used to riding for mile after mile like this."

There were logs laid out in a rough circle in the grass of the clearing. They had obviously been used as seats by travellers in the past, but they were too wet to sit on now. Kesh went a little way into the trees and found a small dry den amongst the undergrowth, perhaps where some animal had previously made a bed. He lined it with his Enahet cloak, wet side out, and invited Maina to sit down. Kesh tethered the horses to the logs in the clearing. He took the luggage off the pack-horse to rest it and carried it over to the little den. He opened the bag of supplies and fetched out bread, salted meat and water. Kesh started to eat standing out in the rain.

These Morthern monks might not be manly but they were certainly gentlemanly, Maina thought. She told him that there was plenty of room for two in the den and Kesh cautiously squeezed in beside her. The breakfast was simple fare but the outdoor air gave them a good appetite and made it taste wonderful. While they ate the rain started to come down harder. Kesh suggested that they should wait a while before venturing out again. It would surely ease up in a while.

They sat side by side, listening to the drumming of rain on the ground and the chorus of dripping noises from twigs and branches. Eventually rain started to drip rhythmically from the roof of the little den onto the animal skin hood of the cloak above their heads. Sitting motionless after a night without rest made the lure of sleep irresistible to Maina. Her eyes felt sore and, at first she first closed her lids just to give them rest but, after one or two further glances out at the rain sodden scene she could no longer summon the strength to open them again.

Kesh was also weary. The head of the Most Honoured Xouthan maiden slumped to rest on his shoulder. He doubted she was aware of it and he shrank from waking her, as it would have embarrassed them both. Consequently, he remained motionless. He was no longer hungry or thirsty and so had little to keep him awake. He tried to go over Ship's plans for the journey, wondering how much this little delay would affect their progress, but the continued drumming of the rain eventually lulled him into slumber also.

Neither of them saw the seacrow come to pick quietly at the crumbs around their feet. They did, however, waken later when this same seacrow started into such a squawking that it seemed to set the whole of the woodland into a commotion. Kesh scrambled to his feet in alarm and stepped into the clearing just in time to see half a dozen horses, some with ragged riders, gallop onto the road and disappear along it in the direction from which they had so recently come. The clearing itself was now empty. Kesh stood open mouthed looking at the space where their horses had previously been. Maina stumbled from the den and together they faced the horror that their lapse of attention had allowed.

"How will we get them back?" asked Maina. "Perhaps we should go to the soldiers at the last fort and ask for help."

Kesh shook his head. "The fort is too far away. It would take all day on foot. The rustlers will be miles away by then."

They both hung their heads at the realisation of the gravity of their situation.

"Your beautiful cam-horses!" Maina breathed, after a while. "I'm so sorry, Kesh."

"It was my fault. I fell asleep. I did not even think about the possibility of rustlers. I am too trusting." Then he exclaimed bitterly "I am so naïve! I am stupid."

"No, no. I should have played my part," said Maina. "We should have taken turns - one resting while the other watched. We will be more careful next time."

"Next time?" Kesh exclaimed. "How is there going to be a next time? We have failed our task. Surely we must return to the Sacred Mountain."

"Not necessarily," said Maina. "We could still go on to the inn. We might get there by nightfall, don't you think? We would only be half a day late and we were going to buy fresh horses there anyway. We still have the bags of coin, don't we? We will have to leave word for Ahbrem. We will have to write a note explaining what happened, for there will be no horses for him to collect, but we will only be delayed by a day at the most. We can still make good our Task."

"But what about our belongings?" asked Kesh. "I cannot

possibly carry the Enahet cloak without a horse to take the weight, especially now it is wet. I must return it to Mattouk Calim. I will have to fetch the pony from the Sacred Mountain."

"Mattouk Calim surely does not expect the cloak to be returned before you are due to end your stay at the Sacred Mountain," said Maina. "We could leave it in the den if we covered it with leaves and branches. As long as it is hidden from view, it will be safe where it is."

"We have just been robbed, Maina," said Kesh. "I do not know how you can be sure that it will not be taken."

"For the sake of the Task I think we have to take that risk. I will have to leave some of my baggage, too. I must leave my priestess's robe behind, at least. I will have to meet the Ship Prophet's people in my travelling clothes. I will leave it with your Enahet cloak. Also, we will not be able to carry all those bags of coin. Perhaps we should take the gold and leave the silver."

Encouraged by Maina's determination, Kesh began to come round to the idea of carrying on with the Task and they sorted through their luggage until they had only bread, cheese, flagons for water and their lightweight cloaks packed into bags which they could strap on their backs. They tied bags of gold coin to their belts, four for Kesh, partly hidden under his jerkin and two for Maina, hanging between the folds of her skirt. They folded the rest of their belongings up in the Enahet animal skins and arranged branches over the heap, finally filling up the rest of the space in the den with autumn leaves. Standing back to admire their work, Kesh was forced to agree that it was difficult to see where the den had been, let alone see what was hidden therein.

Taking up their bags they left the clearing and turned into the road, walking in the opposite direction to that which the rustlers had taken.

CHAPTER TEN

The startled seacrow had risen high above the forest, alarmed by the strangers who so roughly ripped at the reins of the tethered cam-horses and kicked them into a gallop as soon as they had landed on their backs.

He circled around at height, watching the crumb-droppers pack up their belongings and set off on foot along the road. He was disappointed that they had not fetched out more food. He looked down at the long road that cut a swathe straight through the forest and at the slow pace of the crumb-droppers as they walked along it. He grew bored. He felt the call of the sea and decided to turn back eastwards.

He covered the return journey easily and flew eagerly out over the sea to the nearest island. There was a family of bears on the western beach, turning over stones for shellfish. The seacrow followed them for a while picking up tasty morsels too small for the bears' paws to grasp. Then he took to the air again and saw a small fort with a soldiers' encampment around it. The smell of cooking led him to a large tent-like building made with skins drawn over a rectangular timber framework. He hopped under a curtain that hung across the doorway and looked out cautiously from between its folds.

Two small children were sitting at a table, squabbling good-naturedly. A young woman was ladling food from a cooking pot, while a broad shouldered man stood close behind her, kissing her neck and hindering her work.

Suddenly a soldier came up to the doorway and pulled

the curtain back, almost exposing the skulking seacrow. An emissary of the Xouthan Empire stood waiting behind the guard. He had come to see the man betrothed to his Emperor's daughter. He craned his neck to see past the soldier's hulk into the circular island dwelling. The woman's giggling quickly ceased. As her lover turned his head, he was instantly recognisable as the Prince of Benethan.

"Forgive me, your Highness," said the guard, his hand still holding the cloth aside. "An emissary from the Emperor of Xoutha brings you a message."

The prince let go of the woman, thrusting her halfway across the room and knocking over a chair in the process. The seacrow squawked as the chair clattered to the floor, giving away his hiding place. He flapped off quickly skywards. The children's chatter became taut silence.

"Take him to the camp," the prince commanded angrily through clenched teeth. He threw the soldier an accusing look, then regained his composure and drew himself up to his full height. "I will receive him there in due course."

After the wasted journey to the dwelling and a further wait at the camp, the emissary was feeling a little out of sorts. He was pondering on the domestic scene he had just witnessed. The prince's appetite for women was no secret but this woman was a mother. Was it his imagination that he had seen the prince's likeness in the faces of her children? In Xouthan law, a father whose children had a living mother was considered married, and therefore not free to marry any other. This did not bode well for the proposed Xouthan-Benethan alliance.

The prince welcomed him formally when the emissary was announced to him again. This time the prince was sitting on a large ornate chair in the centre of a military tent lavishly decorated with embroidered hangings.

"So what is your news?" the prince asked.

"Your Highness," began the emissary. "Your betrothed, Maina, daughter of the Emperor of Xoutha and its dependencies, is reported to be safely arrived at the community of the Sacred Mountain. This news was relayed to Xoutha by the Most Honoured graduate of the Sacred Mountain returning from her final year of training. Your respected betrothed's return to Xoutha is expected one round less twenty days from now."

"Well, I thank you," said the prince. "That is good news indeed. Um ... take my warmest greetings to your honoured Emperor, and say that I look forward eagerly to my respected betrothed returning safely to her father's house. That is all. You are dismissed." He then added as an afterthought, "Of course you must dine with my officers before you leave." He turned to his military advisor. "Vundmar, find a soldier to show him the way, and then return to me swiftly."

When his advisor arrived back the prince told him, "I need a gift for the Emperor of Xoutha. I do not think the emissary will return with favourable news. One of those stupid Cweel Island soldiers let him see a little too much of my private arrangements, I fear. What do you think would be appropriate?"

"Well, you could drive the Mortherners off the Sacred Mountain," was Vundmar's quick reply. "He would surely love you like a son if you did that."

The prince laughed, "Not yet, not yet, Vundmar. But we could, perhaps, make it a little less comfortable for them. The monastery at Khoulan is not well guarded, I understand. Perhaps we should arrange one or two foraging excursions around there. Look at your maps, Vundmar, and let me know your thoughts tomorrow."

Meanwhile, the seacrow had been so alarmed by the violence in the tent that he flew back to the mainland and decided to seek again the gentle crumb-droppers. Nevertheless, he was wary of people now and kept mostly out of sight for many days.

CHAPTER ELEVEN

Maina's limbs ached and her feet were sore. The sun was sinking towards the horizon, and still they had not reached the inn where they were supposed to swap horses at mid-day. Kesh kept walking resolutely onwards and Maina could not open her mouth to complain, as this method of completing the journey had been at her own urging. Maina stopped a passing cart to enquire how much further they had to go, and the tradesman had assured her that they would reach it before nightfall, yet the road seemed endless.

The forest had given way to open grassland, with clumps of trees dotted here and there, but still little sign of habitation. When they had started on this march, Maina and Kesh had walked side by side. Now Kesh was stopping every so often to wait for Maina to catch up.

At last he said, "I will have to stop shortly and make a fire. As soon as the sun sets it will be time for my meditation."

Maina looked at him blankly.

"Every evening between sunset and darkness, we sit before a flame to meditate," he explained. "You do not do this?"

Maina shook her head.

"The flame represents the burning ship. We meditate on the gift of the Prophet of the Burning Ship, and on the teachings of all the mattouks of Morth, until we reach a state of balancement."

"Ah, the myth of the burning ship," Maina breathed.

"It is not a myth. The burning ship was seen falling into the sea," retorted Kesh. "It was clearly observed by the presiding mattouk of the Khoulan monastery, Mattouk Sahlt."

"It was evening time. Your mattouk saw only the setting sun."

"What you have just said would be considered blasphemy if it had been spoken by a Mortherner," Kesh said, stepping off the road and heading towards a clump of trees. He took a deep breath. "But I know Ship would instruct me to let it pass, as we have to work together on this Task. Furthermore, I think you speak from ignorance rather than a desire to insult the Morthern religion. I will merely point out that there is a difference in speed of travel between a falling object and the setting sun."

"I find it difficult to understand the Ship Prophet," said Maina, abandoning the argument. She was following close behind Kesh as he collected firewood.

"I find he speaks very clearly and simply," said Kesh bending to pick up a small fallen branch.

"I don't mean that I don't understand what he says. I don't understand how he can say the things he says. He is an icon for both our religions, and yet he is a mortal being with his own thoughts and reasoning. How does he reconcile the two religions? Why doesn't he tell us which one is right?"

"Well, I know my religion has more truth than yours, and I expect you feel the same way," said Kesh, depositing an armful of firewood on the ground. "Perhaps the Ship Prophet sees some truth in both."

He gathered stones and made a ring on the ground. Then he took tinder and flint from a little bag and set about making a spark. Maina watched his narrow monk's fingers, not strong and manly but longer than her own. He worked deftly with the flint at the same time as cupping the tinder to keep off the breeze.

"So, in the Morthern religion, is there an equivalent to our fourth law?"

"Fourth law?" Kesh repeated, unable to remember all he had been told about the Xouthan religion.

"Slaughter not except for meat," Maina began.

"The flesh of man thou must not eat," Kesh remembered. "That seems a very reasonable law."

"But you allow men, or those born male at least, to become priests," said Maina, wanting him to recognise the great obstacle she had to overcome in order to accept Kesh as legitimate participant in her religious task. "What happens if a warrior wants to become a priest? Would that be allowed?"

Smoke was now coming from the tinder and Kesh gently put the little flame into the heap of dried grass and twigs in the centre of his ring of stones.

"Monks cannot be warriors, but a warrior could become a monk if he gave up his warrior life," he said. "Now I must begin my meditation. You are welcome to join me, but please understand I cannot speak again until the meditation is complete."

Maina was glad to sit for a while, but the little fire did not throw out much heat. To keep her mind off the cold and damp she began to pray to her gods for protection, as the Ship Prophet had suggested.

"Great Tarn, god of the heavens, protect your servant Maina, and also, Kesh her companion, appointed by the venerable Ship Prophet. Assist us in our Task, speed our journey and protect us from harm. Great Gorlan, mighty god of the sea, protect your servant Maina on the voyage she must soon undertake, and protect Kesh her companion, and all those who sail with her."

She did not notice Kesh cast a sideways glance in her direction and give a little frown. His concentration on flame meditation had faltered at hearing himself mentioned in her vocal prayers.

When it was almost completely dark, Kesh stood up slowly and stretched. He carefully smothered the little fire with damp leaves.

"We must get on," he said. "It is too cold to sleep out in the open. Even if we do not reach the inn, we must find some shelter."

They walked back to the road, and set off along it once more, but more slowly than before, picking their way cautiously around the potholes.

"We should have brought a lantern," Kesh said. "Ship told

us that the magic torch he gave us is only to be used for emergencies."

"There is just about enough moonlight to see the road," said Maina.

They plodded on in silence for a while. Finally, in the far distance, the dimmest of lights, like a tiny star, blinked into view on the horizon.

"I hope that's the inn," said Maina, stepping a little quicker.

It did, indeed, prove to be light from the windows of the inn they sought. Inside, the light seemed bright and there was a fire at one end of a large room full of jovial guests drinking the landlord's ale. Kesh kept on his felt hat to hide his monk's shaven head. As they were still in Xoutha, it fell to Maina to arrange for rooms for the night and to order a hot meal. They had to pay extra for the meal because of the late hour. Maina then asked about horses.

"Ah ..." The landlord started hesitantly. "We used to deal in horses here, it's true. But we stopped that practice a round ago. Too many rustlers in the area you see. We'd buy a pair of nags in good faith and next thing we'd have someone come in and claim them as their own. We'd end up selling them for little more than what it had cost us to keep them in hay in the meantime. It ceased to be a profitable business, you see."

"Yes, I do see," said Maina, with a sigh. "So where would the nearest horse dealer be?"

"There are none this side of the village of Finnan in Enaha, half a day's journey from here or thereabouts."

"On foot?"

"Well," said the landlord. "It will take you best part of the day on foot, I expect."

Maina thanked him and went back to Kesh with the disappointing news.

Overnight, Maina sat alone in her room bathing her blistered feet and contemplating another day of walking. She decided to tell Kesh that she had been wrong, that they should turn back and admit defeat. When she lay down to sleep she thought weariness would soon take her into the world of dreams but she ached in every bone and slept only fitfully.

Kesh, however, met her at breakfast with a broad smile.

"I have been talking to a wagoner," he told her. "He is Enahet and he says we can ride the wagon part of the way to Odout, as long as I take a turn to lead the oxen now and then. It will be slow, but you will be able to rest on top of the cargo. We have to meet him in the yard at the back as soon as we can, so you must eat quickly."

CHAPTER TWELVE

It was thus that Maina was persuaded, in her turn, to continue the journey. The two travellers were unable to find horses to buy but made their way to Odout over many days, sometimes riding on wagons, sometimes on foot.

Odout was a small but affluent sea-port with most of its buildings constructed of stone. It was not unlike Maina's home town. They had arrived there over half a moon later than Ship had planned.

They hurried to the docks as soon as they were in the town, and found the building that housed the offices where passage could be booked to cross to Wadderhick. The doors of the building were locked and no-one could be seen inside. Kesh asked a fishmonger at the nearby market when the office would be open. He was told that the offices were now closed for the winter, the last ship for Wadderhick having set sail two days before.

Kesh began to walk away from the market stall. He walked passed Maina, shoulders slumped dejectedly, face set, staring off into the distance.

"What did he say?" Maina asked him, following behind.

Kesh carried on along the harbour, looking disconsolately out to sea.

"Kesh!" Maina called as she tried to catch up.

At the end of the harbour wall Kesh sank to his knees.

"Harg forgive me!" he exclaimed. "If only I had not fallen asleep and lost our horses. Even without buying fresh horses, our cam-horses would have got us here in time. I have failed you, Maina, and I have caused us both to fail our Task."

He explained to Maina what the fishmonger had told him. Maina assured him again that half the responsibility for the loss of the horses was hers. They sat side by side at the end of the harbour, feet dangling above the water, contemplating their situation. They did not notice a man walking along the harbour wall towards them and were startled when he spoke.

"Might you be looking for work?" he asked in Enahet. Kesh turned to look at him. He went on, "Only we're short of a shepherd in Hittan, just along the coast there." He indicated a settlement that could just be seen across the bay. "The fishmonger said you'd missed the boat. If you're waiting for passage we could give you a job to tide you over, so to speak. There's a cottage goes along with it, if you're willing. The sheep have got to be brought in for the winter, see, so we need to find a shepherd pretty quickly."

"There's the shepherd boy who can show you the ropes," the man went on when Kesh did not answer. "Only, he's just a young lad. He can't do the job on his own."

"What's he saying?" Maina asked.

"Well, I thought it was worth a try anyway," said the man, not getting an answer. He shrugged and turned to go.

"No, wait," Kesh stopped him. "One moment, please."

Kesh translated for Maina while the Hittan resident looked on.

"What do you think?" he asked her. "Is this man sent by Harg to lead us forward, or is this a temptation which will merely serve to delay our return to the Sacred Mountain?"

Maina thought for a moment. She hated the thought of going back, having struggled so hard to get this far.

"Perhaps we should give it a try," she said. "It will give us time to gather our thoughts, at least."

"And somewhere to sleep tonight," said Kesh. In his best Enahet he thanked the man for his offer. He arranged to meet the man when he had finished his business in Odout and walk with him to the village of Hittan.

They waited for him in the appointed place and he arrived well before sunset.

"I'm Bim Toegrath by the way," the Hittan man introduced himself as they set off together.

"Kesh Khoulan," Kesh said, taking the name of his monastery for a surname. "And this is my sister, Maina."

Maina smiled at Bim on hearing her name and he chuckled as he held out a hand towards her. She tried to concentrate on the sounds of the Enahet words but could not follow the rest of the conversation.

"So you're waiting for passage to Wadderhick?"

"Yes," said Kesh.

"Hoping for work over there?"

"No," said Kesh, hesitating. "We are on an errand."

"Oh, on business then?"

"Yes," said Kesh.

"Well, I'm sorry your business will be so delayed. Nothing too urgent, I hope."

"Well, it will have to wait," said Kesh. "Either that, or we give up and go back home."

"And where is home?" asked Bim.

"Just over the border," said Kesh.

"In Morth?"

"Yes."

"I thought I could tell a Morthern accent."

As they walked, the Hittan man explained that the village councillors employed a shepherd, a dairyman, a blacksmith and others on behalf of the residents. The village owned a tract of lowland and grazing rights on the hills behind but the villagers were mostly fishermen and boat builders by trade. Kesh translated for Maina, his voice becoming more and more animated as the information he was hearing confirmed the image of Enahet culture that had been passed on to him through Mattuk Calim.

By sunset they had arrived in Hittan and they were shown the shepherd's house. It was built of stone but roughly cut, not dressed like the stone of the Great Hall on the Sacred Mountain, and the roof was thatched like an unruly head of hair. It was the smallest house Maina had ever seen with one room on the ground floor and a twisted staircase up to a second room above. Bim left them to look round but soon came back with armfuls of dry heather to make a bed and a woman followed behind him with blankets and sheepskins. They left again and returned with firewood and a pitcher of water, a loaf of bread and some slices of cheese and ham. There was a table and two chairs in the room and a cooking pot and other utensils stacked next to the fire. They soon had all they would need to spend their first night in the little house.

Kesh thanked Bim and his wife for their great kindness and Bim jovially said he would repay them many times over if he managed to fetch the sheep off the hills for the villagers before the snows came. He told Kesh he would send the shepherd boy round first thing in the morning to show him where to go. Then Bim and his wife bid them goodnight and Kesh and Maina were left alone in their new home.

Maina looked at the blankets and the heap of heather. It was never going to be sufficient to make two beds.

"Don't worry," said Kesh, seeing the frown on her brows. "Let me have one sheepskin and one blanket and I will be perfectly comfortable. I will sleep down here, of course. The

85

bedroom upstairs will be yours. Help me carry the heather, and we'll make your bed up before meditation."

That night Maina lay in the lowliest abode she had ever experienced, listening to the unfamiliar sounds. She thought she heard squeaks and rustlings in the thatch above her head. It was merely a seacrow settling down to sleep against the chimney but she imagined that unwelcome rodent visitors might come out from the thatch and scurry across her bed. The room filled with a low murmur as a shower of rain hit the thatch and soon after came the tap-tap of water dripping into a tin bucket which stood in the corner. She was feeling very alone and disconsolate but then she heard muffled sounds from below. She guessed Kesh was stirring the fire and found it strangely comforting to hear him nearby. Soon after that she fell asleep.

CHAPTER THIRTEEN

The next morning a young man appeared at the door of the little house and introduced himself as Ginn Gilleth, the shepherd's apprentice. Kesh put on his cloak to go with him to the hills. Maina faced the prospect of a day on her own in a village where she could speak no word of the local language. She begged them to let her go along with them.

"I promise not to hold you up," she told Kesh.

"There will probably be a lot of walking uphill. You may not be able to climb fast enough."

"Then you can leave me resting and collect me on the way back down."

Kesh asked Ginn in Enahet if he minded Maina going with them. He shrugged, and Kesh translated his reply back as "the more the merrier."

Maina wrapped bread and wedges of cheese in a cloth, and filled two small stoppered flagons with water. They followed Ginn and his kirra-dog out of the village, leaving the sea for the hills.

On their way up, with Ginn and the dog ahead of them, Maina asked Kesh if he actually knew anything about shepherding.

"We keep sheep at Khoulan," he told her. "Those who are fit enough take turns with shepherding, but we keep the sheep in a fold at night, and take them out to graze each day. We sometimes get raiders in the area, you see, and there are wolves in the mountains."

Ginn led them to a structure made of stone walls laid out in a square on the hillside, with a small gap for an entrance and, next to it, a longer arm reaching out onto the hillside. Ginn told Kesh that this was the holding pen and that he and his dog would drive groups of sheep towards the long wall whilst Kesh was to move in from the side with two wicker hurdles, which at present leaned against one of the walls. Ginn explained that the hurdles had to be quickly tied across the entrance, once the sheep were inside, to keep them penned up while they went to collect the sheep from the next hill.

Ginn then beckoned for them to follow him further up the hill. From the top, a glorious view of rolling countryside opened out before them, with grassy valleys and heath-covered hilltops dotted here and there with little copses. Behind them the deep blue of the sea stretched to the horizon and all was lit by a golden autumnal sun.

"Din Kick," said Ginn, indicating the ground beneath his feet.

He then pointed to three of the other hills naming them in Enahet, Din Lief, Din Nort and Din Bekella. They were all grazed by Hittan sheep and each would be scoured in turn by Ginn and his dog.

Ginn instructed them to go back to the holding pen and wait. He whistled to his dog and set off down the other side of Din Kick.

Kesh and Maina waited at the pen and soon Ginn's distant whistles and shouts were joined by the bleats of many sheep. The noises gradually drew closer until the sheep rounded the hillside and could be seen coming towards them.

Maina moved away past the end of the long collecting arm, not wanting to frighten the animals, while Kesh crouched behind the wicker panels. With the dog circling the sheep from the outside the flock began to move towards the entrance and, as soon as one sheep found the gap, a stream of woolly bodies began to pour into the pen. One sheep broke off, however, and a small group of animals followed it along the wall towards Maina. She leaped out in front them, arms outstretched, dodging this way and that to force the runaways back into the flock. Kesh watched her, astounded that the dignified woman who, until a few days ago, gracefully bore the full length robes of a Sacred Mountain priestess, was now running around, first one way, then the other, almost matching the speed of the kirra-dog. It verged on comical but was somehow strangely appealing.

When the sheep were all in, Maina came up to him as he was tying the hurdles. She was breathless and flushed and could hardly speak for laughing. She stood before him, pink and glowing and breathing heavily. It was a sight that he found unusually disturbing. She said something about what rascals the sheep could be. He could see her lips move but could find no words to answer.

That evening he lit the fire and sat before it but could not see the flames. He could only see the sheep and Maina's pink and smiling face.

After a while, Maina spoke softly to him.

"Is it alright to put this pot on the fire now? I have prepared a stew and it needs to cook." When he did not answer she said, "You have been sitting a long time. Have you not finished your meditation?"

"I have not yet achieved balancement."

"What is 'balancement'?" Maina asked, picking up a word she had heard him use before.

"Um ..." Kesh hesitated as he struggled to find an explanation that might make sense to a Xouthan with no tradition of meditation. He remembered how their mattouk had explained it to them as students, and began: "The Morthern religion teaches that all men, whether they hold faith or not, are partly good, partly evil. Harg and Denharg are in constant battle for the souls of men. Mattouk Calim told us to think of balancement as being the process of weighing up our souls as a merchant would weigh a gourde-cabbage on a market stall. Our goodness must be the good hearty cabbage, while our evil must be the tiny weight that we must always keep at arm's length. The heartier the cabbage, the further out the merchant must push his balancing weight."

Maina laughed.

"So your soul is like a cabbage?" she teased gently. "Your religion is so full of riddles and parables that I will never be able to understand it.

Kesh sighed and tried again. "Balancement is a state of inner calm within which all emotions are harmonised, releasing the mind to consider problems using reason alone."

"I see. I think I understand that explanation better," said Maina. "So will it take much longer?"

Kesh frowned.

"For you to reach it?"

"I ... I cannot tell," said Kesh. "You must go ahead and use the fire. I will complete my meditation once you have eaten."

"I have prepared enough for two. I have no great experience as a cook but I hope it will be edible once it has cooked for a while."

"Thank you. In that case I must help."

"There is really nothing much to do until it is cooked," Maina said.

"Then I will cook for you tomorrow."

"I will look forward to that. Do all Khoulan monks cook?"

"At Khoulan, all who are able take turns with each of the domestic tasks needed to run the monastery."

"That's good," said Maina, "because stew is the only thing I have been taught to cook. My father forbade me to study cookery further as it would never form any part of my duties. Mealtimes would get a little boring if I cooked every night."

Kesh sat before the fire all the evening and only after Maina had gone to bed, and with much chanting under his breath of 'outer nobility, inner calm, outer nobility, inner calm', did he finally give up trying to achieve a satisfactory state of balancement.

He decided he must do more to tackle the problem that this image of Maina was giving him. If he was going to have difficulty in maintaining balancement while travelling with her, he would have to find a way of overcoming the difficulty quickly or it would put the task in jeopardy. It was inconceivable that he should endanger his vows to Harg or his promises to Mattouk Calim or risk disgracing his family by falling prey to temptation and, it was after all, totally illogical to contemplate abandoning his career, his ambitions and all his training for a Xouthan maiden. She did not share his beliefs, which were the cornerstone of his being, so how could he possibly contemplate spending his life with her?

Kesh took a sharp gulp of air at the speed with which his thoughts had gone, albeit dismissively, from an image of Maina's smiling face to a renunciation of his vows for a lifetime in her company. His grip on balancement was indeed in peril.

Kesh got up, took his cloak from the peg and stepped out into the dark of the street. The seacrow on the roof-ridge woke at the sound of the door. He stretched his wings and launched off the roof to see where Kesh was going in case he had food with him. Some of the sheep were also not sleeping. There was a bleating in the darkness every now and again, coming from their new winter home in the fields behind the houses.

"What would Mattouk Calim advise?" Kesh asked himself as he walked down the narrow street. Of course, Kesh

92

understood what he was experiencing. Although life at Khoulan was lived without any female participants, the monks were well educated about what to expect from coming into contact with females outside monastic life. Obviously, what Kesh had experienced was the physical reaction his teachers had described. He had experienced it once or twice before when his thoughts had strayed from his devotions, and Morthern monks were warned against standing too close to females of their race, but he had not expected this reaction to occur in the presence of a Xouthan. Xouthans seemed so foreign, so alien, almost like a different species. It did not seem possible that he could respond to her in this way.

Nevertheless, Mattouk Calim had warned him to keep his distance form all women and that those with the sweetest natures could be the most dangerous of all. Was Maina sweet natured? Once again her pink smile came into view against the blue of the sky. Kesh tried to clear it from his head and apply reason. As Most Honoured Maiden he had expected her to be aloof and condescending and, at first, she had not been pleasant company but she had been much more friendly and cooperative since they had started out on this journey together. He would have to be doubly careful of her now. And what had his teachers suggested as an antidote? Ah yes, a cold bath.

Kesh made his way in the darkness to the little village jetty that jutted out from the harbour wall. He let his cloak slip to the ground and he shrugged off his traveller's leggings and shirt. He stepped off the jetty into the water and suddenly all the air in his lungs seemed to be expelled at the shock of its chill. He had not been prepared for it to be so cold or so deep. He tried to swim but the muscles in his legs twitched into spasms of cramp straight away and the cold water closed over his head. For a moment he was completely disorientated. In the blackness he could not tell which way was up, let alone in which direction lay the jetty wall. Coughing and spluttering, he surfaced. A crow was calling out in alarm on the jetty path. Kesh knew they didn't land on the water, like most sea birds, so by following the call he could be sure he was not heading out to sea. He managed a few stokes and then could see the jetty wall and the seacrow, silhouetted against the night sky, jumping up and down and cawing. By a supreme effort of will he dragged himself up onto the stonework. He perched on the edge of it for a few moments, sucking in gulps of air. He looked for the seacrow, wanting to thank it, but it had dodged off into the darkness. Kesh shrugged.

"Thanking a dumb beast," he scorned himself. "What good would that do?"

As soon as he was able, Kesh slipped on his shoes and, with just the cloak around his shoulders, he ran back to the shepherd's house. Once inside, he put logs onto the fire and crouched over it shivering, rubbing himself dry with a blanket. Eventually the fire blazed up and he could feel the warmth on his skin. He knelt on the tiny, ragged hearth rug and prayed to Harg to thank him for saving his life and to beg forgiveness for his foolishness, to thank him that there had been no-one around to see his foolishness and, then, to thank him for the cure, for he was no longer thinking about Maina.

CHAPTER FOURTEEN

The next morning Ginn arrived even earlier and spoke to Kesh for a while in the doorway.

Kesh turned to Maina and began hesitantly, "Ginn asks if you would stay and give the sheep their hay and roots, so that we can go straight out to the hills. He says we have to go further today, so it will take longer. He asks if you would meet us at the holding pen after mid-day, and help us drive them down from there. He will show you where everything is." When he had finished translating for Ginn, he asked, "Is that alright? Would you mind staying behind this morning?"

"No, of course not," Maina told him, hiding her disappointment.

Ginn said something more, and Kesh translated. "He says you're obviously a natural shepherd and he has no qualms about leaving you in charge of them."

"Ha!" exclaimed Maina. "Well, thank him and tell him that I will do my best."

Ginn led them to a barn at the end of the field. It was filled to the roof with hay for the winter and next door to it was a shed with a pile of root vegetables. There was also a well in the corner of one of the fields and buckets for carrying water to the troughs. Ginn seemed determined to teach Maina some Enahet. He pointed to the hay and the water and repeated the words for her again and again, with Kesh chuckling in the background until she could say them to his satisfaction.

Then the men left her to fill the mangers and troughs and set off up into the hills.

The sheep were thirsty, and seemed to drink the water almost as fast as Maina could draw it. She spent a while pouring buckets into troughs and then a woman came through the gate into the field. Maina recognised her as Bim's wife. She greeted Maina, and Maina smiled back. She said something else that Maina could not understand. Maina shrugged and repeated the only two words of Enahet that she knew, pointing to the hay and the water. Bim's wife nodded but when she could not make herself understood she took hold of Maina's hand and led her towards the gate. Maina protested but Bim's wife persisted, repeating another word over and over, which she later discovered meant 'tea'. Maina was led into a little house where Bim sat before the fire. There was a table laid with a teapot and little cakes and a kettle sang on the hearth. The air was full of the aroma of baking.

Bim greeted her with what sounded like the same sounds as his wife had used, raising his hand and shifting as if to get up out of his chair.

Maina tried copying the same greeting, hoping that it was appropriate. Bim grinned at her. She deduced that, at least, she had not insulted him. His wife poured water from the kettle into the teapot and indicated a chair to Maina. Maina obediently sat and was soon passed a cup of steaming liquid and offered one of the cakes. They tasted as good as they smelled.

Bim said something to her in Enahet. Maina's face registered anxiety as she struggled to understand him. His wife scolded him, and, as there was nothing else to be said, she held up the cup and said the Enahet word for tea. This was not much help, as Maina could not tell if it was the word for tea or the word for cup. Then she held up her cake. That was less ambiguous and Maina learned the word for cake. Bim joined in.

Maina understood 'cake something something' spoken with the inflection of a question and followed by an 'mmm' denoting deliciousness. Maina spoke her first phrase in Enahet, repeating 'cake good, yes' without the inflection. Bim and his wife laughed delightedly and continued the lesson until the cakes and tea were gone. Then Maina was led back to the sheep.

On a hillside at some distance from Hittan, Ginn and Kesh were sitting down to eat their bread and cheese before starting to collect the sheep. A seacrow alighted just clear of their feet and looked at them, its head on one side, waiting.

Kesh shifted uncomfortably, remembering the crow that had saved his life the night before during his cold bath in the harbour.

"I'm surprised you get so many seacrows this far north," he commented.

"Oh, yes," answered Ginn. "We get plenty but they don't usually come inland until the spring. They nest in the trees, you see. This one must be confused by the warm weather we've been having." Then he added, "Please don't hurt it. They are sacred birds to us."

"Oh, I wasn't going to hurt it," Kesh assured him but a suspicion was creeping upon him that this might be the same crow that had been on the harbour wall and that it was now following him. "Tell me, Ginn, do you have jultie berries in these parts?"

Kesh did not know the Enahet for the jultie bush, so he had used the Morthern name. Ginn did not understand so Kesh described them to him. Once he had told him that they stain the fingers purple, Ginn understood.

"Yes, we have them. Confectioners crystallize them in sugar for solstice day."

"Do you eat them fresh?"

"Oh yes, when they are in season" said Ginn. "They are very good baked in pies too. My mother bottles them in syrup to keep them through the winter."

"Ah," said Kesh nodding and wondering if a seacrow would cat syrupy berries.

Maina was due to meet them late in the afternoon. By then the mild weather that Ginn said had been confusing the seacrow, was turning chilly. The sky had clouded over and a stiffening breeze was coming from the north. Maina was holding her cloak tightly round herself as she waited at the holding pen. She helped the men drive the flock down into another of the little fields behind the Hittan streets.

That evening at the cottage, Maina stood looking into the cupboard at the supplies that the Hittan people had put aside for their shepherd.

"I don't know what to do with most of these things," she said to Kesh. "They all look so strange to me."

 "I will cóok and you can help," Kesh said.

He showed her how to make a sauce for salt fish, while she prepared some vegetables for boiling.

While they were eating she asked, "So, are we going back to the Sacred Mountain or waiting until we can go on with the Task?"

Kesh thought for a moment. "Ginn says the sheep collecting will take two more days. After that, he can probably do the job on his own. We'll wait until the sheep are all in, then we'll decide."

That night the wind brought more cold air from the north. The seacrow perched on the roof-ridge, huddled up against the south side of the chimney-stack and decided that, at first light, he would fly south-west and go home to the monks at Khoulan, where the winters were nearly always mild.

Walking the hills became less and less pleasant for the shepherds, as showers of rain turned to showers of hail. It stung Kesh's face as it was hurled, nearly horizontally , at him by the wind. Ginn took him to a place where they could shelter for a while. It was a little ruined cottage that Ginn said had been the shepherd's summer dwelling in the days when wolves had prowled the hills and the sheep had needed constant attention. When the hail stopped and the clouds had moved on they came out of the little house. The view was breathtaking. The shepherd's hut was higher than all the hills they had cleared so far, and a cavernous valley opened up below them, while to the southwest the view reached into the far distance where a ridge of blue-tinged mountains could be picked out on the horizon. Kesh thought that these must be the Dinash Mountains, on the other side of which nestled his home at Khoulan. To the east, between two of the smaller hills that they had already cleared of sheep, there was yet a glimpse of the sea. It must be a marvellous place to spend a sunny day, Kesh thought, watching the next smoke-grey cloud, heavy with its burden of frozen moisture, moving quickly towards them from the north.

On the way back to the holding pen, Kesh cut extra heather to make himself a softer bed. The sheepskin rug he was sleeping on had proven too hard and too small to allow him to sleep comfortably. Maina helped him to carry the heather down from the holding pen and they arranged it round the fire to dry, before making it into a bed by pushing it up against one of the walls.

The next day, the last of the sheep were brought down and penned safely in their winter home.

"It's time to make a decision," Maina said to Kesh, as they sat down to eat that evening.

Kesh did not answer, so Maina went on. "Kesh, you've been a little quiet lately. Are you missing Ahbrem?"

Kesh hesitated before he said, "Things would, no doubt, be going better for me if Ahbrem were here."

"I do not miss my betrothed," said Maina, "because I don't really know him yet, but I do understand your loneliness."

"Betrothed?" repeated Kesh, too stunned to wonder why she

had suddenly brought the topic up, or why she had assumed that he was lonely.

"Yes. The betrothal ceremony took place the night before we left for the Sacred Mountain. He is quite handsome, and very strong – at least, he looks well built, but we haven't had time to get to know one another yet. My father hopes he will be the man to …" Maina stopped herself from saying 'take back the Sacred Mountain' just in time, remembering that she was speaking to a Mortherner. She finished with "strengthen the Empire" instead. Kesh made no response, so she went on.

"Kesh, I do understand. If you want to go back to Ahbrem, we will go. We have tried to accomplish the task that the Ship Prophet set for us. We have failed. But perhaps it is not entirely our fault. Perhaps the task was just impossible to accomplish at this season of the round. Surely the Ship Prophet will understand. He will know next time not to send his messengers until the spring-time. Perhaps he will forgive us our failure, and set us an easier task."

Kesh was staring at the floor, and thinking how wasted had been his foolish reaction to the glowing, breathless Xouthan maiden that had stood before him that first day on the hills. Not only was it completely inappropriate for such a reaction to occur in a Morthern monk, it was also completely inappropriate for the Xouthan maiden to instigate such reactions as she was, he now found, already betrothed to someone else! If nearly drowning had not completely cured him of the fantasies that had temporarily plagued him, surely this news should do it.

"Kesh, look at me," said Maina, lowering her head to get into his field of view. "Do you want to go back?"

Kesh raised his eyes with difficulty, still not trusting in his ability to maintain inner calm when meeting her gaze. He was relieved to find that she was just the formal temple maiden he had first met on the Sacred Mountain, and not the enchanting shepherdess breathlessly chasing sheep, who had so disturbed him.

"No," he told her. "I do not want to go back. In fact, all this stumbling across hillsides has left me rather tired." He did indeed feel suddenly drained. "I think I will need to rest a day or two before I can contemplate any more travel. I would really like just to go to my bed. Perhaps we can reconsider after a few more days here."

"Did you not tell me that Ginn thinks there will be heavy snow before long?" Maina asked. "If we leave it any longer we may have no more choice in the matter."

"Are you telling me that you want to go back?"

"I don't really want to go back, but I don't want you to stay if you are finding it difficult."

"I can assure you that spending a little longer here is not in any way difficult for me," said Kesh.

"Good," said Maina. "That's settled, then."

They finished eating and cleared the table. Then Maina picked up the lamp, said goodnight, and went upstairs.

Kesh lay gratefully down on his new heather bed and blew out the candle. He slept well for a while, but the single blanket was not sufficient to keep out the cold that night.

Kesh got up and threw more wood on the fire, and took down his cloak from the peg to spread out over his blanket before he was able to sleep in comfort.

CHAPTER FIFTEEN

The next day, Kesh and Maina woke to a light covering of snow. They helped Ginn to feed and water the sheep. Then Ginn asked Kesh if they would both help the villagers with decorating the hall for the winter solstice festival, which was by this time, only a few days away. Ginn took them to a large building on the north side of the village square. Inside, many of the villagers, including Bim and his wife, were already busy with wreaths of greenery and berries, or chains of paper and ribbon with which the hall was going to be decorated. Long trestle tables were set up for these activities, whilst around the sides of the hall, barrels, bottles, crates and baskets of various provisions of food and drink were being stacked. It was obvious that a great feast was being planned. Kesh and Maina were introduced to many new people, whose names it was impossible to remember, and shown how to make the wreaths and chains. Bim's wife took Maina under her wing and her lessons in Enahet continued while they worked side by side.

That night, a snow-storm blew in from the north. The windows rattled and draughts blasted through every gap in the thatch. Maina gave up trying to sleep and felt her way in the dark back down the stairs. There was still some fire in the grate and Maina sat as close to it as she could get, feeding it with bits of wood from the basket next to the hearth.

"What is the matter?" said Kesh from his bed by the wall.

"I can't sleep," said Maina. "I'm too cold."

"Put your cloak over the bed," suggested Kesh.

"I've tried that, but I'm still not warm enough."

"Nor am I," Kesh admitted. "I think I will have to move my bed nearer to the fire. Perhaps we should bring your bed down here too."

Kesh lit his candle and they fetched the bedding down from the upstairs room, together with the lamp. Kesh arranged the heather in a bank to keep out the draughts, and then they made up two beds on the fire side of the pile, with two pillows in the middle, and their feet facing either side of the room. It was impossible to keep out the draughts completely, as the fire had to draw in air in order to burn. Nevertheless, they managed to warm up sufficiently to lie down and sleep once more.

The next morning, the world outside the cottage window had turned white, covered in a thick blanket that hid all ugliness, lending beautiful curves to sharp corners, and hiding dark muddy tracks with brilliantly glittering purity. Maina went upstairs to dress, and found powdery snow had blown in through the hole in the thatch. It had covered the nearest corner of the floor with a layer of tiny crystals that looked like glittery white dust. It showed no signs of melting.

When Ginn arrived he took one look at their footwear and went away again to borrow some boots for them. He came back with an assortment of boots, woollen socks and gloves which he handed to them. Once bundled up in their borrowed winter clothing, they followed Ginn to the sheep enclosures. Maina gasped when she saw how few sheep were in the wooden shelters at the ends of the fields.

"We have lost so many!" she cried.

"They will probably be alright," Kesh told her. "They are most likely up against the north walls. We will just have to dig them out."

Ginn brought shovels and they spent the morning shifting snow carefully away from the cavities made by the woolly animals where they huddled together for warmth. Only one sheep seemed to have succumbed.

"She was old," said Ginn. "She probably wasn't carrying lambs this year anyway."

When Kesh translated this comment, Maina thought it was a heartless way to look at the loss. Kesh refrained from pointing out that one of the main dishes at the forthcoming feast would be roast mutton, and that some of the sheep they had brought down were already hanging in the butcher's pantry.

More snow fell before they had finished moving the sheep into the shelters. They left them with enough food and water to last the day. Then they invited Ginn into the shepherd's cottage for tea and a bite to eat. Despite the extra clothing, they came back indoors with hands and feet numb with cold. Kesh had made up the fire with fresh logs before they had gone out but they had burned away almost completely. It was a while before the kettle was singing. They sat around the fire making conversation while they waited.

"Now we have snow, it won't be long before the trappers come down to sell their furs in Odout," Ginn said.

"Oh?" said Kesh, inviting him to go on.

"They wait for the snow so that they can use their sledges. They go faster than carts. They have snow oxen to pull them. Have you ever seen snow oxen? They have feet like dinner plates and they run over the surface of the snow without sinking into it. All the Hittan children run out into the street to watch them go past. It's quite an event. Then the next day they all come back through again with their sledges empty, on their way back north."

Maina could not understand more than a few words, so Kesh had to translate.

"Where do they come from?" he asked Ginn.

"Somewhere to the north," said Ginn. "I don't know exactly. I expect they travel around a lot, hunting."

"Do they speak Enahet?"

"The traders speak some Enahet, yes, but it's not their native tongue."

Kesh was thinking that he would like to talk to these traders, and wondered if somehow going north with them would help with their journey to find the Ship Prophet's people.

"So when exactly do they come?" he asked Ginn.

"If the snow lies, they usually reach here about a half moon or so after the first fall."

The next day was the day of the solstice festival. Maina feared that, as a trainee Xouthan priestess, it would not be fitting for her to go with the villagers to their temple to witness the sunrise. Kesh decided that it might be better for him to stay away too, although curiosity burned a scar of regret into his heart. This did not, however, affect his enthusiasm for joining in with the non-religious aspects of the festival. After seeing to the sheep, Ginn, Kesh and Maina went to the hall to help with final preparations. Wonderful aromas were coming from the kitchens at the back, where mutton was roasting, pies were baking and puddings were boiling. They helped to lay the table with plates and flagons, and then were sent to the kitchens to wash and peel vegetables ready to go into the steaming cauldrons of water.

Villagers began to arrive dressed in colourful costumes, with decorations made from ears of grain and sprigs of dried berries pinned to their clothes or in their hair. Bim's wife explained that these were to represent the harvest past which, when planted, would bring the harvest future in the next round of the sun.

Bim's wife asked Kesh if Maina had brought her festival clothes with her, and Kesh explained that they had been forced to leave their luggage behind when they lost their horses. The result of this conversation was that Maina was led away by the hand and taken round several of the cottages in the village to beg for spare clothes. Then at Bim's house, Bim was sent off to the hall while his wife and two daughters dressed Maina. She relinquished herself to the control of these cheery women, who giggled when they decided this or that fitted well, and shrieked with laughter when an item was tried on and failed to come up to standard. Eventually, holding her skirts up out of the slushy snow, she was led back to the hall, where she found that Kesh had also been decked out in berries and ears of grain. His hat had been taken from him and Maina noticed that his hair had grown a little since their journey had begun. It stuck out from his head like the bristles on a soft brush, the same length all over, about a thumb's width now. It was unlike any other man's hair, but Maina decided it looked well on him. It softened his features, making him look less monkish, less like an honourary woman and more like an ordinary person. She wondered whether Ahbrem would have liked this new style on his friend.

Kesh told Bim's wife that Maina looked wonderful, and thanked the family for their generosity. The villagers were all standing near the doorway of the hall, waiting for the festivities to begin. They watched while the village councillors, including Bim, filed in and took their places at the top table. Then the villagers were called to take their places. Maina and Kesh were placed side by side, with Bim's wife and daughters opposite, and Ginn next to Kesh. Ginn introduced his family, his mother and father seated next to him, and his elder sister and younger brother seated opposite. Before the food was brought, Bim's wife gave Kesh a bottle decorated with ribbons and berries. She told him that it was a gift to be shared with Maina and that they must both drink the contents with their meal. Ginn handed Kesh a jar of preserved fruits, jultie berries he guessed, and Kesh became embarrassed,

"But we have no gifts for you," he told the company.

"Don't worry. Our sheep safe home is your gift to us," said Bim's wife. "And before the snows too. I think we should have a toast to our shepherds."

"To our shepherds," echoed Ginn's mother, while Bim's wife opened the bottle she had given Kesh, and poured some of its contents first into Kesh's glass, and then into Maina's. She finished up with a wink and a grin at Ginn's mother, who grinned back at the excellent joke they were sharing. Kesh had missed the joke, but then his Enahet was still improving, and as long as these good people were happy to welcome them, he was more than happy to be enjoying their company.

The villagers were taking turns to bring plates of steaming food out from the kitchens and lay them down the centre of the trestle tables for the villagers to help themselves. Soon, they were tucking into roast lamb and vegetables followed by puddings and pies and sauces, more than anyone could eat. The surplus was not going to be wasted, however, as any food left on the serving plates went back to the kitchens to be packed up ready to be shared out between the villagers later. After the food had all disappeared, except for sweetmeats such as the candied jultie berries that Ginn had described to Kesh, it was time for entertainment. Villagers took turns to step onto the platform behind the councillor's table and sing songs, recite poems or tell stories. Maina understood little, but realised that she might be asked to perform. As a guest, she could not refuse. She climbed up to the platform when her turn came and sang a Xouthan children's song, the only song she knew off by heart. The villagers clapped politely and then it was Kesh's turn.

He sang an Enahet traditional ballad that he had been taught as part of his Enahet lessons at the monastery. His voice was rich and unexpectedly powerful for so slight a figure. He threw it up into the rafters of that humble hall, so that it came back to the ears with the illusion of sweet harmonies.

There was thunderous applause when he finished, with the villagers banging the tables and stamping on the floor. Bim's wife nodded her approval at Maina and grinned again, and Maina felt proud to be associated with him. The Hittan villagers really seemed to like him.

Kesh, for his part, was a little embarrassed by this enthusiastic reception. After all, Morthern monks were taught to sing for the glorification of Harg, not for their own glorification in the eyes of their audience. He hung his head and raised his hands to deny the applause, but smiled and thanked the Enahets with bashful glances from side to side as he made his way back to his seat while the plaudits continued. He would hardly meet Maina's eyes as she tried to voice her appreciation. Then, more drink was poured into their glasses and Kesh forgot his embarrassment as the councillors' table was moved away from its central position and a group of musicians took to the stage. Dancers filled the empty space below them and the entertainment went on long into the night.

CHAPTER SIXTEEN

Very early the next morning, Maina woke with a start. She was cold. A sharp pain shot through her head as she opened her eyes. It was not properly light, but it was sufficient to see that she was still wearing the clothes lent to her for the celebrations the night before. At least, she still had *some* of these clothes on, but they were only loosely fastened. She decided she must have been too hot and thrown off the rest in her sleep. A sprig of berries dropped from her hair as she sat up. She reached for the corner of the blanket that she was lying on to pull it round herself. She noticed that Kesh seemed to have thrown off a good deal of clothing too, and was lying close by on the heather. She thought a Morthern monk would not like to be seen with so little to cover him so she reached for another blanket and spread it, as gently as she could over him, hoping he would not wake.

She crouched on the little hearth rug wrapped in the blanket and closed her eyes, trying to recall the reason why they had not changed into night clothes or made themselves proper beds. She remembered hazily that it had been very late when they had arrived back at the cottage after the festivities, and the hearth had contained only cold ash. Kesh had relit the fire and they had sat in front of it with blankets round their shoulders, shivering and very tired. Before the fire had properly burned up, they had pulled up pillows and lain down on the hearth-rug, back to back for warmth, but still wrapped in blankets. She could remember feeling irresistibly sleepy but nothing more. It was surely the alcohol they had consumed which had made them feel too hot in the night, for in this wintry weather the room did not get very warm even when the fire was blazing.

Maina knew she would not be able to sleep any more so she coaxed the feeble embers back to life and made tea. She sat on the floor, nursing the cup of steaming liquid in both hands to draw as much warmth as she could from it. Kesh slept on, his face childlike in its unconscious state. Maina thought of Wyn's little brother, her own nurse-brother, and how sweet he had looked when sleeping. How she wished she could be at home with them all now, safe in the care of her nurse-mother and Bradmutt, who had always been so kind to her. But when she had been a child she had been impatient to grow up, always dreaming of dancing with handsome princes, or of being whisked away to live in a magnificent palace with a wealthy king for a husband. Now she was betrothed to a prince, yet all she could dream of was being back with the people who had shown her love and had cared for her as a child.

Kesh stirred, turned on his back, and sighed contentedly. At least someone was happy. Perhaps he was having a good dream.

Her own clothes were still at Bim's house. Maina went upstairs to find something else to wear. She brought the clothes downstairs and dressed behind her blanket, to make the best of the fire while Kesh was still asleep. Soon they would have to go out and see to the sheep. Maina poured a second cup of tea from the teapot and touched Kesh's shoulder. He woke smiling but winced as soon as he tried to sit up.

"We shouldn't have drunk so much of Bim's wife's wine," Maina told him.

"The room is spinning," Kesh complained, collapsing back onto his pillow.

"Drink some of your tea," Maina coaxed. "It will make you feel better."

He took a sip of the tea and carefully lay back down.

"I am suffering only in body. My spirit feels wonderfully light. I feel as though I have had a truly blissful dream, yet I can remember nothing of it."

"You did seem to be dreaming," Maina told him.

"It was an enjoyable feast last night, was it not?" Kesh asked. "Or was that a dream too?"

"It was enjoyable, yes. Your song was ..." Maina faltered, finding it difficult to find adequate words, "very beautiful."

"I am sure that it is not my place to comment on the looks of a temple maiden," said Kesh, "but I feel compelled to say how very fine you looked in your festival clothes last night. You were the finest Enahet lady there."

"Um … thank you," Maina responded, surprised that a monk would comment on any lady's appearance, but pleased nonetheless.

They sat for a while sipping their tea, then Maina said, "If we are to be here much longer, I should make more effort to learn the language. Bim's wife is very good at telling me the names of things, but what I really need is to understand the structure of the language, so that I can speak proper sentences.

114

I wondered if you would be willing to teach me."

"Of course," said Kesh. "It would be an honour."

"Perhaps when we get back this evening you could give me a lesson."

She excused herself then and went upstairs, telling him he should get dressed but not wishing to be present when he discovered the sparsity of his clothing.

Later, while the shepherds were carrying hay and water to the sheep, Ginn asked Kesh what he thought of his brother when he had met him the night before.

"He seems a very likeable young man," said Kesh.

"My mother wants me to take him on as apprentice shepherd."

"Would that not be a good thing to do?" Kesh asked.

"I am not sure we would work well together," Ginn said. "He has never been very willing to take orders from me."

"That is often the way with brothers, I understand," said Kesh. "But surely he will listen to you on matters of shepherding. After all, you will have the authority of the council once you are officially appointed shepherd."

"Perhaps," said Ginn, "but my brother is still very young. I think perhaps he should continue his schooling for a little while yet."

"I suppose that is for your brother and your parents to decide," said Kesh.

"You would not be offended if he took your place?"

"I would not be offended. We must move on as soon as we can travel, anyway."

Ginn nodded and spoke no more.

When the sheep were taken care of, the three shepherds went once more to the hall, this time to help clear up, and afterwards Kesh gave Maina her first real lesson in Enahet.

CHAPTER SEVENTEEN

More than a moon passed before the trappers came through Hittan on their way to Odout. They announced their passage through the village with hoots and shouts, and the village children ran out into the street to watch them pass. Kesh and Maina ran to the end of the sheep pens to marvel at their snow-oxen and at their enormous sledges piled high with skins and furs and containers for provisions. Kesh told Maina he wanted to speak to the trappers and got ready to walk the few miles to Odout in their tracks.

Maina was alone for the evening. She went round to Bim's house to ask if she could help with anything. Bim's wife was preparing the evening meal and invited her to share it with them. She set Maina to peeling vegetables while she made pastry for a pie.

"Any news for us, Maina?" Bim's wife asked.

"How do you mean?" asked Maina, thinking she had misunderstood the question.

"Well, you seem to be glowing with good health. I am thinking that perhaps our little gift has worked for you?"

"Gift? Are you asking me about the bottle of wine?" Maina asked in clumsy Enahet.

"Very special wine," Bim's wife told her.

"Fertility potion," said her daughter, but Maina did not

117

understand those words in Enahet.

"There is a house in Wadderhick," Bim's wife explained, "where young couples go to find children if they have no children of their own. Sometimes these couples pass through Odout like yourselves, yes?"

Maina nodded. She had understood the words, if not the meaning.

"But our potion - our 'wine' - is a better way of solving the problem. You get your own children. Little Maina, little Kesh."

Maina thought she was beginning to catch their train of thought but, surely Kesh had told Bim that they were brother and sister as instructed by the Ship Prophet. Why would they give a drink intended to produce children to Kesh and his sister?

Maina thought she would check that Kesh had indeed told them what the Ship Prophet had instructed. She started by pointing to the two girls in the room and repeated the Enahet word Kesh had taught her for sister.

Bim's wife laughed.

"Not ga*dill* she said, emphasing the second syllable as Kesh had done "*Ga*dill," she said with the emphasis on the first syllable. The girls are ga*dillz* but I am *ga*dill to Bim. It is makky word for woman. It means I am his woman, his wife."

She repeated the word 'makky' once more.

118

Maina began to realise that Kesh's grasp of Enahet, although good, was not quite perfect. A mistake had been made. These good people had mistaken them for a married couple. No matter. No fertility potion would have any effect on a temple maiden and an honorary woman such as Kesh, other than giving them the headache they had both experienced.

Kesh arrived back at the cottage very late and told Maina to pack. He had arranged for them to go north with the trappers the next day and then to cross with a trapper guide to Wadderhick over the winter ice, which should have thickened sufficiently over the last moon or so.

Maina's first reaction was to resist this suggestion. She was just beginning to feel comfortable in Hittan, just beginning to be able to communicate. Kesh reminded her that they had been given a Task by the Ship Prophet, and to turn down the chance of furthering their progress would not be a good thing to do. She had to agree but was nevertheless dismayed at having to leave so suddenly.

"You can still use your Enahet to communicate with the trappers," Kesh told her. "They will take us to their encampment up the coast to start with. Their wives are waiting there. It will be good if you are able to talk with the women, only not so many of them will have learned to speak Enahet, perhaps."

"As we are on the subject of learning Enahet, I have learned a few new words myself this evening. For example, I learned that the word for sister should be pronounced ga*dill*. Apparently, the word *ga*dill is different, it means a woman or a wife. It is a makky word, Bim's wife said."

"Mmm … 'makky' would be 'casual' or 'slang' in the sacred language," Kesh told her.

"So you told Bim I was your 'woman'", Maina said.

"Oh!" said Kesh. "Sorry."

"…which is why they assumed we were on our way to Wadderhick to obtain a child from a 'house' there. I think she meant an orphanage. Apparently, couples often pass through Odout on their way to Wadderhick for that purpose."

"I see," said Kesh.

"…which is why Bim's wife gave us special 'wine' intended to produce children."

"An aphrodisiac?" suggested Kesh.

"I don't think so," said Maina. "She only talked about producing children. I think it was meant to be a fertility potion. Anyway, it wouldn't have affected a Morthern monk, even if it had been an aphrodisiac, would it? You are an honorary woman, afterall, and obviously in love with Ahbrem."

"In love with Ahbrem?" Kesh repeated incredulously. "Why ever would you think I am in love with Ahbrem?"

"Well, he's certainly in love with you," Maina told him. "All the maidens noticed. He follows you around like a hungry kirra-puppy."

"Ahbrem is my servant," said Kesh, drawing himself up to

his full height. "He follows me around in order to be close by when I need his assistance."

Maina did not answer for a moment. Then she repeated, "Your servant? Did you not say that, at Khoulan, all who are able take their turn?"

Kesh sank into the chair behind him. Maina's criticism had finally deflated the illusion he had been clinging to. "You are right, of course. I was told, before we set off for the Sacred Mountain, that he had been allocated to travel with me as my servant. He is, after all, a year behind me in balancement training. However, I later learned that he had been instructed to keep an eye on me. In reality, he was appointed my moral guardian. I don't mind, really. He has always been my best friend. I am only just beginning to realise how much I relied on him for guidance."

"But Morthern monks are still honorary women, are they not?" asked Maina. "They are allowed onto the Sacred Mountain only because they are accepted as honourary women."

"I do not really understand what you mean by that term."

"The monks do not bear arms, so they never break the fourth law, and they also ..." Maina hesitated to speak explicitly to a fellow religious devotee, "prefer the company of men."

"You mean you thought ..." Kesh began to understand. He took a deep breath. "Denying ourselves the company of women is not the same as 'preferring the company of men', as you put it. "

121

"All I know is that Xouthan men would not be capable of perpetually denying themselves the company of women," said Maina, "unless they did happen to prefer the company of men."

"We achieve our devotional state by meditation, by attaining and maintaining balancement each and every day," said Kesh. Indeed, those monks who, as you put it, 'prefer the company of men' are highly revered, for they have to maintain balancement in the face of constant temptation. Only ..." Kesh trailed off at this point.

"Only?"

"Oh, nothing," said Kesh, not quite ready to confess that he had not meditated on the evening of the festival. Ginn had taken him from the hall to dress him and to pin solstice decorations to his clothes, and he had not been home to sit before the fire at sunset. 'Surely,' Kesh thought, 'one missed night could not have made a difference.'

It was getting very late and they were still not packed so little sleep was had that night. Maina wanted to say goodbye to Bim and his family and to Ginn before they left, and to thank them all for their kindness, so they went round to the Toegrath's house early the next morning.

"But you don't need to go," Bim's wife told her, holding her arms out to embrace her. "Stay another moon and you will see."

"We cannot," Maina said sadly. "Kesh has arranged for the trappers to pick us up today."

122

Kesh asked Ginn anxiously, "Your brother will help you with the sheep, will he not?"

"Yes," Ginn answered. "I have agreed to take him on as apprentice but I have told him that, if he doesn't do what I tell him, I will cancel the contract."

Kesh and Maina went back into the cottage to collect their travelling bags. Already it looked empty and impersonal. It was not until they were leaving that Maina realised how homely it had been. A jar of jultie berries sat on the window-sill. Maina asked Kesh if he was going to leave them there.

"I suppose I had better pack them," he said. "I would not like Ginn to think his gift had not been appreciated."

"Why did he give you a jar of fruit?"

"I had asked whether they had jultie berries here," Kesh said. "Actually, it was to feed a seacrow which had been begging for crumbs out on the hills. I thought it might have been following me and I remembered that Ahbrem fed jultie berries to a crow near Khoulan. He convinced me that it was the same crow following us because it carried the stain on its beak. It followed us all the way to the Sacred Mountain and Ahbrem kept feeding it like a pet. I haven't seen the Hittan crow since that day on the hill though."

Kesh squeezed the jar into the top of his bag and the two travellers stood waiting by the cottage window for the sounds of the trappers, ready to go out into the street to meet them.

CHAPTER EIGHTEEN

The seacrow had flown southwest, struggling to keep ahead of the wall of smoke-grey storm clouds that was closing from the north. It had taken him more than two days, despite flying cross-country and ignoring the roads and settlements where he might otherwise have picked up some easy crumbs.

As he soared over the peaks of the Dinash Mountains, with the rain lashing against his feathers, balancing on the updraught of air sweeping up the mountain sides, he looked across to where the Khoulan monastery sat serenely on the fertile lowlands between the mountains and the sea. There was smoke coming from the monastery buildings. This did not alarm the seacrow. The weather was chilly and smoke to a seacrow meant cooking and food scraps to eat. But as he drew closer, it became obvious that the smoke was coming not from a chimney but from the still smouldering timbers of one of the four buildings that formed the quadrangle. The haystack, which had been in the corner, was completely gone, while the feed store lay empty, its splintered door leaning crookedly on twisted hinges.

Approaching the monastery slowly from the north was a group of about a dozen riders on very large cam-horses, led by a rider bearing the king's standard. In the centre of the monastery courtyard was a coffin draped with a deep blue cloth bearing the royal insignia on one corner. Two more undraped coffins waited under the shelter of the cloister eaves. Monks on the top of the north wall of the monastery shouted the instruction for the gates below them to be opened. This was unusual, as the gates were normally left open throughout the daylight hours. With visitors approaching, the seacrow hoped there would be food on offer before too long and he alighted on the ridge of an unburnt part of the roof.

The king handed his spear and sword to one of his soldiers as he approached the monastery gate. Each soldier then deposited his weapons against the outside of the wall before riding behind the king into the courtyard. Once inside, the entourage parted, the riders guiding their horses to take up positions in two lines on either side of the quadrangle, at a respectful distance from the coffin. The king dismounted, removed his helmet and stepped forwards.

"Dear, gentle Uncle Calim," he said quietly. Then he raised his head and shouted, "Those Xouthan dogs will pay for this!"

The Khoulan monks said nothing. They had begun to gather in the courtyard and now stood in small groups facing the coffin of their dead mattouk with bowed heads.

"Who is leader here now?" the king asked of the silent clerics.

The scripture master looked at the music master with raised eyebrows. The music master quickly shook his head and looked down at the ground. The scripture master was left to speak for the community.

"Kesh of Khoulan was appointed our mattouk designate," he told the king.

"Excellent," said the king. "And where is my nephew? I do not see him here."

"Kesh of Khoulan is on sabbatical with the Community of the Sacred Mountain," the scripture master told him. "We sent word, of course, but the answer back was that Kesh of Khoulan is presently away completing a task for the Prophet of the Burning Ship. A messenger has been dispatched to find him ..." The scripture master coughed and quickly corrected himself. "That is, I mean, to give him the news. We hope every day to see his prompt return."

"Perhaps we had best not wait on a man whose whereabouts do not seem to be known." said the king signalling to his men.

Six of his followers dismounted and stepped up to the coffin. Some of the monks recognised that it was the king's eldest son acting as lead bearer and were pleased to see their last mattouk so honoured.

"Let's get on with it," the king said to the monks. "Where do you want him?"

After a little hesitation amongst the monks, the scripture master again took the lead.

"This way," he said, and turned to go out of the north gate. He led the procession round the walls to the burial ground on the eastern side of the monastery, where a grave had been dug in readiness against the eastern wall.

The coffin was rested at the grave side while the scripture master recited the traditional funereal texts. The music master gathered the choir to deliver the haunting Morthern 'Chant for the Dead'. Then the coffin was lowered into the ground.

A final prayer was said, petitioning Harg to accept the soul of his departed servant, as the rich red Khoulan soil was thrown back into the grave pit. Garlands of greenery were then heaped onto the resulting mound. The heavy mountain of cloud that had chased the seacrow from the north could wait no longer and burst its first wintry splashes onto the heads of the funeral party just as the wreaths were being laid.

"Will you come in for refreshment?" the scripture master asked the king nervously.

"Thank you," said the king and he followed the scripture master back into the courtyard. The empty trestle table that had borne the coffin was quickly taken apart and carried into the refectory, where the mattouk's table was already laid with bread, cheeses and cold meats underneath a bright white cloth. The monks had prepared cold food in advance, as the exact time of the king's arrival could only be guessed at. The music master and the scripture master both sat with the king and his son to eat.

"I want you to come back with me to Ahbresk," the king said, including both monks in his gaze. "You will be safer there. You are too near the coast here. Too short a ride for marauders landing on the beaches. I can find you temporary accommodation at the palace until we can build you a new monastery."

"Oh, your majesty, that will not be possible," said the scripture master bravely.

"But I will make it possible," said the king. "What do you mean?"

"We are a Community of the Sacred Mountain. The shadow of the Sacred Mountain touches the bell tower of the meditation hall on solstice day. We are already as far from the Sacred Mountain as we can be."

"Very well," the king sighed, a little annoyed. "Then I'd better send you a cohort of soldiers to make sure you don't get attacked again."

The music master coughed uncomfortably, not quite brave enough to speak.

"It's alright," the king assured him. "They will build their barracks outside your sacred ground."

At this point a young monk arrived with a large teapot. The king waved him away.

"Have you nothing stronger?"

The scripture master nodded to the monk who returned with a flagon of wine form the cellar. This proved to be more acceptable.

"Is there anything else you need, besides protection?" the king asked the scripture master.

"Our grain has been taken and all our hay burned."

"Take note, Emish," the king said to his son. "I may not remember all I am told if this wine is as good as it tastes."

"It is our best vintage," the scripture master said.

"Anything else you need?" asked the king.

"Merciful Harg spared our kitchen stores," said the scripture master.

He went on to describe the attack, which had come at night.

"We think it started with lighted arrows sent into the hay stack. It was burning fiercely before anyone awoke. We think burning hay must have wafted up onto the roof where the mattouk's quarters were housed. Two monks went up to get him out, but they did not return. The fire was too fierce, or perhaps they were suffocated by the smoke. The rest of us drew buckets of water from the well and passed them along a line. Two brave young fellows climbed up onto the roof of the meditation hall and threw water down onto the mattouk's quarters. They succeeded in quelling the flames eventually, but not before the three inside had perished. It was not until morning that we found the grain store empty and arrowheads in the yard. We did not realise that the fire had been the result of a raid until it was all over."

"You can rest assured your mattouk's death will not go unanswered," the king said grimly.

Neither monk spoke to remind the king that a peace-loving mattouk of a community which did not allow its members to bear arms, nor even allow arms to be born within its gates, would not want his death to be avenged. They shifted uncomfortably in their seats, both thinking the same thought, but neither opening his mouth. This was, after all, a family matter for the king and neither dared to comment on it.

"Well, thank you for your hospitality," said the king after

his second flagon of wine. "I will leave four of my guards to stay with you until the soldiers get here. Would it be possible to house them within your walls?"

"If they continue to leave their arms outside, as they have done today," answered the scripture master.

"Master," the king said, fixing the old man solemnly in his gaze. "I want to appoint you temporary mattouk to take charge until my nephew returns."

The scripture master shook his head energetically. "No, no, Your Majesty. I am too old."

"Then it must be you, music master," the king said, turning to the other senior cleric.

He also shook his head. "I am not worthy of that task, your majesty."

"Then you will have to decide by vote. Let each monk in the community write down the name of the man he would follow. Let no man write down his own name. Count the votes for each name. Announce the results. Repeat the process until one man has the votes of more than half your community and let that be a binding decision. You must have a leader by the time I send your soldiers, for their captain must know which of you to answer to."

In the courtyard one of the king's men brought an arrowhead to show him and spoke to him in the Morthern language.

"Your Majesty, these arrows are barbed like the Cweel arrowheads," he said. "I'll warrant these were islander marauders."

"That's as maybe," said the king, "but you can be sure who put them up to it. I heard the Xouthan snake has betrothed his daughter to that obnoxious chieftan's son, Thrull of the Southern Isles, the one who goes round calling himself the Prince of Benethan. That's where this attack has come from, make no mistake. The Xouthan emperor wants the Morthern monks turned off the Sacred Mountain and access denied to all Mortherners, as it was before the last war. We will have to put a stop to his ambitions before they go any further. I want a plan that we can put into action by the first bud of spring. Emish, my son, we have some talking to do."

The seacrow watched the king and his son leave the monastery and ride northwards across the lowlands, bowing their heads against the sleety rain. They followed their standard bearer, but had four fewer soldiers with them. The crow came down from the roof to glean what he could from the scuffed-up earth of the courtyard. He then flew up to the roof again to spend the night against the monastery's kitchen chimney. He crouched up against the south side sheltering from the wind. He was disappointed to find the weather almost as bad at Khoulan as it had been in Enaha.

The next morning he set off to fly south for Xoutha, where the winters were always milder.

***

Xoutha was peaceful. Its people were unaware of the Benethan raid in Morth or of the Morthern king's assumption about Xouthan involvement. The emperor's daughter was

131

not expected home for many more moons and the emperor knew nothing of the Task that had taken her off into foreign lands. The rumours that the Prince of Benethan already had a wife and a family on the islands had not yet reached his ears. He looked forward eagerly to his daughter's marriage, when Xoutha would gain an ambitious and energetic ally and when hopes of a grandson to rule the empire would come one step closer to realisation.

CHAPTER NINETEEN

Maina and Kesh heard the shouts of the trappers as they drove their snow-oxen into Hittan village. They quickly stepped out into the street to wave them down. The trappers pulled up their snow-oxen with a flourish and took Maina and Kesh on-board separate sledges, perching them on top of the provisions they had bought in Odout. Maina was wrapped in furs by the driver of her sledge. He warned her in Enahet that they would be travelling swiftly and the wind would chill her if she did not keep the skins wrapped tight. She sat on a cushion made out of a bolt of cloth.

The driver gave a shout and a shake of the reins. They trembled in the air just above Maina's head. The oxen lurched forward and were soon running at full tilt. Hiding from the wind that whistled past her ears, Maina pulled the furs up to her nose and watched the scenery pass, snowy cliffs and beaches against an inky sea. She tried to quell the pangs of regret at leaving the friendly Hittan people and her anxiety at venturing out once more into the great unknown.

The land was transformed into a world of featureless blinding whiteness that made the sea look deep and dark. However, the beauty of this contrast soon began to lose its power to fascinate. Lack of sleep began to take its toll and she found herself dipping into dreams and then waking in a mild panic before remembering where she was.

The sledges pulled up after a little while. Kesh was getting bored and had cajoled his driver into letting him have a go at driving the oxen. Maina had no such inclination. The snow was rushing by beneath them far too quickly for her to want to be balanced on that narrow board at the back of the sledge.

By evening time, they had reached the encampment where the trapper women and children were waiting. The driver took the harness off the snow-oxen and let them wander off. Maina commented on this and was told that they always came back for their morning feed and that, even if they didn't, they could be easily found by following their trails. They had boney plates on their noses with which they pushed aside the snow to get at whatever was underneath. They were rapacious eaters and would consume lichens, mosses, grass, heather or any other vegetation they could uncover. Their noses left marks in the snow like wobbly snail trails, radiating out from the point at which they were released and Maina could see that they would, indeed, be easy enough to follow.

Maina was taken into one of the tents of the encampment and introduced to her driver's wife and family. The wife was told that the guests were paying generously and to be sure to cook enough supper for both of them. She answered him in their native language and Maina could not understand anymore of the conversation but she seemed happy enough to accommodate them. Her driver went out again, leaving Maina with his family. She offered in Enahet to help with preparing the meal but the offer was refused and she was asked to sit by the stove to wait. She looked around at the tent, a huge domed construction made of wood and skins and surprisingly warm for a temporary structure. The chimney of the stove reached up through a hole in the top of the dome. Bed rolls were stacked all around the sides, along with boxes and barrels of provisions. Above her head, around the stovepipe, hung sausages and dried or salted joints of meat suspended from the wooden roof supports. Two small children who had been playing on the other side of the stove, now openly stared at her, one head round each side of the stove-body. She smiled and said hello in Enahet but got no response, just the steady stares. She waited. Eventually her driver returned, this time with Kesh in tow who was told in Enahet where to hang his outdoor furs. They ate. Maina sat on the women's side of the tent and Kesh opposite with the driver and his son. It was a stew, tasty enough but with more meat and fewer vegetables than Maina was used to. Afterwards, Kesh was taken out to sleep in another of the tents, as they could only squeeze in one extra sleeping space in each. Maina slept fitfully next to the trapper's wife, with her driver snoring on the far side of the stove.

The next morning, they were given a kind of tea and breakfasted on salted meats. Then they went outside and Maina watched as two planks fastened together with a triangular gusset of leather were wedged open and pressed into the snow to form a v-shaped trough which her driver filled with crushed grain. He gave a piercing whistle and very soon snow-oxen came running out from the nearby woods to jostle one another for a share of the grain.

"Precious," her driver said, indicating the grain bag. "Traded. Also, if we let them eat too much they cannot run."

Kesh came to look at the trough.

"Is it not a truly wondrous contraption?" he said, his face glowing with the enthusiasm. "So simple and yet so effective! Do you know, I am now seeing things that even Mattouk Calim has never seen? He fascinated us students with tales of his travels but he only went as far as Odout. He saw the trappers but he did not travel with them as we are doing now. I am indeed a fortunate man."

The snow-oxen were harnessed while they ate and led to the front of just two sledges, which had been provisioned and loaded with a folded tent and a stove together with the trapper's spears and bows, ready for the next stage of the journey. The trough was lifted out of the snow and a few remaining grains were emptied carefully back into the grain sack.

The journey that followed was speedy in velocity but slow in time. Many miles must have been covered each day but always there were many more to go. Instead of the days drawing out after the solstice, they seemed to get shorter because they were travelling north. One morning a blizzard blew in before they woke, preventing further travel. The whole day was spent crouched in the tent, feeding the stove only just enough to keep it going so that the fuel would last until they next came to woodland. The next morning, one side of the tent was buried under a snowdrift and had to be carefully dug out before it could be packed. The trappers told them they were lucky to be held up only one day. Trappers were sometimes stuck out in snow for half a moon at a time.

At last, the days seemed to be drawing out again and the snow began to get wetter. By the power of a magic beyond Maina's understanding, the sledges were now travelling with the sun rising on their left hand side and setting to their right. She did not recall them making any turns. The travellers were taken south to an encampment of Tejwan nomads, who were of a different culture to the trappers and lived by herding their own variety of snow-oxen rather than by trapping and trading. The trappers stayed one night and then asked Kesh for payment. He gave them what they asked and they looked pleased but surprised.

"I think you were supposed to haggle," Maina told him

The trappers in turn paid the Tejwans for their hospitality and took their leave. Only one of the Tejwan nomads spoke any Enahet so it was difficult to communicate with them. Kesh managed to explain that they needed to get to Wadderhick. The Tejwan chief drew a map and, through the one Enahet speaker, told them to walk always towards the mid-day sun and eventually they would reach their destination.

Kesh asked how long it would take them to walk there.

"Many days," was the reply.

"Does anyone here have horses for sale?"

The reply was a shake of the head.

"Are there any traders who might travel there soon?"

Another shake of the head.

"Is there a settlement nearer than Wadderhick?" Kesh asked.

"Yes, several."

"How long would it take to walk to the nearest settlement? Could we do it in a day?"

"A man might do it in a day, but …" the translator and the Tejwan chief both looked at Maina, taking in her slight frame and pale face.

"Then we had better make a start," said Kesh.

He bought strips of dried meat from the chieftain's wife and she threw in two of the pancakes that served as bread in those parts. They filled their flagons at the nearby stream, where Kesh had seen the nomads collecting water, and then they were ready to start.

CHAPTER TWENTY

They walked all day through slushy snow across almost flat countryside. Just when Maina thought she was going to have to tell Kesh she could not walk another step, they saw a plume of smoke reaching up into the sky ahead of them. As they came to the top of a small rise, they found themselves looking down into a river valley. The river was a wide, dark band against the snow, strangely luminous in the gathering dusk. On the other side, dotted across a darkly wooded slope were the lights of a scattered community. As they drew closer, dogs could be heard barking somewhere on the far side, the sounds echoing across the valley. The imagined warmth and hot food in these houses drew them on. They followed the road down to the river where footprints seemed to disappear into the blackness of the water. They both gazed across forlornly.

"It is a ford," remarked Kesh.

"So it would seem," replied Maina.

"The snow has been melting. It may be deep and dangerous."

"What's the alternative?"

"Wait here till daylight. At least we will be able to see where we are going."

"But that will be so long to wait," said Maina. "I'm exhausted. Cold and hungry too. I'm not sure I can keep moving that

139

long yet I feel that, if I stop moving, all warmth will drain from me."

"Well ..." said Kesh, thinking. "Perhaps there is a bridge. Perhaps we should walk along the bank and look for one."

"I can't walk any more, I'm sorry," said Maina. She swayed a little and made Kesh think she was about to sink into the snow. "And I don't think there will be any bridge," she went on. "This is the main route south. If there is no bridge here, then there is no bridge." She made as if to sit, one hand out behind her to feel for the bank.

Kesh grabbed her by the shoulders. "You cannot sit in wet snow Maina. Here, put the bags together and sit on them."

She sat and he stood, both of them listening to the river splashing over the stones, watching the lights twinkle on the other side, dotting the slopes of the black ridge that now seemed to tower against the sky as the darkness grew.

"What about your flame meditation?" Maina asked.

"No wood here," Kesh replied.

"Plenty of wood over there," she commented helpfully.

"So I see."

"I'm getting colder already," said Maina, trying to stand up. Kesh caught hold of her arm and helped her up. "I will have to keep moving or else lie down and sleep forever."

"I am not sure this is proper behaviour for a Khoulan monk

but I will offer you my arm, if it is of any help."

For the first time in all the miles they had covered together, they now walked close, side-by-side with arms linked. They stepped slowly along the riverbank, first walking downriver and then turning and walking back up. As they passed the point at which the track disappeared, a post loomed ahead in the gloom and attached to it was a rope that ran steeply down the bank, dipping into the water. Kesh let go of Maina in order to investigate.

"I think it is a guide to get across the river."

"The water is deeper here," remarked Maina. "I don't think this is a guide to the ford. Perhaps it's for a ferryboat. We have a ferry like that across the river near my home. It's operated by the ferryman pulling on the rope."

"I do not see any boat," said Kesh.

"It will be over the other side for the night," Maina told him. "Perhaps we could shout. The ferryman might hear."

They tried shouting across the river but got no response. Their voices echoed back at them and seemed to get lost in the dark. Indeed, there were no lights at all on the opposite bank at the level of the river. It seemed unlikely that the ferryman lived at the riverside.

The prospect of spending the night walking up and down in the snow did not appeal to Kesh and he was uneasy in his mind because Maina did not seem well.

"I will walk across and fetch the boat," he announced.

"Kesh, it is too dangerous," Maina replied.

"I could take the magic torch that Ship gave us."

"He said only to use it in emergencies," Maina reminded him. "He said it will only last a little while."

"I think this may be the emergency that the torch was meant for," said Kesh. "We cannot stand around in the snow all night."

"Please be careful," Maina begged. "Find a stout stick to test the depth as you go."

"As you pointed out before, the wood is on the other side."

"Let's look around at least. There might be old posts or sticks buried in the snow."

Maina started to scuff the snow around with her foot, while Kesh searched his bag for Ship's magic torch. Next to the post that bore the tow rope, Maina found an old post lying on the ground. It was not ideal. It was stouter and shorter than a staff should be but Maina insisted that Kesh take it.

Kesh stood on the bank where the track led into the water and felt around with the post. He picked out a stone near the surface and put one foot cautiously onto it. He then searched with post and torch to find the next foothold. Again, Maina begged him to be careful. She stood on the bank watching the tiny light bobbing up and down as Kesh felt his way across step by step in the midst of the splashing water.

Kesh made slow progress but stepped successfully from one

large stone to the next until he judged he was about two-thirds of the way across. Suddenly, one foot slipped and his boot filled with icy-cold water. The shock of it nearly took his balance. It was so cold that it made his bones ache. He could hardly believe that water could be so cold and still be liquid. Soon the other foot was wet too and in the wet boots his feet had less grip on the stones than in dry ones. He thought about taking the boots off altogether. After all, his feet could not get any colder. But he could not carry boots and stick and torch, so the boots had to stay on or be lost. He slipped and stumbled and struggled over the remaining stones, breathing prayers to Harg to fetch him safely to the other side. Eventually, he felt the mud and snow of the opposite bank and gratefully hauled himself up onto it.

He sat on the wet snow for a moment, as he had told Maina not to do, in order to get his bearings and to empty each boot of muddy water. He then walked a little way along the bank and found, as expected, a boat tied up to a post and the other end of the thick rope coming up out of the water to meet that same post.

'Here is the means to fetch Maina across the river,' he thought to himself but his training forbade him to simply steal or borrow the boat. 'Now I must find the ferryman.'

He found the place where the track from the ford came up out of the river. It climbed up the hill steeply, bearing to the right. Kesh followed it but he switched off the magic torch, as its light seemed to be growing weaker already. He soon came to a small house made of mud with reed thatching. A light showed inside and Kesh knocked at the door. A man opened it and looked Kesh up and down, taking in the sodden boots and the strange clothing which, though it might have been of

143

a similar quality, was subtly different to his own. This man did not speak Morth or Enahet, or the sacred language, so Kesh resorted to sign language.

He put two hands together by the side of his face and tilted his head against them to indicate sleep. He took a single gold coin out of his pocket to indicate that he was willing and able to pay. At this the man nodded and stepped out of his house to point to lights further up the hill. Kesh put up a hand to stop him, which he ignored, until Kesh frantically waved his hands to attract his attention again. Kesh held up the index fingers of his two hands next to one another, which was the Morthern way of indicating two people. This did not seem to be understood, so Kesh tried holding up two fingers of the same hand and then, muttering 'Harg forbid that Maina shall ever hear that I have described a Xouthan priestess thus', made a sand-glass shape in the air with both hands, starting wide, sweeping down to a narrow waist and curving out again. Then he pointed in the direction of the river, arching the path of his finger in the air in the hope that this would indicate that she was on the other side.

Mercifully, this seemed to be understood and, after collecting a coat from his house, the man turned to walk down to the river. He unhitched the boat and pulled on the wet rope. The boat slid out easily into the darkness and soon they were on the far bank. Kesh's feet were numb with cold in his wet boots and he slipped clumsily as he tried to get out. He called Maina's name but got no reply. Stumbling along the riverbank in the dark, he began to fear that she had wandered off and collapsed somewhere in the snow, but eventually he found her, still sitting on the bags, hunched up and shivering.

Kesh hesitated. His training rendered him totally unable to

put his arms around her to warm her as she needed, especially in front of this stranger. The ferryman brushed past him. He scooped Maina up as if she were no heavier than a bag of feathers and carried her to the boat. Kesh picked up the bags and followed, wondering why he now felt resentment towards the stranger.

The ferryman took them into his own home to sit before the fire while he went out again. He returned with a woman who beckoned them to follow her and they went up the hill to another house. Here they were given hot tea and wrapped in blankets before a blazing fire, while the woman warmed up a fish soup which she served to them with chunks of bread and cheese.

"Are you feeling better, now?" Kesh asked Maina.

She said she was and thanked him for asking but she still looked pale. After Kesh had sat before the fire for his meditation period, the woman showed them to a bedroom where there was a proper bed for Maina and a couch for Kesh. Here they passed the night in better comfort than they had experienced since they left the village of Hittan.

CHAPTER TWENTY ONE

The seacrow had been living in Xoutha for more than two moons, hiding from the winter cold. He had begun to grow restless.

The worst of the weather would surely be over now. Time to fly. He should have gone inland to look for a mate. Instead, he first flew north to the Sacred Mountain and perched on the balustrade of the balcony of the community's Great Hall.

Ahbrem was on the balcony, leaning on the railing, looking out to sea deep in thought, but he recognised his little friend immediately.

"Sakki, welcome!" he greeted him. "Where have you been?"

He put his hand in his pocket and pulled out a draw-stringed bag of nuts that he had kept since the journey from Khoulan. He shared them with the seacrow.

"Much has happened since I saw you last, Sakki. Bad things are brewing up in Morth at present. Bad, bad things. There will be battles fought before too long and the mattouk designate is the only man with influence enough to stop them." He hesitated momentarily, wondering if the seacrow could understand anything he was saying. Nevertheless, he continued, "There are rumours of a plan to repeat the historical attack on Ghaba but you can be sure that it will not end there. The Xouthans will seek revenge and war will be declared. Then young Morthern men will be sent to become soldiers and if they are not home by autumn the crops will rot unharvested in the fields. Many of them will never go home because they will lose their lives in battle and many families will be thrown into mourning. The whole land will sink into darkness. I wish you could find Kesh for me, little friend. We have such dire need of him now."

At this familiar name, the bird had taken off from the balustrade. He had balanced a moment on the updraught from the mountainside. Whether he had caught a scent, or a thought, or simply went to find a mate, Ahbrem never knew, but he watched the bird fly inland in the direction in which Kesh and Maina had first travelled.

The seacrow had flown on and on away from the coast. He did not wish to go further north for fear of bad weather, but, being a west coast crow, he was driven eastwards by the urge to move inland to mate. He did not, however, find any cause to stop his eastward progress. No female crows came near him, tempting him to tarry. Truth was, he was a little bit too early for them and, though he often stopped to poke about at the backs of inns and settlements, there were no really good places to find food. He flew so far eastwards that he eventually found the sea again but this time a little further down, south of Odout. He happily breathed in the familiar salty air. He opened his wings to the lifting currents, soaring out over the grey water. He flew out to an island and landed to follow a flock of gulls along its beaches, picking at their leftovers amongst the pebbles. When he took to the air he was again drawn eastwards but the vast expanse of water was a danger to a bird that could not land on it. He flew out a little way but, seeing no land, he turned back and set down on the little island once again. He spent another day there but spring fever got the better of him and, early the next day, he set off.

He flew many, many miles and grew extremely weary. He began to fear that he would never see any land again. He flew low, skimming the waves, unable to summon the energy to rise up out of their reach. Eventually, he came to a sharp rock reaching skywards from the angry foam at its base, where the sea was patiently working to pound it out of existence. There was no food but he rested and drank out of little pools of rainwater tainted by salt spray. He did not want to have to fly so far again, so the only way was eastwards, in the hope that land would be nearer in that direction. He no longer dreamt of females. He thought only of the sanctuary of a good beach, where food might be found under surf polished stones.

By the end of the next day, he had come to a group of islands. He rested on the nearest one and ate well by catching live food for himself in rock pools on the shore. When he felt stronger, he took off again. He circled and gained height and saw to the east a dark strip of land, stretching left and right as far as his eyes could see. Before night fell, he was on the beach just north of Wadderhick and, on the next day, he set off inland to look for a mate.

***

After spending a night in the relative comfort of the riverside community, Kesh suggested that they should rest a day or two with the people there but Maina wanted to press on.

"You looked ill last night," Kesh argued.

"I was just cold and tired," she told him. "I am not ill. I don't want to stay here. I want to find a place where they speak Enahet. I look forward even more to meeting the Ship Prophet's people so we can speak the sacred language."

They bought a large sausage which was hanging from the ceiling by their host's fireplace and Kesh, holding up a piece of the bread he had been given with breakfast, offered another coin. The lady brought out a whole loaf wrapped in a calico cloth, which he put into the top of his bag. He would have bought more food but he could only buy what he could see, by pointing at it. They refilled their water flagons and set off southwards once again.

Kesh walked more slowly than the day before, trying not to hurry Maina, still convinced she was not well. They followed the track through the trees and up the hill on the south side of the river. When they reached the top, the landscape ahead looked altogether more inviting. It was undulating countryside with hills to the south and it was dotted with wooded areas. There were patches of pale green where the snow had melted from the grass of the pastureland, and it reminded Kesh of the hills around Hittan.

As the sun passed its zenith, the track led them into woodland, and they were soon on a south-facing slope where there was no snow at all. Kesh took his cloak off and laid it down by the side of the path. They ate some of the sausage and bread and rested for a while, before moving on. The path went deep into the wood. Every now and then Kesh stopped to make sure Maina was still following.

"You are looking a little better now, I think," he told her. "Perhaps your illness is on the wane."

"Kesh, I was not ill," said Maina to his back. "I … I think I am with child."

Kesh stopped in his tracks and turned around.

"With child?" Then, after a brief pause, "Is it not customary in Xoutha to wait until after marriage?"

"Indeed, it is," said Maina. "Nevertheless, I think I am suffering the symptoms described by our teachers as being indicative of a coming child."

"So the Prince of the Isles did not deem it necessary to wait?"

"He did not come near me," said Maina. "This is not Lord Benethan's child. If it were his, I would be big as a house by now."

"Then … whose child is it?"

"Kesh, you have been with me almost every minute since we left the Sacred Mountain. Whose child can it be?"

"I do not know," said Kesh, thinking of all the people they had met on the way. "Ginn Gilleth's?"

"No, it is not Ginn's," said Maina, actually laughing at the ridiculousness of blaming her unfortunate condition on such an innocent.

"So you are telling me it is a miracle child?" said Kesh. "A product of Enahet magic, perhaps, or is it an act of Tarn?"

"An act of Harg, perhaps," muttered Maina.

Kesh was affronted by this blasphemy and said nothing.

"I thought it was Enahet magic at first," Maina started slowly, sorry that she had offended him. "But now I have had time to think it over, I am not so sure. Kesh, do you remember the night of the solstice festival?"

Kesh frowned, trying to anticipate the coming words.

"When I awoke the next morning, I noticed that I had thrown off some of my clothes."

Kesh backed away from her a step, but she went on, "I noticed that you also had … discarded some clothing. Do you remember, Kesh? I had pulled a blanket over you but you must have noticed, when I went upstairs, that you ... Do you remember?"

Kesh took two more steps backwards.

"No!" he said in disbelief and then he began to remember, "You witch! You harlot! You seduced me! You broke my vows!"

Kesh turned away but carried on shouting at himself, throwing his hands up into the air.

"The masters warned us. They told us it was so. The sweetest maidens are always the most dangerous. They are always out to break your vows, they said. Women see you as the ultimate challenge, they said. We make ourselves unattainable and therefore we become the most desirable of men. Why did I not take note?!"

He turned back to Maina.

"Why?" he asked her. "Why did you do this to me? Out of hatred for Morth? Or do you find the prince you are betrothed to so repulsive that you used me to escape your promise?"

He turned his face skywards, looking up through the tracery of the winter branches, as if looking to find an answer in the heavens.

"You have destroyed me. I was going to become language master at the monastery. I was going to inspire the Khoulan boys with thrilling tales of my adventures, just as Mattouk Calim had once thrilled me. I was going to teach them Enahet, I was going to teach them about the world beyond Khoulan." He turned to face Maina once again. "Did you know that I am mattouk designate? I was meant to take over mastery of the whole of Khoulan once Mattouk Calim retires. Now I am sullied, I am not worthy to step through its doors." He paused as he looked at the open-mouthed woman before him but he got no response. His head dropped and he stood disconsolately addressing the earth beneath his feet, "My dreams are dust!" He turned his back on her and walked away.

Maina sank to her knees on the path. Was it true? Did she so fear Benethan that she had unwittingly encouraged Kesh to do this to her?

She had already spent many nights worrying about what the consequences would be if her suspicions were true, if she really was shortly to give birth. The betrothal was certainly in jeopardy, as Benethan would be expecting to marry a virgin, but that was a problem for another day. Knowing that there was an orphanage not far away, she had already decided that she would leave her child at Wadderhick. Was it possible, therefore, that this event would have a worse effect on Kesh than on herself?

'But wait a moment,' she said to herself. 'Kesh did not tell me that the Khoulan monks were not proper honorary women until after the festival. I did not know, had never imagined, that he could be seduced. So how can I have set out, unwittingly or otherwise, to do that?'

Furthermore, she was sure neither her teachers at the Sacred Mountain, nor the Ship Prophet, would have sent her out on her own with Kesh if they had known he was not a true honorary woman. If they had known that he was just an ordinary man, who relied solely on a little meditation every night to keep him from temptation, they would never have allowed her to go out on a task alone with him.

She looked up and drew breath to put these points to Kesh but she saw only the empty pathway between the trees.

She got to her feet and went a few paces along the path.

"Kesh?"

She went a few more paces, a little quicker this time, and called out loudly. The only answer was a bird flapping out of the tree-tops. A few more steps but still Kesh was nowhere to be seen. Well, she would just follow the path, she decided. She walked for a while but no Kesh. Then she came to a fork in the path. To the right was a wider grassy cart track but the narrower path on the left looked more used. She bent down to look closely at the grassy track and could see no sign that any feet had passed that way, so she chose the other route. But as she walked further without seeing, or hearing, any sign of Kesh, the doubts began to mount. Was she going the right way? Had Kesh deliberately left her behind? Did he really mean to abandon her in the middle of a wood in a foreign land where she could neither understand what was spoken, nor make herself understood? Had he really been that angry with her?

If so, his anger was misplaced. His accusations were unjustified and she must find him and regain his friendship. She was growing increasingly uneasy about the path she was following. Tears stung her eyes but a sense of indignation kept her from openly weeping. Then, with bleary vision, she saw a figure coming towards her. Her heart leaped but she realised almost immediately that it wasn't Kesh.

"Kip-tee," the man said as he approached.

Maina froze but the man came on towards her.

"Tond son," the man said. "Kin sinah?"

"Do you speak the sacred language?" Maina asked a little shakily.

"Mmm, i traheh," the man said. "Kin sinah?"

He started to walk around her, studying her. Maina saw that he was carrying an axe, his hand round the balance point near the axe head and that he had a large bark-stripping blade in his belt. He was probably just a woodsman but her fear grew. He paused a moment in his tour, standing close behind her. His breath was in her ear. It stank of stale pipe smoke. A wave of revulsion made her spine tingle as she felt him lift a lock of her hair. He sniffed it, then let it fall. She stayed absolutely still until he had completed his tour and stood facing her once more.

"Beet uha Enahet?" she asked in desperation.

"Enahet? A little," he said in Enahet. "I learn in school."

"Have you seen a man?" she asked him. "I have lost my friend."

"No, no man," he said.

"There was a fork in the path," Maina said, her voice trembling. "I don't know which way he went."

"Fork?" the man repeated.

Maina pointed behind her and gestured with her hands to show the paths dividing.

"Ah," the man nodded. "You come my house. I find your friend."

Maina did not think that going to his house sounded like a good idea. She stalled for time while she tried to think of a way of avoiding it without annoying him.

"How will you find him?" she asked.

"I know woods," he said. "Where birds ... ," he replaced the

Enahet for 'fly' with a flapping of his hands for wings, "there man walk. You go my house?"

"Can I come with you to look for him?" Maina suggested, thinking this would be better than going to the stranger's house.

"No," he told her. "You stay this path. I look other path. My house, this path." He pointed back along the path the way he had come.

"Very well," said Maina. "So I will walk along until I come to your house, while you look along the other path. Is that right?"

"Very good," the man said and started walking away from her. He looked over his shoulder to check that Maina was doing as she was told.

Maina turned and walked slowly up the path. The track narrowed and the trees touched their bare branches overhead. She came to a pile of logs left across the path. They were green and dripping with mosses, as though they had been there a long time even though the path on the other side looked just as well trodden. They were surely there to bar the way, to discourage visitors. She grew more uneasy. She stepped over the logs and walked on. Eventually, the trees opened out and a cottage could be seen on a rise. Maina did not want to wait in front of the house. She did not want to be seen until she could see the woodsman. She wanted to know whether he had Kesh with him before she showed herself.

The path continued past the cottage and she followed it until it went into the trees again. She stood on the far side of a thick-trunked tree and waited. As she had feared, the woodsman was not away long, not long enough to have looked far along the other track.

"Lady?" he called out in Enahet. "Lady, where are you? I have found your friend."

Maina chanced a cautious sideways glance around the side of the tree trunk but the woodsman appeared to be alone. He went into the house and continued calling for her. He came out again and started along the path, still calling. She could hear him getting closer. She pressed herself harder against the tree and held her breath, silently praying to Tarn to maintain her concealment. The woodsman came along the path almost as far as the very tree she was pressed against. She heard his rasping breath, more rapid now, and held her own, knowing that if he merely turned his head he would be sure to see her. The woodsman stood listening and quietly drew the long blade from his belt. Should she fight? Should she submit? She must think of her child now after all. The woodsman stood stock still but she imagined that his ears and nose were twitching, waiting for the sound or smell of her to come to him. Her heart thumped so violently she thought that sound alone would be sufficient to give her whereabouts away.

At this moment Kesh appeared, walking up the path towards her tree. He spotted Maina and was about to step towards her when Maina shook her head and put her finger to her lips to silence him. He looked from her, to the woodsman and back. He nodded imperceptibly and walked on up the path.

"Good afternoon," he greeted the woodsman in Enahet. "You have not seen my wife, have you? I have lost her in the wood."

"Your wife?" repeated the woodsman, sliding the blade surreptitiously back into his belt. "No, I see not anyone."

"She is slender with long hair. She must have gone down this way," said Kesh, indicating the part of the path leading away from Maina back past the woodsman's cottage. "Is this your house?"

The woodsman followed him.

"How you lose her?" he asked Kesh.

"Oh, we had a little tiff," said Kesh. "You know how it is!"

"I understand this, yes."

Maina glanced around the tree trunk as the voices grew more distant. She saw the backs of both men. She stepped out quietly onto the path and then ran down it as fast as she was able. After a little distance she had to slow down to catch her breath and, as soon as she did, she began to regret that she had left Kesh alone with the woodsman. He still had the blade in his belt. What if he attacked Kesh to get rid of him? How could she help Kesh get away? She kept on walking, feeling more and more guilty but reluctant to turn back and risk a second encounter with the man she had just escaped. She started to argue with herself. Perhaps this man had no evil intentions. Perhaps he had just been trying to help. But he had lied about having Kesh with him when he had been calling to her and he had lied to Kesh, denying that he had seen her.

Maina found herself at a junction where the path she was on joined another, giving her an equal choice of left or right. The best course of action, she decided, was to hide again and wait a while to see if Kesh was following her or if the woodsman was going to be the first to find her. She stepped off the path and hid behind another tree but it was not a large enough tree to hide her completely. Furthermore, a seacrow alighted on the path and stared at her, resentful perhaps of her hiding in his domain. She found herself putting her finger to her mouth again, as if she expected it to understand her command to stay quiet. Perversely, it started to flap and squawk. She shrank against the woodland side of the tree as footsteps thudded on the earth. She breathed a sigh of relief as she saw Kesh coming into view but he approached from the right. He had not come down the path she had just trodden.

"This part of the path goes round in a loop," he explained. "Come quick. Let us find the way out of here. I think we have to take that track that goes down the hill."

CHAPTER TWENTY TWO

The crow had taken flight and was now squawking above the path that came down from the woodsman's house. Kesh grabbed Maina's hand and pulled her along, going back the way he had come. They ran a good distance with the squawks of the seacrow following, taking the grassy track down the hill. Eventually, the squawking grew more distant before finally stopping. When they came to the bottom of the hill they found the landscape opening out into a valley with a river running through it. There was an arched bridge where the track crossed at a narrow gorge. Once they were on the other side, Kesh stopped and Maina bent, hands on knees, to catch her breath.

"Are we close to the sea?" asked Maina, panting. "This wood is full of seacrows."

"We are not too far from the coast," Kesh told her. "But the seacrows may be moving inland for the breeding season. You do not fear them, do you?"

"Fear them? No! Why should I?" she said.

"I understand the Xouthans regard them as harbingers of bad fortune."

"Just superstitions. I don't believe in them."

Kesh smiled, amazed at how this heathen priestess could sometimes show such level-headedness. Suddenly, he sank onto his knees before her.

"Maina, I am so sorry," he said, hanging his head. "I said awful, terrible things to you. I did not mean them. Please, if you can find it in your heart, I beg you to forgive me."

"That does not matter now, Kesh." Maina told him, holding out her hand for him to get up. "I thought you had left me, but you came back for me. That's all that matters. I now realise how much I rely on you. I can't complete the Task without you. I can't even travel safely on my own. I need you, Kesh, or I will never get back home alive."

"I am so sorry that I lost you. I was so absorbed in my complaining, I was being selfish. All I could think of was how my life would change. As soon as I realised you were not following me, I came to my senses. You are my responsibility now, you and your child. I will never abandon you again, I promise. We will forget the Task. We will go back to Enaha. There is a shepherd's house in the hills …"

"I can't," Maina interrupted him. "I would love to go back to Enaha and live with you but it isn't possible."

"What do you mean?" he asked.

"Kesh, I have responsibilities too. I have a duty to fulfil my promise to my father. I have to marry the Lord Benethan, for the sake of the empire. The child must go to Wadderhick, to the orphanage."

"No!" said Kesh.

"It is the only way. We can complete the Task while I wait for the birth and then we take the child to Wadderhick on our way back to the Sacred Mountain."

Kesh was silent for a moment, mulling over what she had said but he could not accept her plan.

"I cannot let any child of mine languish in an orphanage in a foreign land," he told her. "You may not be able to fulfil your responsibilities towards her, or him, but I have nothing else left to me now. I will take the child to Enaha and bring her up on my own."

"Kesh, I've been thinking about your hopes for the future. I think you should still go back to Khoulan to become a teacher."

Kesh shook his head but she went on before he could speak.

"I think your vows are still intact. Am I not right in thinking Morthern monks hold purity of the soul as the principle criteria for the office? Well, I think that your soul is still completely pure. The gods may have used your body to produce this child but it is clear to me now that you knew nothing of it. You did not intend to do the deed, neither do you have any memory of having done it. It was, rather, done to you by the Enahet potion and by my presence next to you that night. I should have had more sense. I should have behaved more responsibly. You were partly right, at least some of the blame is mine."

Kesh shook his head again.

"No, no," he said. "If I had as much sense as Ahbrem has, it never would have happened. He never would have allowed me to sleep so close to a woman. Not even in the same room. And he would not have allowed me to drink so much at the festival, potion or no potion. If he had been with us we would not have lost the horses. We would have caught the last boat, we would have delivered the message to Ship's people and been on our way back to the Sacred Mountain by now. I am not worthy of the life I had planned for myself. I will relinquish my position as mattouk designate, I will recommend that Ahbrem take my place."

"Don't give up on your dreams just yet, Kesh. There is still the Task to complete. Becoming a mother does not bar me from completing my training and, if I can still become a temple priestess, I don't see why you could not still become a Khoulan teacher. If you help me to complete the Task, you will have earned your right to the title of Mattouk Designate of Khoulan."

"But I have broken my vows."

"Then retake your vows," Maina told him. "From this moment on you can vow to remain celibate again. It is only the same as a warrior vowing to give up his arms. Is it not true that a Morthern warrior can become a monk if he promises never to take up arms again? I know that you are pure in your heart, Kesh, and pure in your intentions."

Kesh frowned. Having spent all afternoon running round in circles in the woods, desperately looking for Maina, he had grown accustomed to the idea of relinquishing his mattoukhood for a life in her company. But his offer had been rejected. He was floundering about in total confusion, now. He felt a dire need for meditation, whether or not he could still claim the right to call himself a monk.

"We had better travel on," he said. "We have to find

somewhere to stay tonight, whether we go on with the Task or not."

They walked on, following the road that led away from the bridge. As the sun was sinking towards the west, they saw a settlement in the distance. They were confident that they could reach it well before dark so stopped to rest a while. Kesh lit a fire and, after his meditation, they shared the last of the bread and sausage. A seacrow joined them and Maina threw it some crumbs.

"Right," said Kesh. "Let us see if this one follows us."

He searched in his bag for the jar of jultie berries and opened it. He rested one wet syrupy berry carefully on a nearby stone. The crow hopped forwards and tried to pick it up. The berry burst immmediately, squirting purple juice on both beak and stone. Undeterred, the bird swallowed the remaining flesh with relish. Kesh offered some berries to Maina, ate one or two himself, and then resealed the jar.

CHAPTER TWENTY THREE

The travellers and their new pet seacrow reached Wadderhick after another three days of travelling. Many more people spoke Enahet in the port as seafarers and traders regularly crossed the sea to Odout. Maina felt at more ease with people she could talk to and they stayed several days at an inn, throwing crumbs out from their windows for the seacrow with the berry-stained beak.

They found a draughtsman who had mapped the land to the south. They purchased a copy of his map and planned their route to the land of the Ship Prophet's friends. The shortest road took them up into the mountains. They had been in view in the distance since the day after Kesh had forded the swollen river in the dark. Sailors in the port tried to sell them passage southwards, assuring them that it was the quickest way to arrive at their destination, but Maina's fear of the sea drove her to think up excuses for not boarding a ship. She convinced Kesh that, in her present condition, she would be unbearably seasick. He agreed that they should take the mountain road and they gathered supplies for the journey. Kesh bought two elderly cam-horses, and a bag of tilly-oats to supplement the wayside grazing which he thought might be sparse this early in the season.

On their last day in Wadderhick, Maina asked Kesh if he would go with her to visit the orphanage. She persuaded him that she needed to see the place, even if he did not want the child to be left there. She was charmed by the children but not by the conditions they were kept in. Her instinct was to take a child away, or indeed all the children, rather than to plan to leave a child in that establishment. She had to agree with Kesh that the orphanage was not going to be the answer to her problem. They put two of Ship's largest gold coins in the alms box and left.

"Do not worry," Kesh said to her. "We will find another way. I will take her, or him, with me to Morth. I will find a nurse-family. If the baby is male, he can go to Khoulan for schooling. We take boys as young as seven rounds there."

Maina was, nevertheless, anxious about this obstacle to her plans and spent the first part of the ride to the mountains deep in thought. She half hoped that the problem would just go away, that the child she thought she was expecting would prove to be a figment of her imagination, that the symptoms she had been experiencing were merely a result of the hardships they had faced on the journey. On the other hand, she found herself praying to Veyer, goddess of fertility, to protect her unborn child. With time, her prayers to Veyer outnumbered her prayers to Tarn to end her dilemma.

Kesh remained his usual cheerful self. He stopped to talk enthusiastically with traders going in the opposite direction on their way to Wadderhick. He asked them questions about the places they had come from, trying to get a feel for the territory they themselves were heading for.

The terrain became more hilly as the day wore on and the horses flagged as the cart track climbed the slopes. They passed by some peasants working on a piece of land by the roadside, and Kesh tried asking if they knew where they could find lodgings for the night. There was no response to his request in Enahet but, when he tried the sacred language, one of the men seemed to understand.

He asked Kesh what their business was and Kesh told him that they had a message for the kings of the south from a possible kinsman. At this the farmer straightened up and gave Kesh his full attention.

"Is that so?" he said. "The kings want to mine the rocks around here. My father says no. He sent me to give them that message. I spent some time in their country. That's how I came to learn their language."

"What can you tell us about them?" Kesh asked.

"I witnessed how easily they live," the young man answered. "Everything I saw excited me – new machinery, new ways of doing things. I think we should join them. My father is very ill. If he dies, I will say yes to the mining."

"Why does your father not want the mines?"

"He thinks they will ruin the land, and bury the good cropping soil under heaps of spoil."

"And you do not agree?" Kesh asked him.

"Once we have a share of their wealth, we won't need to worry about losing a little of our land."

"I see," said Kesh, not wanting to reveal what his instincts told him. "So are there any inns on this road?"

"Not for quite some distance," the farmer told him. "If you want to reach a bed before dark, you'd best come up the mountainside with us. We will be finishing for the day quite soon. My father will be pleased to see some fresh faces. He doesn't come down the mountain now at all. Only those who can run back home before the mountain sands run out are allowed down here."

"Mountain sands?" Kesh repeated.

"It is an old time-piece. It has been used for many years to judge who can safely come down from the sanctuary of the fort. If we come under attack, a trumpet is blown by a look-out. Anyone who can beat the sands is judged to be able to outrun an attacker, unless the attacker also happens to be practiced at running up mountainsides. The elderly, the sick and the very young are always kept at home."

"I don't think I'll be able to run up a mountain," Maina said.

"Guests are not required to pass the test," the farmer laughed. "My name is Hernst, by the way, son of chief Ackhart of Ahn Dehar." He bowed to Maina, and Maina and Kesh gave their names.

"What about the horses?" asked Kesh. "Will they get up the mountain?"

"Yes," said Hernst. "But you may need to dismount and lead them up the final ascent. It is a rather narrow path, and steep."

Maina began to have misgivings about agreeing to climb the mountain, but the farm workers were loading their tools into an ox-cart and it was soon time to go.

"I hope you have some stories for my father," Hernst said to

Kesh. "He loves to hear stories."

"You could sing him your song," suggested Maina.

Kesh shook his head. "I can only sing it in Enahet."

"I can assure you that it sounds most beautiful in Enahet, even when the listener does not understand the language."

CHAPTER TWENTY FOUR

The travellers were led off the road and along a track, into a large belt of evergreens. Off this track, hidden amongst the tree trunks, was a barn. The ox-cart and tools were stowed on one side of it, while the oxen were fed and watered and tethered in stalls on the other. Hernst suggested that the travellers start the climb up the mountain with him while the others finished tending to the animals. They rode behind him along a needle-strewn path through the trees until they came to a look-out spot where the view opened out below them like a counterpane stretched across a lumpy bed. The sun was sinking in the sky and mounds and ridges were accentuated by shadow, bringing into relief the shapes in the landscape that remained secret by the mid-day sun.

Kesh admired the height of the look-out post and was told that they were not yet halfway upto the fort. They were advised to dismount as the path steepened and soon the woodland opened out into a landscape of beck-heather and rock. In places, the path itself was fashioned into narrow steps too small for the horses' hooves so that they had to be led through the heather alongside. In other places the rock seemed to be shattered into flattened shards that slipped over one another underfoot, making the going difficult for horse and two-footed traveller alike. Maina plodded silently upwards, thinking how much more terrifying the path was going to seem in descent. The workers they had left behind seeing to the oxen overtook them, stepping lightly from rock to rock like mountain goats, but Hernst walked up slowly, stopping to wait for Kesh every now and again, and then waiting with Kesh for Maina.

It began to grow colder and as the path rounded the mountainside, the wind whipped into their faces from the west. They stopped to catch their breath and Hernst pointed out the road and the belt of trees they had recently passed through. Seacrows were circling the tree tops below, disturbed by the newcomer, the stranger crow, who had chosen not to follow its crumb-givers further up the mountain. Ahead loomed a great wall built around the whole mountain top and the path led to a large gateway blocked by a door made up of whole tree trunks lashed together. Hernst shouted and, after a while, with much creaking of rope and scraping of wood on rock, the door began to open. They were led through it into a tunnel built through the enormous wall.

'This was not a peaceful land,' thought Maina. 'These people lived in fear.'

They were given food and Kesh sat before the fire to meditate while Hernst asked Maina about the Ship Prophet. He confirmed that the four kings in the south did indeed match her description and that he thought they may well be of the same kind. This was very encouraging for Maina. The longer their journey, the more she feared that it would be in vain. Now she had new hope that the Task could be completed successfully.

Afterwards, they were taken to a timber building constructed on a base of stone and mountain rock. It was decorated inside with ornately embroidered hangings. Here they were shown into a modest room with a pallet against one wall on which lay Hernst's father, Chief Ackhart. He was pale and thin and covered in bruises, scars and scabs.

Hernst translated as the chief spoke into his ear. "He wants

171

me to explain that these bruises appear whenever he is touched. He wants you to know I am not beating him. He still has some sense of humour, you will observe." The old man tugged at his sleeve and Hernst continued, "He would very much like to hear how you come to be passing by. He wants all the news you can give him."

Whether it was pity for the sick man or the mountain beating it out of him, Kesh decided to tell these two men the truth about who they were and why they were there. The conversation lasted late into the night, punctuated by the Enahet song and a Morthern lament from Kesh which the old man told his son he wanted sung at his funeral. Kesh was much moved and felt that his trust had already been rewarded.

The next morning, they left the fort with Hernst and the field workers. Maina felt unusually queasy and took Kesh's arm several times on the path down, while Hernst led both their horses. Kesh also admitted to feeling a little less than fit but blamed it on the exertion of climbing the mountain the evening before and on the short night and consequent lack of sleep.

They said goodbye to Hernst at the turning onto the road and thanked him warmly for his hospitality. He refused their offer of payment, saying they had already paid with their songs and stories. Hernst told them to visit again whenever they were passing and went off to work in the fields while Kesh and Maina turned the horses southwards. The road climbed higher up, to a pass in the mountains. On the far side they stopped to absorb their first view of the land of the four kings. Even from this distance it was a busy landscape, criss-crossed by many roads and dotted with tall smoking chimney stacks.

The travellers went down the pass to the undulating lowlands and reached the first settlement quite quickly. They passed a smithy and saw, through the open doorway, the red glow of his fire and a gush of steam as some hot metal object was thrust into a trough of water. There were horses and people waiting outside for his services. A little further on there were bakers, cobblers, butchers and other trades people all busy buying, selling or fashioning some kind of product.

A little further down the road was another settlement. Here, were all the kinds of traders they had seen in the first village but in addition, a basket weaver and a potter. They came to the fourth such settlement before midday. No question of a day's walk to get to the next bed, as in Tejwan territory. All these villages were full of busy people. They met many tradesmen on the roads, but Kesh soon stopped expecting a conversation from their fellow travellers. Although many of them seemed to understand a little of the sacred language, they were always in too much of a hurry to stop for gossip. The travellers stopped at an inn for food at midday, and found it full to bursting with noisy customers supping large jugs of ale. Their host wanted an unusual quantity of gold for his fare and Maina suggested they should buy supplies for the rest of the day from a baker's shop. Even there the food cost much more than it would have done in the north or in Enaha.

Further southwards down the road, they passed a large hillock of black soil and saw a line of men with blackened hands and faces coming out of a gate, while a line of less blackened men seemed to be waiting to go in. They were told that this was a coal mine. Neither Morth nor Xoutha had coal mines and although they did have mines which went deep underground for metal ores, neither of them had seen a mine operating on this scale before.

Two more days of travelling southwards brought them to the City of the Four Kings. Here, they asked directions for the palace. The city was bigger than any settlement either of them had ever seen. Riding from the outskirts to the centre took longer than riding between settlements on the road south. While they were plodding along the main route, their mounts were suddenly startled by a mechanical flying horse which exited rapidly from a street to their right and then glided off ahead of them. It appeared to float just above the road but made a good amount of noise in doing so. The seacrow flapped up above the buildings and flew away into the sky. They asked a bystander about this strange device and were told that it was probably ridden by one of the kings themselves, or by one of his senior officers, but they could not explain how it worked.

The country held so much strangeness that Maina began to dread meeting the four kings. Kesh was taking in the wonder of the city with his usual wide-eyed enthusiasm. They found the palace and stood outside its walls discussing how they would introduce themselves. They had a sealed letter from the Ship Prophet but he had asked them to deliver it personally to one of the kings and then only if the king looked sufficiently likely to be of his kind. Therefore, they had to remember exactly what the Ship Prophet had told them to say and word their request for an audience carefully.

They approached the large main gate that was set prominently in the high wall and Kesh pulled on the bell-rope. A wooden slat was pulled aside to reveal a pair of eyes in a partial face.

"Yes?"

"We have been sent to request audience," Kesh said. "We have a message from a man, a human, who calls himself Ship."

"No one gets audience. Go away."

The slat closed again.

"Wait, please," Kesh said. He raised his voice and shouted to the closed gate, "Just give the name Ship, please. We will wait."

They did wait. A long time passed. The sun moved towards the west. Maina sat on the ground, her back to the wall. The horses grazed the raised banks on which the wall was built.

"They are ignoring us," she said. "Try ringing the bell again."

Kesh pulled on the rope again and shouted but got no reply.

"We had better go and find lodgings," he said.

Maina stood and picked up her bag. She had just got hold of the cam-horse she had been riding when the slat was pulled aside again. A face cautiously appeared, the eyes looking sideways at the travellers by the wall. It was a human face.

The slat quickly shut again and, although Kesh shouted, "We have a message from Ship," there was no response.

"We could wait just a little longer," said Maina, letting her horse lower his head to the herbage again.

As the sun was beginning to set, the slat opened up once more and the face of an ordinary person announced:

"You are cordially invited to dine with the Four Kings."

CHAPTER TWENTY FIVE

The commotion and arguments which the mention of Ship's name had caused within the palace and which had given rise to the delay in deciding what to do with these visitors, were smoothed out and now lay hidden beneath a veneer of order and regal dignity. The kings had all agreed that the only way to decide whether these visitors had anything to do with the man they had once known, the one who had been called Ship by his friends in a previous life, was to question them thoroughly.

The visitors were shown to rooms the like of which they had never seen before, with walls of a brilliant whiteness and smooth as polished marble. It was suggested that they might like to bathe in preparation for the dinner. Maina was taken aside by a female servant and shown how to operate equipment called heaters and taps, in a room where water flowed from she knew-not-where straight into a large bath and was able to drain again through a hole in the base. This servant asked her diplomatically if she had any "more formal" clothing. As Maina had long since abandoned the robe she had originally packed for the occasion, she had to admit that she did not.

The servant left her to bathe while she went off to find something that might be suitable. When she returned she helped Maina to dress and arranged her hair in an elaborate style. In the mirrors that hung on all the walls, Maina saw a reflection of the young woman she had been many moons ago, the emperor's daughter. Outwardly she looked like that young woman but inwardly she knew it was a very different person looking back at her from the glass.

She was shown out into a corridor and found Kesh waiting. He also looked very different out of his travelling clothes. Maina had only ever seen him in his peasant guise or in his monk's robes before. Now he stood in civilian clothing and looked fine enough to be a prince himself. He held out his arm for Maina just as Thrull of Benethan had done when he had led her out to dance at their betrothal all those moons ago. Maina was glad enough of some physical support as they were led through many corridors and then out along an internal balcony. This walkway looked out over a great dining hall where a long table was already laid with candles and flowers, plates and cutlery, all set out on a cloth so white it seemed to be luminous. They came to the top of a flight of stairs from which Maina could see a dais and four human men all dressed in extravagant silks, furs and feathers.

As they descended these steps, Maina clutched Kesh's arm tightly, afraid that she might stumble and lose all dignity. At the bottom a footman asked for their names and titles. Kesh gave his name as Kesh of Khoulan in Morth and Maina, not wanting to give away her identity completely, was announced as a student priestess of the Sacred Mountain.

They were shown to seats on one side of the table while, on the other side, the four kings sat in a line and openly stared at them. The first two courses of the meal were eaten gratefully by the famished travellers but, after that, too many courses were offered and they were glad to answer questions and only pretend to eat.

"So how did you come to know this Ship?" the first king asked.

"He is our Ship Prophet. He lives on the Sacred Mountain," Maina answered.

"And do you know," the second king hesitated mid-question, "how he came to be there?"

"He arrived in a ship which now lies at the bottom of the sea," Maina told them.

"It was a ship which fell from the sky in flames," Kesh said. "To us he is the Prophet of the Burning Ship."

Maina frowned and shook her head, as if to apologise for her companion's outlandish ideas.

"He is an icon for two different religions," she explained. "We Xouthan's don't believe in ships falling from the sky. We think the Morthems saw the ship against the fiery colours of the sunset glow."

The kings looked at one another but made no comment.

"How long ago was this?" asked a third king.

"Many generations," answered Maina.

"We thought he was immortal," said Kesh. "He is very, very old but he says that now he is ageing and will eventually die."

"That is why he has asked that one of you come to visit him," said Maina.

"We have a letter," said Kesh, bringing out the rolled epistle that had lain in his bag so many moons.

There was a long silence during which the kings passed the letter from one to another. The travellers exchanged an anxious glance. Neither knew what Ship had written.

The kings muttered to one another and then one said:

"We will give this matter our consideration. We will let you know in a day or two what we intend to do. In the meantime, please accept our hospitality. The east wing is at you disposal and we will instruct our servants to see to all your needs."

With that two servants stepped up to take the chairs the travellers had been sitting on, from which they understood that they had been dismissed.

They were led back to the corridor where they had met again after dressing. Kesh was taken into rooms on the left and Maina was shown the rest of the suite of rooms on the right, which included a bedroom, a day room and the bathroom. The servant helped her to undress and put a silk gown round her shoulders. It was Anthrakat silk, elaborately embroidered. She recognised the style and knew how expensive it was to buy. It was all very luxurious. The rooms reminded Maina of her home in Xoutha, only they were bigger and more lavishly furnished. She felt she should be enjoying her surroundings, revelling in the sumptuous extravagance, as she once would have done, but it meant nothing to her now. Once the servant had withdrawn, she looked around her at the pointless opulence. She went to her bag and took out the book of Sacred Texts that Bradmutt had given her. She leaned against one of the walls, opened the book and began to read, muttering the first few lines and then reading out aloud.

"When trouble threatens all around
Seek the solace of a good, true friend."

"Well, I would if I could," she said to herself.

She slid down the wall and sat on the floor hugging her knees, feeling very alone. She knew she would not be able to sleep. She wanted to talk to Kesh, find out what he thought the kings were saying. She had spent so much time with him over the last few moons. In fact, she had only been separated from him for that short time when she was lost in the woods. Now he was on the other side of that grand corridor, he might as well have been in a different country. She could not possibly step out and go to him. There would probably be servants about and it would not look good.

Then her thoughts strayed to the servant who had helped her to bathe. She would surely have noticed her condition. Her child was still small enough to hide under her loose travelling clothes and also under the flowing gown she had been dressed in for dining with the kings but, naked, the shape of her swelling belly was becoming obvious. Would the servant gossip? Would there be speculation flying around the palace as to whose child this could be? Were the reputations of the monk and the maiden already being destroyed?

She was tempted to go to Kesh but knew she could not and it would not be wise for him to come to her. Nevertheless, as she sat against the wall, she was willing him to knock at her door. Surely, by now he would know her well enough to sense when she wanted him with her. But no knock came and eventually discomfort forced her to get up from the hard

181

floor and to try the overly soft bed.

***

The weather in Morth was easing. Birds began to sing in the gardens of the capital city and the king's plans for a repeat of the historical raid on the Xouthan Fort at Ghaba Head were well advanced. His eldest son, Emish, requested the honour of taking revenge for his great-uncle Calim's death. The king consulted with his military leader, General Byack. Having weighed up the risks he reluctantly gave his consent. The plan was, after all, for a surprise attack to mirror the raid on the Khoulan monastery and the risks to the attacker were judged to be far lower than would have been the case in open battle.

Archers, footsoldiers skilled with spear and sword and the crew of three naval vessels were moved into place in the port of Fullabish, which was the most southerly in the country and closest to the Xouthan border. The timing of their sailing was calculated to deliver them to Ghaba just before dawn. The raid was a success for the Mortherners, in that many Xouthan soldiers perished and the fort was heavily damaged, but a stray Xouthan arrow slipped into Emish's throat between his breast plate and his helmet, and he was slain.

On hearing this news, the initial despair of his father quickly turned to fury and he sent a declaration of war to the Xouthan Emperor. Maina's father was also in a state of furious indignation at the sudden unprovoked attack on Ghaba and readily accepted that a state of war now existed between the two of them. The emperor sent word to the Prince of

182

Benethan, inviting him to visit Zoradetra.

Thrull was welcomed at the palace and a dinner was given in his honour in the presence of the whole court. After he had drunk a couple of goblets of their finest wine, the emperor broached the subject that was uppermost in his mind.

"You are my future son, Thrull, Prince of Benethan. Indeed I love you like a son already. I hope you will not mind if I ask of you the kind of favour I would ask of my own son, had I been fortunate enough to have one."

"I would be honoured, Sire," said Benethan, slightly wary of what was coming.

"You may have heard that our troublesome neighbours in the land of Morth have declared a war against us. Indeed, the sly she-dogs attacked our fort at Ghaba before they had even warned us that they were contemplating war. Notwithstanding, we are ready for battle and mean to take the fight back to them on the border as soon as all our troops are rallied. I would therefore like to take this opportunity to invite you, Prince of Benethan, my future son, to take up arms by the side of your future kin and people and to fight the Mortherners along with us. I plan to retake the Sacred Mountain and perhaps a few southern counties of the Morthern lands. What say you to a corner of the mainland to call your own?"

"I like the sound of it very much, my noble father," answered Thrull.

"So will you fight with us?"

"Yes, gladly, but I have only a handful of well trained men."

"The number of men is of no consequence. To see your men stand shoulder to shoulder with the Xouthan warriors will give them all stout hearts."

"In that case, just send me word and I will send you back my finest."

"Dear Thrull, I will be forever grateful."

Thrull turned away from the emperor, smiling to himself. Could his little raid on Khoulan have been the catalyst for this? It was beyond his wildest expectations.

In the coming moon, troops from both Morth and Xoutha moved towards the border lands like iron filings to a magnet and there they prickled at one another from look-out towers and guard posts all along the line of the Visca Mountains.

**

No one was sleeping in the palace of the four kings on the night of Kesh and Maina's arrival. Kesh was standing by an open window holding the crust of bread he had slipped into his pocket at dinner, wondering what had happened to his pet since he had been startled by the mechanical flying machine. The four kings were still at the table in the grand dining room and sat long into the night, talking about the possible meaning of the visit and the letter that the visitors had brought. At first, they argued about who should go with them, not one of them being willing to travel over the sea to see the old man. Then, when one of them volunteered to go, another was driven by jealousy to also volunteer, until each had convinced himself that he would be the best one to make the journey. It took most of the night for them to finally decide on a workable plan and to choose which one of them should execute it.

In the morning an envoy was sent out to find a sea captain who was willing to sail to Anthrakat and the kings went into their stable to choose a horse to carry the chosen king through Anthrakat and Xoutha to this Sacred Mountain. Over that day and the next, items were packed and unpacked, as the chosen king tried to decide what he would need for such a journey and what could be carried on one horse. Then it was decided that a second horse should go, as a packhorse, and everything that had been unpacked was packed up again. By the evening of the second day, it was announced to Kesh and Maina that the king calling himself Kevin was to accompany them and that they would board a ship to sail to Anthrakat on the following afternoon.

Maina was relieved to be leaving this place, where there was nothing to do but wander around her rooms or walk up and down in the garden. Most of the time, she had been left entirely on her own. At dinner on the second night Kesh told her that he had found someone who played the peg-lute and he had been learning to pick out a tune. She wished she had Kesh's talent for making friends and getting involved with the things that were going on around him.

Meanwhile, the seacrow was avoiding the city and its terrors. When he had been startled by the noise of the mechanical flying horse he had flown right to the edge of the conurbation and there found a group of seacrows foraging on a beach.

They seemed happy enough to allow the visitor to feed with them. He had even flown inland a little way with one of the females, who had allowed him to flirt with her because she was intrigued by his foreign-sounding voice, but she had abandoned him as soon as her usual mate turned up. Her mate was a well-fed, sleek feathered cockbird and Sakki was no match for him. He had returned disconsolately to feed on the beach with the juveniles and he remained there all the time that his crumb-droppers stayed in the palace.

Maina soon realised that the king's announcement about sailing to Anthrakat meant that she was about to be taken on a long sea voyage and her relief at the prospect of getting out of the palace began to turn to anxiety. She spent the night in earnest prayer to Gorlan for the safety of the whole ship full of heathens she would shortly be travelling with, begging protection from storms and sea monsters and leaky ship's timbers and all the myriad of other occurrences that came into her head that she could foresee leading to their demise.

Dressed once more in their own clothes, now washed but faded and shabby, Kesh and Maina rode their Wadderhick horses in the party that rode from the palace of the four kings to the dockside. Together with the king called Kevin, they boarded a large sailing ship. It was a hive of activity, busy with deckhands stowing luggage and sailors getting ready to cast off. The cam-horses were as nervous as Maina and had to be cajoled into stepping onto the gangplank. The passengers stowed their packs in tiny cabins each fitted with a bunk and a locker but little else. The horses were taken to a stable below decks that already stank from the animal excrement of previous trips. Back on the main deck, the enormous masts reached up as if to pierce the blue of the sky. When the sails were unfurled, they would dwarf the body of the ship.

Maina joined Kesh leaning on the railing. He was watching a seacrow picking at detritus on the harbour wall.

"Is that our crow?" she asked.

"I am not sure," Kesh said. "If he follows the boat, I will be more ready to say it is."

The crow did indeed follow the ship, landing frequently to pick up offerings of food and to take shelter from rough weather. They soon lost sight of land and passed through a barren world of only sea and sky. There were no signs by which to judge whether they were actually making any progress. Maina had to put her trust in the ship's captain to find his way from one side of the featureless ocean to the other. She found she fared better if she was out in the fresh air when the ship was riding heavy waves. She spent all the stormy days clinging to the rails, lashed by wind and rain, but at least not feeling so nauseous. She anxiously watched Gorlan's fickle mistress fling up her arms in furious indignation each time the ship's bow pierced her heaving forms. While the sea was yielding the ship was surviving, but would the sea eventually cast it aside in a fit of temper and break its back with a single powerful blow? Or would she send a wave so huge that, on entering it, they would all be swallowed into the body of the ocean? She remembered being blown towards the rocks on the maidens' journey to the Sacred Mountain. How bruised and broken they all would have been if the boat had not been turned around and swept out to sea in time. Perhaps the most dangerous part of the journey would be at its end. Maina shuddered and offered up more fervent prayers to Gorlan and also one to Veyer, to protect her child and bring it safely through this voyage.

Kesh spent most of his time playing dice with the crew, or practising on a peg-lute he had borrowed from one of them, but sometimes he came and stood with her by the rail and looked out over the sea. They talked deeply at such times, exchanging childhood memories, discussing events they had witnessed in the past, comparing attitudes taken by their two cultures, growing in understanding and regard with every conversation.

One day when the weather was fine, Kesh found his companion looking unnecessarily serious.

"Maina, the sea is calm, the sun is shining but you still look pale and anxious. I am worried about you."

"It is not only the raging sea I fear."

"What then?"

"You remember me telling you that I was brought up by Bradmutt and his wife because my mother was dead?"

"I remember."

"Well, she died through giving life to me," said Maina. "Kesh, she died in childbirth and I can't help … "

"I understand your fears. But, Maina, you are not your mother. You do not have to fear that you are treading the same path. You are Maina. You are unique. Your destiny is not going to be the same as your mother's. You are not married to an emperor and you are not High Priestess. At least, not yet. Your life is already different."

"Whether I live or die, I cannot be a mother to this child. And he is not going to have Bradmutt and Martha to look after him. What will become of him?"

"He will not have Bradmutt and Martha but he will have me. I will make sure he has the best of care."

"But to be sent to a monastery at seven. It is so young."

"I was not much older than that when I first went to Khoulan. It was not so bad. After a little while, Khoulan became my home and the monks became my family. And when Ahbrem joined the monastery, I had all the companionship I could ever need. He was like every brother to me, both my follower and my guide. Anyway, the child ..." Kesh's voice trailed off.

"Yes?"

"Oh, nothing. I was just day dreaming."

Maina turned away from him and looked around her.

"You're right. The sea is beautiful today." She lifted her eyes. "And the sails are so white against the blue of the sky. I could almost get used to sailing if the weather would stay good."

"Perhaps we have come through the worst. Perhaps we will see land before we see another storm."

"That would be wonderful. I do hope you're right."

Maina looked daily for signs of a new coastline in the west

but was always disappointed. Then, after what seemed like a moon's worth of watching, she heard the shout from the look-out that signified land had been sighted. She could soon see for herself that a dark line now separated sea from sky on the distant horizon.

They disembarked at a small port on the Anthrakat coast. Although this country bordered Xoutha, Maina had never before set foot within its boundaries and she did not speak the local language. Luckily the king called Kevin spoke a few words. He arranged lodgings and gave instructions for the horses to be fed and thoroughly groomed after their caging in the stinking stables on board the ship.

The next day they set off inland, crossing the Plain of Anthrakat which, as Maina remembered from her lessons, was flat and semi-arid. It was good for growing certain crops, in particular the bush that fed the grubs that made the silk of Anthrakat. Settlements threaded up shallow river valleys and the lands around them were the only areas where there was enough moisture for their crops to grow. They followed a road up one of these valleys, and then along one of its tributaries. It led them towards the belt of mountains which partly encircled Morth, made up of the Dinash mountains to the north and the Visca mountains to the west, running all the way to where the Sacred Mountain dipped its toes into the sea. At the apex of the curve, where the Dinash became the Viscas, Anthrakat became Xoutha and Maina trod on home soil once again.

CHAPTER TWENTY SIX

Tensions between Morth and Xoutha had risen through several moons until, with the arrival of the king's youngest son, Tarleck, and a large contingent of fresh troops, the Mortherners burst over the border at the Sangbem Pass to avenge the death of Emish. The pass was at the eastern end of the Viscas, as far away as they could get from Zoradetra and Xouthan reinforcements. Tarleck did not have his father's permission to take part in any military activity. He was only supposed to be helping with the training of the new recruits, but General Byack found it difficult to keep him away from action. Tarleck did not bow to the general's authority as did the other men and seldom listened to his advice.

Having overcome Xouthan defences at the guard post on the Sangbem pass, the Mortherners made camp on the first piece of level land in Xoutha, an area known as Sankat in the Anthra province near Larkat. Geographically this was part of the plain of Anthrakat and lay close to the border with Xoutha's eastern neighbour. The incursion was witnessed from a watch emplacement high up on Mount Sangbem and a rider was immediately dispatched west along the border with the news.

On hearing of the Motherner's incursion into Xouthan territory, the emperor ordered all his troops to mass and be ready for a great march eastwards, knowing that it would take a day at least for them all to reach and rally at Larkat. He also sent word straight away to the Prince of Benethan but knew that it would take a full day for his messenger to reach him, and at least another for Thrull's men to ready themselves and sail to the mainland. It would then take the best part of a further day to ride eastwards to Larkat. At best, the islanders would reach it two days after the emperor's own men could be ready. He spent a night in anxious discourse with his advisor, Bradmutt, and between them they decided that they should not wait before answering the Morthern insult. A few of Thrull's islander warriors would not affect the outcome of the battle but they might be some use in rallying the troops should it go badly. Meanwhile, the Xouthans should show those Morthern upstarts that their trespass onto Xouthan territory would not be tolerated.

Thrull of Benethan received the emperor's messenger with careful politeness and returned him to Xoutha with a promise that he would dispatch a band of his best the very next day by ship.

"Defend yourselves before you trouble to fight for Xoutha," he told their captain at their departure. "I want you back again, alive and fit. Remember, your presence there need be no more than a demonstration of allegiance. See how the battle goes. Bring me back news of how Xoutha fairs. We have to be sure we are joining the winning side, when all is said and done."

So the Xouthan troops moved east ahead of the promised islander warriors. A battle coalesced near to the Mortherners' camp, on the Sankat plain below the mountains, only a short march from Larkat.

The Mortherners fought fiercely, led by General Byack. Tarleck was the first to fall. Keen to avenge his brother, it had proved impossible to keep the hot-blooded youth away from the fight. On seeing Tarleck downed, the general threw himself into the battle without fear. It seemed better to die with honour on a Xouthan sword than face the anger and desolation of the King, if he had to be the one to tell his monarch that he had lost him a second son. The general pushed forwards into the centre of the fray and there met Bradmutt, the Xouthan military chief. These two older men were evenly matched, both experienced and powerful. There was a long and tortuous struggle but eventually both lay fatally wounded, splayed out on the ground.

Once the warriors on each side began to realise that their leaders had both fallen the urge for battle proved to be fully spent. Those few left alive amongst the corpses melted silently away, either slinking off towards the mountains or fleeing back into the fields of Xoutha.

***

What Kesh and Maina found, when they arrived there later with King Kevin, was a piece of open land all spread about with death. In places there were mounds where corpses were heaped one upon another. A group of riderless horses had gathered to graze on a patch of sparse vegetation, empty saddles on their backs, reins trailing on the ground. The travellers dismounted and allowed their own cam-horses to join with them.

Maina and Kesh each recognised the livery of some of the fighters and realised with horror that their people had been fighting one another. They went from corpse to corpse, brushing hair from faces, gently lifting shields and helmets, drawn by grief to look at the features of the dead. Kevin watched from a respectful distance, bending every now and then to discourage their seacrow pet from investigating the bodies.

Maina knelt by the corpse of a large man in the centre of the fray and saw the bloodied, lifeless face of her nurse-father, Bradmutt. Bradmutt who had officiated at her betrothal. Bradmutt, whose warm hand had steadied her as she stepped on to the boat of maidens bound for the Sacred Mountain. Bradmutt, whose gift of a book of the Sacred Texts had travelled with her everywhere. Slow tears rolled down her face. There was a Morthern sword protruding from his chest. It had been driven directly into his breastplate. Maina tried to pull it out. It offended his honour but it was lodged tight. She could not shift it. She watched as the disturbance of the breastplate released from beneath it a mass like a dark, red-berry coloured jelly. As it slumped to the earth she realised it was Bradmutt's blood, congealed. She let go the sword handle with a cry of alarm. Then Kesh's voice came to her from close by.

"Here is my cousin Tarleck!" he exclaimed with dismay. "He is … he was … younger than me."

They continued to look for familiar faces until, with his head close to the ground, Kesh announced that he could hear the drumming of horses' hooves. He ran up a little nearby rise to see who was approaching. Maina and Kevin both followed. They could see tiny shapes like black mosquitoes moving towards them across the plain. They could tell that the shapes were horses and riders approaching at a gallop but they could not identify them. Maina thought she could see the outline of bulky furs as worn by island warriors and feared they might be coming to plunder the possessions of the dead.

"Where can we hide?" asked Kesh.

"There is nowhere on this open plain," said Maina. "Whoever is coming, they are likely to want to murder at least one of us."

"Then we must run," Kesh said.

"Your horses can't outrun theirs," said Kevin. "Look how quickly they're moving towards us."

Kesh edged infront of Maina.

"If Morthern monks were but permitted to bear arms, dear Xouthan priestess, I would defend you now."

"Then I am glad that you are not. I don't want anyone dying over me – certainly not you, and not even one of them," said Maina, waving a hand towards the approaching riders. "There must be another way." She stood in silence thinking for a moment. "I have an idea. You know the Enahet believe that seacrows release souls through the eye-sockets of the dead? Well, if I remember my lessons well enough, I understand the island folk have similar beliefs, in that they think that seacrows are angels from the Dark World."

"Dark World?" Kevin repeated.

"Where evil-doers go after death," she explained.

"The Realm of Denharg," muttered Kesh.

"If I may borrow your black cloak, King Kevin, I will try to frighten them off. You must both play dead, I am afraid.

With luck they will not harm a solitary Xouthan woman. Kesh, do you think you could catch your seacrow? If I can hide him under the cloak, I could try releasing him once they get here and it might just frighten them away."

"I have an idea too," said Kesh, feeling in his bag for the jar of jultie berries that were still unfinished.

"Lie down amongst the dead and I will put one of these on each of your eyes," he told King Kevin, "but you must not move, whatever happens." He repeated with emphasis, "whatever happens."

With King Kevin stretched out on the earth and looking suitably dead, Kesh held out one of his berries high in the air. When Sakki came to claim it, he deftly took hold of the seacrow's legs.

"Sorry to do this to you, little friend," he said. "But it is in a good cause."

The crow flapped and complained indignantly for a moment but Kesh tucked his head gently under his arm and he fell quiet.

"Take him from me and hold him as I am doing," he told Maina.

He then draped the black cloak around Maina and the bird and pulled the hood forwards to partially hide her face. Once he was satisfied that the cloak concealed the bird sufficiently well, he knelt down by Kevin and placed a berry carefully on each of the king's eyelids.

"Remember, you must stay absolutely still, whatever happens," he repeated.

Then Kesh stepped over the corpses and went went to lie next to his cousin, placing a jultie berry on each of his own eyelids.

Maina stood waiting nervously, praying to Tarn for protection and for good fortune for their plan. She asked her dead mother for forgiveness, as she was about to invoke her name. She prayed for a mist to come down to provide a better disguise but the sky remained stubbornly clear and the sun shone down incongruously on the bodies behind her.

For quick horses, they seemed to take a long time to arrive. Maina stood on the little rise for many slow moments, with her arms folded in front of her, holding them up almost horizontally in order to hide both the belly and the bird. When the advancing riders finally pulled their horses up in front of her, the slight elevation resulted in her head being level with theirs. She was face to face with six large men in fur and armour. It was with some relief that she discovered that Thrull was not one of the party. She hoped that none of these men had been at the betrothal ceremony with Thrull, or they might now recognise her.

"I am the spirit of the High Priestess Aleyandra," she said in Xouthan, her voice shaking in terror. She took a deep breath and said more loudly. "I guard the dead."

The men stared at her in silence but their faces were breaking into sneers. The man nearest to her turned his head away a little and looked at her out of the corner of his narrowing eyes.

Undeterred, Maina turned towards the battlefield and parted the folds of the big black cloak. She released the seacrow's head from under her arm and when he saw daylight he spread his wings and flapped off skywards. She thought for a moment that he was just going to fly away but he circled round and caught sight of his friend with the berries. He swooped down and landed on Kesh's chest, reaching for one of the purple berries from his eye socket. Dark juice immediately squirted and ran down Kesh's cheek.

"Ughh!" came a voice from behind Maina and the horses started to shift their feet.

"Join the dead," Maina invited, as the seacrow plucked the berry from Kesh's other eye.

"I'm not watching this," said one of them and turned his horse around.

The crow came in to land on King Kevin's forehead to eat his berries. Instead of lying quiet, as he had been advised, the king gave out a bloodcurdling scream of alarm at the touch of the wiry feet on his face. He sat bolt upright, waving his arms around in the air. His alien limbs, pale and hairless, appearing suddenly at the touch of the bird, was sufficient.

"The spirits rise!" one of the islanders cried. "Run for your lives!"

The horsemen all turned tail and spurred their horses into a wild gallop. Maina cautiously turned and saw them disappear towards the horizon. Having taken off in fright, the crow now went back to beg his berries from King Kevin, but they were lost amongst the corpses. Kesh sat up slowly, the purple

198

juice stains looking like two black and bleeding eyes.

"Have they gone?" he asked.

"I think so," said Maina.

"We had better get to the Sacred Mountain as quickly as we can," he said. "We must send word about what we have seen. Burial parties must be dispatched to give the dead a proper burial before those marauders get their courage back."

"Kesh, I don't think I can ride at a gallop," she said. "My belly is too big. You must go alone."

"Take my horse," offered Kevin. "It'll go faster and further than yours, I think. I'll look after Maina."

"Are you sure?" Kesh asked, not only because the king was being generous but also because he found it hard to entrust Maina's safety to anyone else since he had grown used to being her companion.

"Certainly," affirmed the king. "Go and do what you have to. Maina will show me the way from here."

"Very well," said Kesh, leaning down to catch hold of the reins of Kevin's elegant cam-horse.

He led the horse back to Maina and Kevin.

"How long will the stains last?" Maina asked him.

"Huh?" Kesh had forgotten about the berries and lifted a hand to his face as if to feel the stains. "Several days, I suppose."

"Well, be aware of your appearance," Maina told him. "You may not even be recognised at first. You also have some hair on your head now, don't forget. You don't look much like a Morthern monk."

"I will bear that in mind," he promised. "Well, goodbye."

He stepped forward to kiss Maina on the cheek. She was so surprised that she stepped backwards. Kesh did not normally show affection towards her and in front of one of the four kings, it was particularly unexpected.

"Goodbye," she said. "We'll see you again soon."

He mounted and urged the horse into a trot, a canter, a gallop and was soon as small as the mosquitoes that had ridden towards them a little while before. She watched him for a long time, realising that she had unwittingly just passed through a great portal in the passage of her life, that their long journey together was now over, that they would never be together in that way again. Kesh must have realised the end was upon them sooner than she and had chosen the kiss to mark its passing. She now bitterly regretted having stepped away.

"I'll take the cloak back if you've finished with it," the king said, breaking into her thoughts. "Perhaps we'd better get going, too."

CHAPTER TWENTY SEVEN

Kesh kept the horse at a steady gallop down the military road that ran eastwards along the line of the Viscas. He may have been heading for home, in the sense that he was heading back to the Sacred Mountain, but he was a Mortherner on the wrong side of the mountains when the two countries were in an obvious state of war. He could speak precious few words of Xouthan and was aware that the words he could speak would carry a heavy Morthern accent. He could not go for help to any of the guard posts that this road served, as they were all Xouthan. He was forced to ignore any road users who greeted or called out to him and gallop past as fast as the horse would go. His greatest fear was that his way would be barred by Xouthan military guards out to capture Mortherners retreating from the battle. Luckily for Kesh, the Xouthans were too disorganized and understaffed to guard the road in that way. Kesh reached the path to the Sacred Mountain unhindered just as the sun was setting.

The horse could gallop no more and stumbled on the rough stones up the steep slope. Kesh dismounted and led him up the path in failing light. When he reached the wall of the mountain community he rang the bell at the gate. After a few moments a temple maiden leaned over the top of the wall to look down at him.

"What do you want?" she asked cautiously in Xouthan.

"I am Kesh of Khoulan," he told her, answering in the sacred language. "I must speak to the Prophet of the Burning Ship."

Her face disappeared and Kesh was left alone in the growing dark. He waited a good while, until he thought he must ring the bell again. A breath of air and a faint whirring sound passed his ear. As Kesh looked back up at the top of the wall, he saw the shadowy shape of the seacrow alighting on the coping, just as another face appeared above the wall.

"Kesh?"

Kesh struggled to make out the shapes in the dark and recognised the face of Ahbrem. He was never so pleased to see his old friend.

"Ahbrem!"

"Kesh, is that really you? You look so different."

"It is I, truly, brother," he said. "Can I come in?"

"Mercifull Harg!" Ahbrem exclaimed joyously and got down from the wall to open the gate.

"We are at war," Ahbrem whispered to him as he drew Kesh inside. "I am not supposed to be here. We Mortherners are all supposed to be expelled but Wyn and Ship have been hiding me here to wait for your return. I was beginning to think you must both be lost. Where is Maina, by the way? Is she not with you? She is not …?"

"She was well when I left her half a day ago," Kesh said. "She is following behind with one of the four kings."

"One of the kings? Is he …?"

"Like the Prophet of the Burning Ship? Yes," said Kesh. "But, Ahbrem, we came across a battlefield where many of the dead lie untended. Dear friend, my cousin lies there. Tarleck, our king's youngest son. He must be taken home for burial immediately."

"The king's youngest?" Ahbrem repeated. "Kesh, he was the king's *only son* since the attack on Ghaba Head last spring."

"Both dead?"

Kesh stood silent for several minutes. The first emotion to wash over him was devastating grief at the news of the death of his older cousin. This was closely followed by a sudden terror, as his expectations for his future life collapsed again. For the second time in this turbulent round, he was losing his grip on the dream of becoming language master and eventually mattouk at the monastery. Both the king's heirs were dead. Who would he choose to take their place? Kesh was now the only living member of the next generation of the king's family.

"Come and eat, Kesh," said Ahbrem, taking him gently by the arm. "You must be hungry and you look worn out. Were you in the battle? Come, Wyn will bathe your face."

"No, I am alright," said Kesh and told him about the jultie berries. "A burial party, Ahbrem. We must fetch Tarleck back before those marauders get to him and before the Xouthans bury him in a nameless grave. We must get word to Morth straight away."

"Yes, yes," Ahbrem said. "Do not worry. I will go myself

203

tonight. I will take word to Morth. Come and rest now."

"The horse," said Kesh. "It belongs to one of the Four Kings."

"I will take it to the stable," Ahbrem told him.

"And I must look out for Maina and the king."

"Wyn will look out for them," Ahbrem told him. "Do not worry, Kesh. We will take care of them. Come and rest."

Kesh allowed himself to be led to the kitchens, where Ahbrem left him with Wyn who was warming a pot of stew. The appetising smell reminded Kesh that he had not eaten since breakfast and, despite his great sadness, he found himself eating hungrily. As he was finishing his meal, a knock came on the kitchen door. Wyn went to open it and Ship stepped through. He looked older than Kesh remembered and was leaning on a wooden stick but a smile played around his mouth, making him look rather pleased with himself.

"Well, my boy, you came back," he said. "But you did take a little longer than I expected."

Kesh got to his feet but resisted the urge to hug the old man. Instead, he fell on one knee before him.

"Most honoured Prophet of the Burning Ship."

"Sit down Kesh. You look exhausted. Are you injured? Is Maina alright? Where is she?"

Kesh explained again about the jultie berries and about

leaving Maina and the king behind in order to hasten with the news of Tarleck's death. He did not tell the whole of the story of their journey, however. Whether through cowardice or out of respect for Maina, he left the more sordid details of their adventure for another day.

"I feel the need to go back to Khoulan," Kesh told Ship, after he had explained all that he felt was necessary. "If it is acceptable to you, I would like to go as soon as I have seen Maina and the King safely back."

"Indeed, they have great need of you now, Kesh. They have been waiting many moons for their mattouk designate to take up office."

"Take up office?"

"Oh, you did not know?" Ship faultered. He began again gently, "Just before the winter, there was a raid on the monastery. It was the raid that started this war."

"Mattouk Calim?"

"He perished in the resulting fire, along with two others," Ship told him in a low voice. "I'm so sorry, Kesh. He was your uncle, wasn't he?"

"My great-uncle. He was uncle to the king."

At this point, his tiredness and lack of meditation caused the shock of this further loss to overwhelm Kesh. Hot tears filled his eyes. Ship put his great arms around him, and, given this permission, he sobbed on his mentor's shoulder like a child. Wyn withdrew quietly and a short while later Ahbrem silently entered the room.

"I must go to Khoulan tomorrow, Ahbrem," Kesh said as soon as he saw him. "Can you help me prepare before you go? I need my robes and my head must be shaved."

"Wyn has become very skilled at the task," he told him. "I will send her back in to you. The king's horse is stabled and Wyn has instructed a watch of maidens to wait above the gate."

"No sign yet, then?"

"Not yet," Ahbrem said. "I must go now to arrange for the retrieval of Tarleck's body. I have come to wish you farewell."

"Will you go to Khoulan?" Kesh asked.

"Eventually, but first I will ride to our military post near Sangbem. The officer there should be able to send a detachment across the border before dawn, if I can get the message to him soon enough."

"Then I pray Harg will speed your journey," said Kesh. "Take care. Fare you well."

Ahbrem put his arms out to grip Kesh by the elbows.

"Until we meet ..." he said, and turned to go.

CHAPTER TWENTY EIGHT

Maina rode beside the king along the Xouthan military road south of the mountains. She should have been afraid of returning islander marauders. She should have been afraid of parties of belligerent Mortherners coming down from the mountains, who might have been even more of a threat to them, but she was not thinking of any such dangers. She thought only about how she was going to break the news to Wyn of her father's death and how she was going to face the shame of returning to the Sacred Mountain in her present condition.

Of course, Kesh might tell the Ship Prophet what to expect but that did not make it any easier to face him herself. How was she going to explain? Even with the excuse of the Enahet magic potion, falling asleep next to a man after taking alcohol was an unforgivable mistake for any temple maiden to make. What could she possibly say for herself? Her only excuse was that she, and the Xouthan Priestesses who had taught her, had misunderstood the nature of Morthern monkhood.

She could see why this misunderstanding might have been promoted for, at the end of the last war over the Sacred Mountain, a compromise had to be reached in order to allow the Morthern monks access without breaching the rule that forbade men to go there. That is when they had become 'honorary women'. But all that would be under threat now there was a new war.

The best that Maina could hope for was that knowledge of her expected child could be restricted to a chosen few and kept secret from all others. The Ship Prophet would obviously see for himself, as would Wyn and any maidens or priestesses who saw her enter the community. Besides them, she was soon going to need the services of a midwife. Often, priestesses acted as midwives but she had no way of knowing if anyone within the community had the necessary skills. No woman in the community would ever have had the need of a midwife before now. Again she realised how afraid she was of going through this process. If her own mother had died, was it not more likely that she …?

An involuntary moan escaped her mouth and she put her hand up to stifle the sound.

"What's the matter?" King Kevin asked.

"Nothing, nothing," she said.

"You are not looking forward to reaching the Sacred Mountain?"

"It will be good to be back among friends," she said.

"But?"

"I am a little anxious."

"About the baby?"

"Yes," she said, but did not want to discuss her fears with the king. It was not hard to think of something more immediate that she was dreading.

"And I have to give my nurse-sister some bad news," she

said. "Kesh will not have told her. He did not know Bradmutt and I did not tell him that he was Wyn's father."

"I see," said Kevin, as if he understood. "I'm sure you will break the news as gently as anyone could. She would rather hear it from you than from a stranger, I'm sure."

"It's kind of you to say so," she said, genuinely encouraged by his remark. "Thank you."

By sunset Maina and the king had covered about half the distance to the Sacred Mountain. They rested a while and discussed whether there might be an inn where they could spend the night but there were no inns on that part of the military road, only tracks every so often leading up to guard posts on the border. They decided to press on, with the darkness closing in around them.

It was well into the night when they reached the path that led up to the Sacred Mountain. They led the horses up in the dark, straining to see where they should put their feet. Maina remembered that Ship's magic torch was in Kesh's bag and she wished she had asked him for it. After a while, Maina's breathing became so laboured that King Kevin offered to lead her horse so that she could ride. He handed her the reins of his own horse and it meekly followed on behind, with the packhorse taking up the rear. As they reached the Xouthan gate in the community wall, Maina looked eastwards along the line of the mountains and fancied she could see the first wash of dawn fading out the inky blackness of the night. She pulled on the bell rope and straight away a maiden called down to her from the wall.

"Is that you, Maina?"

"Yes," she answered. "Who is that? Krista?"

But the maiden had already come down the steps and was opening the gate. She embraced Maina and then stepped back as she found a swollen belly had come between them.

"Oh!"

"Krista, not a word. I will tell you everything later. Please tell no one."

Krista recovered her composure quickly.

"Welcome back, dearest friend. Come in, come in, you must be exhausted. Wyn is in the kitchen, I think, waiting for you. Go to her. If you don't mind, I will go to my bed now. I have been awake for many hours. I will see you in the morning."

She did not tell Maina that she had been asked not to go to the kitchen herself. Krista had guessed that the request might have something to do with Morthern monks and the fact that no one was supposed to know that there were any monks on the mountain during this time of war.

Maina remembered her way through the dark corridors to the kitchen with difficulty. It seemed to have been such a long time since she had been there. King Kevin followed meekly. Maina opened the door quietly and saw by candle light two figures with their backs to her. The nearest was a woman bent to a task and the other a man in a pale blue monk's robe, seated with a towel around his neck. Maina stood watching for a while. Kesh, her Kesh, was gone. In his place, a Morthern monk, already reabsorbed into his old life and no longer part of hers. Skeins of his dark hair lay discarded on the floor.

"There, I think it is done now," said Wyn, lifting the towel to dry the bare head.

"Wyn, it is the middle of the night," said Maina.

Wyn turned suddenly at the familiar voice.

"Maina!" she exclaimed with joyous relief. "You are back safe at last."

Like Krista, she tried to embrace her nurse-sister and discovered the belly.

"I have a great deal to tell you, sister," said Maina.

"So I see," said Wyn.

"But first will you tell me why you are playing barber in the dead of night?"

"Oh ..." Wyn faultered and turned towards Kesh.

Kesh stood up in the shadows. He turned around solemnly. He acknowledged King Kevin with a formal bow of his head and then addressed his travelling companion.

"Maina," he began.

He took a step towards her and came into the pool of light from the candle. His hollow cheeks were drained of colour. In the dim light the stains around his eyes, combined with the nakedness of his scalp, gave his head the appearance of a skull. Maina drew a sharp intake of breath, but resisted the impulse to step back.

"Mattouk Calim is dead," he told her. "I have to go back to Khoulan tomorrow. I must leave at first light."

"Oh," said Maina. "I am sorry to hear that."

"Where am I to sleep, Wyn?" Kesh asked.

"I will show you where Ahbrem has been hiding," Wyn told him. "Maina, I will not be long. Please wait for me here."

She included King Kevin in her gaze and Maina suddenly realised that she had not introduced him. She apologized profusely for not having been more prompt.

While Wyn was out of the room, Maina swept Kesh's hair up off the floor. With her back to King Kevin, she slipped one lock of it into her pocket. She threw the rest into the fire.

Wyn came back and busied herself warming stew and making tea for the new arrivals. All the while they were chatting lightly but Maina was thinking of the awful news she had to give Wyn as soon as King Kevin was settled for the night.

The time eventually came when the two women were alone. Maina took hold of both of Wyn's hands and they sat down facing one another.

"Wyn, I have some terrible news," she said.

Wyn's face wrinkled into a puzzled frown.

"At the scene of the battle there were many dead," she said. "So many dead." Tears began to roll down her face once more. "Both Xouthans and Mortherners. Wynn, your father … our father …"

"No!" gasped Wyn.

"He was lying at the very heart of the battle. He had obviously died very bravely. Wyn, you can be assured that you need have only the very greatest pride …"

Despite her being the bearer of these terrible tidings, Wyn embraced Maina and they wept together, mourning their great loss. They talked until the dawn had turned to day. Maina told Wyn about the Enahet potion and how Morthern monks were not really honorary women at all.

"I have discovered that much for myself," Wyn said. "Sister, I have spent much time with Ahbrem while he has been in hiding here. He …"

"Wyn!" exclaimed Maina and made Wyn explain herself.

"He has expressed … um … regret at having taken the vows of a Morthern monk. He has said, if things were different, that … "

"Yes?"

"Oh, just that ...well ... that I would be the woman he would choose." She sighed. "But it is impossible. And now there is the war so even if we gave up our vows and our current plans, we would never be able to live together in peace."

"Oh, Wyn," said Maina. "Are you in love with him?"

"I think I am," she answered sadly. "What about you? Do you have feelings for Kesh?"

"Alas, I do."

"Would you say you loved him?"

"With all my heart and more with every passing day," she said, relieved to have admitted it at last. "I haven't told him, of course. There is no point. I have to go back after the baby, and marry Thrull of Benethan and Kesh has to go back to be the mattouk at the Khoulan monastery."

"Maina," Wyn breathed. "Will the Lord Benethan not realise that you are no longer a maiden?"

"I hope not. There are ways of fooling a man, I understand," said Maina. "A little vial of red paint spilt in the right place at the right time has sometimes helped, I have heard. And if he does find me out, it won't be until after the ceremony, so it will be too late."

"Maina, I have to tell you ... I am afraid there have been rumours," Wyn said. "There is word that the Lord Benethan already has a woman and children living on one of the islands."

"Then I will feel less ashamed of cheating him," said Maina.

"You will still marry him?"

"I must, for my father's sake."

"But your father would not make you marry a man with children."

"But I could not be the one to tell him. He would think I was just making up an excuse to avoid marrying Thrull. And he knows you are my dearest friend, so you could not tell him either."

They fell silent for a moment and then Wyn said, "I feel ashamed."

"Why, Wyn?" Maina asked her.

"Because you have just told me of my father's death and all I can think about are my feelings for Ahbrem."

"Oh, Wyn, we cannot invest every thought in mourning, and anyway, suffering one sadness reminds us of another," Maina told her, mixing her Xouthan proverbs. "I know your father was concerned for your happiness. He would want to save you from your dilemma."

Wyn smiled faintly. "He would tell me to stop moping around and find myself a proper man. A Xouthan man, of course."

"Well, my father doesn't want me to marry a Xouthan but a Morthern man would certainly be out of the question," said Maina. "Our countries have been enemies for so long, he would never contemplate such a match, even if it were possible to marry a monk." She paused a moment. "I wonder how he will cope with the loss of his chief adviser. He depended on Bradmutt for so much, you know. I am afraid

215

the loss might break his spirit. He told me that Bradmutt was the one who hauled him out of the pit of despair when my mother died. There is no Bradmutt to save him this time. I am afraid he will be tempted to give up. I am afraid he will just put Thrull in charge of the empire and withdraw into himself. That would not be good for Xoutha and it would not be good for Morth, either, I fear. I wish I could be with him when he hears the news but I can not go to him yet." She looked down at her belly.

"We must see out the end of our round on the Sacred Mountain," Wyn said. "Will your baby come before then?"

"I think so."

"So what will you do?"

"Kesh plans to find a nurse-family in Morth and, if it is a boy, he will take him into the community at Khoulan, once he turns seven rounds."

"I see," said Wyn. "Maina, I understand it can be very hard to give up a child."

"I have no choice," Maina answered quickly. "I have other responsibilities. I must keep my promise to my father and I must serve the interests of Xoutha."

CHAPTER TWENTY NINE

The daylight in the kitchen made the forgotten candle flame seem pale as it spluttered and drowned in a pool of its own wax. There was a knock on the kitchen door and Kesh came in.

"Is there a spare loaf of bread I could take for the journey, please?" he asked Wyn.

She gave him a loaf, some cheese, cured meat and fruit and apologized that the bread was a day old. He assured her that it was a feast compared to what they had been living on before they reached the palace of the kings.

"Well, goodbye, again," he said to Maina.

Wyn turned her back and pretended not to be watching their parting.

"Goodbye, Kesh."

He looked so different with his bare head and robe.

"No doubt Ship will call you in as soon as he wakes. I haven't said anything about ..." Kesh's eyes drifted to Maina's belly. He took a deep breath. "I will come back as soon as I can. I will see you again, soon."

"Yes," said Maina simply, as though she did not quite believe him.

"So … my prayers are with you."

"And mine go with you. Fare you well, dear Kesh."

"Farewell."

He turned and left the room. Wyn came up to Maina and they clung to one another for a few moments silently.

Wyn made tea and took a cup of the hot brew up to the Ship Prophet. It wasn't long before he sent for Maina to go to his study. As she stood outside in the corridor, her hand poised to knock, she felt just as apprehensive as she had done on the first occasion.

"Welcome, my child," Ship said as soon as she was through the door. "It is very good to see you. I was so worried about you. You were away so much longer than I expected."

Then, of course, he noticed her belly. "Oh," he said, just like Krista, just like Wyn.

"Oh, my child," he said quietly. Then with increasing emotion, "What did they do to you? Oh, I should never have sent you. It is all my fault. Who was it? Where did it happen?"

"Well, I think it was Kesh."

"Kesh?" the Ship Prophet said incredulously. "You *think* it was Kesh?"

"Well, I was asleep and Kesh remembers nothing."

Maina told the story of the Enahet potion once again, not forgetting to blame the Xouthan's mistaken beliefs about Morthern monks, Kesh's mistake in introducing her to the Enahets as his 'woman', and most of all her mistake - lying down to sleep next to a man when they were both drunk.

Ship sat listening with his hands over his face, groaning and shaking his head now and again, but never interrupting. She finished by explaining Kesh's plans to find a nurse-family, so that they could each go back to their duties. At the end of her story Ship still had his face in his hands, silent. Then his shoulders began to shake a little and Maina thought he might be crying. But the shaking turned into unsuppressed laughter.

"Oh Maina, Maina," he said.

She found this laughter the ultimate scorn on her failings and hung her head in shame.

"I had hoped that sending you and Kesh on a task together would force you to become friends," he said between ripples of laughter. "But I never envisaged you coming back with his child in your belly! You straight-laced Xouthan priestesses and those endlessly repressed Morthern monks. Who would have thought it?"

Ship calmed himself and began to consider practicalities.

"I am sorry. I am not really laughing at you, merely laughing at my own woeful inability to judge character. In reality, I appreciate the gravity of your situation. So we must send to Xoutha for a trust-worthy midwife, then? One who can keep your secret safe for all time?"

Maina nodded in silence.

"I will see what can be done. Now, Wyn tells me you have not slept yet? You had better go to your room and rest. I have to prepare to meet my old friend as soon as he wakes up." Ship's voice grew more serious. "Thank you for bringing him to me. I am very grateful and amazed that, despite all those setbacks, you still accomplished your task. You and Kesh are very special people. I think you will both serve your religions and your countries supremely well. They are very fortunate to have you."

Maina left Ship's study feeling dazed by the alternate ridicule and praise but, ultimately, just thankful that the confession was over. She went to her old room and climbed gratefully into the bed.

Ship waited for news that Kevin was awake. When one of the maidens came to tell him that Kevin was up and eating breakfast, Ship asked her to invite Kevin to take tea with him in the study. A short while later a knock came on the door and in stepped his old crewman, hardly looking any older than when he had last seen him.

"Captain Shipham," he said and saluted.

"Kevin, please, I'm not your captain now and I haven't been for many years. Please just call me Ship."

He shook Kevin's hand warmly.

"You don't know how good it is to see you," he said. "After all these years! I thought the landing vehicle must have crashed and killed you all. I heard no news at all. Nothing.

220

And then, after all that time, a rumour from a tradesman. His supplier imported from overseas and had heard tales about unusual beings. Hairless beings! That's when I decided I must send someone out to find you."

"They seemed to have come the long way round. Why didn't they just sail across?"

"It's a long, long story, apparently. I haven't heard the half of it myself, as yet. The wonderful thing is that they reached you, eventually, and it really is you!"

"We saw the ship streaking across the sky in a ball of flames. We never imagined for a moment that you could have survived. We would have sent out a search party, if we'd had any idea … We had a kind of memorial service for you and for Angela and Candace."

"I can never forget Angela's accident with the airlock but Candace was with you on the lander," Ship said, a little shocked. "Whatever happened?"

"Her seat-harness failed, we think. Such a simple thing. She was just too badly injured and she was the only doctor. We did what we could but she died a few days later."

"I'm very sorry to hear that."

"So there we were, four men stranded on an alien planet and we'd managed to lose both of the only women on the crew."

"Four Adams and no Eves." Ship said wryly.

"There's no saying Candace would have wanted to become Eve, of course. She never seemed to have much time for any of us."

"She just liked to be professional, that's all. She was alright underneath."

"I suppose she might have been different with you."

"As ship's doctor she had some power over me too, you know."

"God, I haven't thought about her for years. Seeing you brings it all back. How many years is it, anyway, in Earthtime?"

"I have no idea," Ship told him. "Once I had stopped kidding myself that they were ever going to send a message, let alone a rescue party, I buried the synculator on the beach. That was my only way of calculating Earthtime. I buried it exactly fifty rounds after we arrived here. It was my way of marking it."

"Fifty rounds?"

"I have been calling this planet's short year a 'round of seasons' to avoid confusing it with an Earth year. And it was many, many rounds ago that I buried the synculator."

"Yes, I understand how being stranded on this planet might have made you want to destroy the one thing that reminded you of Earth. And the years ... the rounds seem to go by here so quickly. The Penethellans seem to go through so many generations in the blink of an eye and we've only just started to age."

"Penethellans? Why do you call them that? They don't call their planet Penethella."

"The ones who live on our side of the ocean do. What do your lot call it then?"

"The Mortherners call it Plax-e-har and I believe the Xouthans call it Redhera."

"Redhera sounds a bit like the Anthrakat word for land."

"I think it translates more like 'ground' or 'soil'."

"You mean earth. Are you telling me the Xouthans call their planet Earth?"

"Maybe that's it! Perhaps every alien culture calls its home planet Earth." Ship laughed. Then he asked Kevin, "So, what have you four been doing with yourselves all this time?"

"Doing? Well, we are helping to develop their technology. I believe the Penethellans who are working with Dougie are very close to creating a large-scale coal powered generator. We've had a small generator in the palace for a while, but this will be quite a breakthrough. It could revolutionise their capacity for industrialisation. It could take them forward in leaps and bounds."

"I see," said Ship.

"How about you?"

"Me?" said Ship. "I'm afraid I can't claim to be helping their development at all. In fact, I have tried to do as little as I can to interfere. You'll probably notice they seem to be back in the middle-ages here. But then, I rather like it."

"You don't miss life's little luxuries?"

"Well, I did scavenge a few things from the ship. When I was first here I dived down to it a couple of times from a little boat I borrowed. The emergency lighting system came out in easy pieces, and I used it for the corridors and the waterfall."

"Waterfall?"

"Yes. My first visitors seemed to bring some sort of parasite with them that made me very itchy indeed so, after that, I made them climb up the way I had come the first time. The only way I could find to get off the beach was up a waterfall. It empties into a cave down there. Anyway, the washing seemed to cure the problem. I put a couple of speakers down there too and changed the warning messages, but actually I think it rather frightens them. I don't always use it."

"And have you er … um … ever married?"

"A Penethellan, do you mean?"

Kevin nodded.

"No, I've never felt inclined," said Ship. "Being that bit older probably helps. I don't feel the need like I did back on Earth. You?"

"Me? No. Bit too hairy for me."

Ship nodded with a wry smile.

"Ted did, though. He went off for a few rounds with one of the locals. She actually shaved herself all over for their wedding day. She looked terrible! I thought he'd back down but he went through with it. She grew her hair back and he stayed with her until she died."

"No children?" Ship asked.

"No, there have never been any children. I don't think we're compatible, sadly. For one thing, they're arranged a bit differently down below, as you probably know."

"Oh, really?" Ship raised his eyebrows and nodded at this younger man's information, not really wanting to see the image that it conjured in his head and ashamed of his own ignorance. He changed the subject.

"Anyway, I think they'll be ringing lunch bell any time now. We could start making our way down to the dining room."

CHAPTER THIRTY

Kesh rode all day for Khoulan. There were guards on the gate. He was shocked to find them there but with his robes and shaven head they would have let him in even without checking with their master. As it was, scripture master Hamlin came to the gate and embraced him as soon as he saw him. Hamlin told him that, although he was honoured to serve the community in high office, he was very weary of being mattouk elect. He explained that it was the name they had given to the new office introduced to bridge the time between Mattouk Calim's death and the return of the mattouk designate.

The next day, Ahbrem arrived at the monastery with the body of Tarleck and a military escort. They stayed one night but were due to take Tarleck on to the capital for burial. Before they left the next morning Kesh and Ahbrem walked together round the outside walls to visit Mattouk Calim's grave.

"I see you have brought Sakki with you," Ahbrem remarked, as a seacrow hopped across their path.

"Sakki? What makes you think it is Sakki?"

"I would know him anywhere. Anyway, he still carries the stain of those jultie berries you fed him from your eyelids."

"His beak is a little stained," agreed Kesh. "Perhaps he has been eating berries in the wild."

"Too early in the season," said Ahbrem.

226

"Anyway, if it is the same bird as the one that was with us on the battlefield, it cannot be Sakki. That one had come with us over the sea from the Land of the Four Kings."

"I am certain that it *is* Sakki. He is a very special bird you know. I sent him off to find you and he brought you home to us. It took him several moons but he did it. He took off eastwards, the way you had gone, and he came back from the east with you."

"I suppose I have to admit that big black bird saved all our lives, although he will not know it."

"I think he knows more than you give him credit for," said Ahbrem. "We should take special care of him, pay him suitable regard."

"I will bear it in mind," said Kesh. "Perhaps the new mattouk will have to designate seacrows as sacred to our religion, as with the Enahets."

"An excellent idea! Give them all the protection of religious veneration."

They laughed together, only half joking.

Kesh sighed. "I missed you, Ahbrem. I made some serious mistakes without you to guide me."

"Nonsense. You successfully completed a very difficult task. I would have just been in the way."

"I do not think so. Anyway, it is good to be back with you."

"This must be Calim's grave. The one by the wall?"

"So I am told."

"I will pick some greenery to add to its adornments."

"That is a good idea. I will do the same. Following your lead again," said Kesh. Then he blurted out, "Ahbrem, stay for my installation."

"My first duty is to deliver Tarleck's body to his father's house. After that I will come straight back. I will be back in time for your installation. Besides, the king will undoubtedly want to witness the installation of his nephew as mattouk."

"The day after receiving the body of his only remaining son? I think not."

***

Two days later, Kesh was at the centre of a ceremony to install him as mattouk. Before an audience consisting of the whole of Khoulan, the two most senior monks solemnly placed a robe of rich deep blue over his shoulders, covering up his pale blue monk's robe. The king had ridden from the capital to see his nephew installed and he sat on Kesh's right hand at dinner that night while Ahbrem sat on his left.

"So how does it feel to be facing this way round?" the king asked Kesh.

"Strange," Kesh replied.

"Ha!" the king laughed. "You will get used to it. Soon you will be giving out orders as though you had been doing it all your life."

"I feel I must warn you that I would like to make some changes to monastic life at Khoulan," Kesh told him.

"Such as?" he asked warily.

"Such as allowing monks to marry, if they so desire."

The king raised his eyebrows. "Do you have someone in mind?" he teased.

"As a matter of fact …"

The king's eyebrows rose higher.

" … I just think that the monks need the opportunity to experience a more realistic taste of life. Young men graduate from here and go out to help and advise those in the surrounding communities without really understanding anything of what normal life entails."

"Well," the king shrugged after considering for a moment, "What you say is true, of course. I will not argue against your proposition. You may have some opposition amongst the clerics in the capital, however. It would be a radical change to make."

"I realise that," Kesh said, "But having your support will make a considerable difference to my chances of persuading them."

"You will be coming to the capital to officiate at Tarleck's funeral tomorrow, of course."

"Yes," said Kesh. "My first. I wish it were not my beloved cousin. I hope I can do him justice."

"I am sure you will," said the king. "You will see Emish's grave." The king put his hand to his brow and hid his face for a moment while he recovered his composure. "We are putting them side by side."

"I am so sorry for your great loss," said Kesh.

"Kesh, you know that I now have no-one left but you."

Kesh nodded. "This evil war …" he began, but the king interrupted him.

"I want to name you as my heir."

"But my duties …"

"Your duties need not change. I do not intend to die just yet. You must quickly name a mattouk designate, however, so that when the time comes you will have someone ready."

"I already have someone in mind," said Kesh. "Someone who has already made the pilgrimage to the Sacred Mountain." He looked in Ahbrem's direction but Ahbrem was in conversation with the music master seated next to him.

"Good," said the king. "Excellent. It is a pity that there is no one else from the royal family coming through for the mattoukhood but it cannot be helped. I will make the announcement two moons hence, when the mourning period is complete."

"Very well. Thank you. I am deeply honoured." Kesh said, though he hardly relished the thought of taking the king's place and was hoping that some miracle would take the burden from him before he was obliged to take up the crown.

Kesh worked hard over the next moon visiting the mattouks of other communities and clerics and experts in religious law. Using the king's name he influenced those in power to consider his idea but he did not gain a majority for change. His last chance, though he was reluctant to take it, was to persuade the king to force the issue. At the end of the moon he was riding to the capital once more to ask a favour of his uncle.

He arrived at the palace and was formally announced. He waited until the evening meal before he dared to broach the subject. The king sat at the head of a long table and Kesh sat to his right. All the other seats were empty.

"I am sorry your aunt is not dining with us tonight," the king said. "I am afraid you remind her too much of our loss." He dropped his voice. "You know that it was Tarleck who should have gone to Khoulan to represent the royal family but his mother could not bear to part with him so young. When my brother offered to send you in his stead she accepted with alacrity. Now, however, she thinks that if Tarleck had become a monk he would not have gone to war. She does not blame you. Do not think that. But she says she is not ready to face you over the dinner table yet. She has asked that you go to visit her before you leave, though. I thought a private dinner was therefore best. I hope you do not mind that none of the court is joining us."

"No, no, not at all," Kesh assured him.

The king's words went some way to explaining one of the puzzles that had haunted him all his younger days, namely the question of why he had been sent to Khoulan at a tender age with so little warning.

"So what is the business you wanted to discuss with me, mattouk?"

"Sire, you will remember the change I wanted to introduce in order to allow the monks to marry?" he reminded the king. "Well, I have made some progress with the clerics but they are not yet all in favour. I am here to beg for your help in this matter. I have come to ask you to make a royal edict in favour of the change."

The king shifted uncomfortably.

"Khoulan is the most influential monastery in Morth, the principal monastery of the Sacred Mountain. If the mattouk of Khoulan can not instigate change, it is not the king's place to force the matter."

"Uncle, please."

"You do not know what you are asking. I have to listen to what my clerics tell me. They pray for my soul. They help me to keep the people … happy. I am not in any position to risk offending them."

"This matter is very important to me," Kesh said. "If you refuse me, then I am not sure that … I will want to become your heir."

"Kesh," his uncle said quietly. "You are threatening me. I have just lost both my sons. My wife is destroyed by grief. She will not leave the palace. All I have left is you, and you threaten me?"

"No," Kesh groaned. "I take it back. Please forget I said that. It is not in my nature to serve out threats, believe me. But, if I was willing to choose that path, you can see that this matter means a very great deal to me."

"I do see that," said the king. He took a breath. "Very well, I will talk to the clerics on your behalf to see if I can persuade them. But I am not willing to war with them. I have enough battles of my own to fight, now those Xouthan murderers have joined forces with the island savages."

"Thank you," said Kesh. "I am most grateful. What news is there of the war, by the way?"

"Little news, and none of it good," said the king. "We are rallying troops and training more recruits. We have to make good our losses before we can avenge them."

CHAPTER THIRTY ONE

The senior priestess educator, Priestess Hannala, was summoned by Ship to his study. When she stepped inside she found the Most Honoured Maiden was already with the Ship Prophet. She noticed her condition immediately. Maina told her story over again and Ship asked Hannala if she would be able to find a midwife who could come to the community for a while. They decided the best way forward was not to reveal her identity at all but simply to say that she was an unmarried Xouthan woman who had come to the community for help. She was to be called Munwa. Hannala chose the name because she thought it would be close enough to her own name for Maina to respond even if she was in a state of distress, although she did not explain this reason to Maina.

Maina grew more and more anxious about the coming birth but Priestess Hannala had grown-up children living in the north of Xoutha, although their father was long dead. She assured Maina that the experience was not to be feared and that very few women met Maina's mother's fate. The midwife arrived and told Maina that everything seemed to be progressing as it should and that she thought the birth would come within the moon. Maina was told to rest and enjoy the peace and quiet of the mountain community while she still had time to herself.

Maina and Wyn spent much time together discussing what they thought would be going on in Xoutha.

"They will have taken Bradmutt's body back to Zoradetra by now," Maina told Wyn. "You should go back for your father's funeral."

"But we are supposed to be in isolation here," said Wyn. "I am not supposed to even know about his death. We have to wait until our round of training is complete and we can sail back to Zoradetra on the maidens' boat. I will mark his passing in my prayers."

"Maybe we could arrange a small service here. Perhaps Hannala would officiate for us. We could pray for him together and sing the funeral invocations, just the three of us."

A few days later they held a private service in the Great Hall, their figures dwarfed by the empty space around them. Towards the close, while the three were singing the final invocation, Maina put her hands to her belly. A sudden pain had strangled the harmony of her part.

"Do not worry," Hannala told her. "There is plenty of time yet. We will get you upstairs then Wyn can fetch the midwife."

"But is this not too soon?" Maina asked.

"They come when they are ready," Hannala told her.

Before they had got to the top of the staircase another pain made Maina stop and catch her breath.

"This is too quick," said Maina, frightened.

"Quick is good," said Hannala, hiding her own fears as well as she could. "Wyn, I will manage from here. You go and get the midwife."

Wyn seemed to hesitate.

"As soon as you can," Hannala prompted.

Hannala helped Maina to her bedchamber and tried to make her comfortable. Wyn arrived with Mrs Plumtin who immediately sent Wyn away again to fetch clean bed linen, towels, soap and warm water. Maina was quiet, almost too quiet, Hannala thought. She seemed to remember screaming the house down at her first birthing. Maina appeared to be bearing the pain stoically, as if she only wanted it to be over, over and successful, with her own life intact and a healthy baby to hold. Except that Maina did not intend to keep the baby. Hannala was worried by the fact that Maina intended to give her baby up. She understood why Maina wanted to go back to her father and make good her promises as if nothing had happened but Hannala doubted that Maina knew what she was asking of herself.

The hours passed slowly. In Maina's bedchamber the three women waited around her for the next bite of pain, for the child to come a little nearer to their world. Too quick, indeed! They need not have worried! Maina's face looked gaunt and tired. The midwife gave her a thick sweet tea to drink but it erupted out of her again as the next pain came. Wyn bent to clean up the mess and Maina felt guilty at being the source of such revolting excretions and causing all this work for the women around her.

Eventually, in the dead of nightn when Maina thought she had no strength left, the babe finally slid out into the world. The midwife wrapped it in a shawl and placed it in Maina's arms. A son.

"Oh, he has his father's eyes!" said Hannala, leaning over to admire him.

He lay quietly looking up at Maina and at the new world of free-moving beings. Looking up at her with eyes that Hannala thought were like her beloved Kesh's. Her child, her son.

"Ah, look at him," said the midwife. "Sweet little innocent! A child born in innocence will save the world – isn't that what the prophet Sandbert said?"

"He did, Mrs Plumtin," said Wyn. "Indeed he did."

Wyn set about collecting up the dirty laundry. She found herself resenting Kesh for what he had just put Maina through. She began muttering under her breath, "Born in innocence, perhaps, but maybe not conceived in innocence. Waiting until my sister was drunk, indeed!"

"Well, he's a little darling, my dear," Mrs Plumtin said to Maina. "You should be very proud."

Kesh arrived that very evening, having ridden hard all day from Khoulan. Wyn let him in at the Morthern gate, and told him Maina's child was born. A strange mixture of excitement and disappointment reacted inside him like a surfeit of overly rich foods. He was disappointed that all his efforts over the past moon to avoid his child being born out of wedlock had come to nought, but he was desperate to see his son. Wyn took him to Ahbrem's old hiding place and made him put on a hooded white robe. He was led up the stairs to Maina's room disguised as a temple maiden even though the midwife had already been sent away.

He was shown into the modest bedchamber and saw Maina tenderly cradling a small bundle. Maina smiled and held out the bundle to him. In the dim candlelight it seemed like it was all blanket and no baby. He hesitated, but Maina told him how to hold the child, just as he had told her how to hold the seacrow. Still he hesitated. Wyn took over and told him to sit down. He sat on the edge of the bed by Maina's feet and Wyn gently put the babe into his arms. He sat very still and looked down at him.

"He has your eyes," said Hannala.

As she leaned over to admire the baby she smiled encouragingly at Kesh.

"Oh," said Kesh, a little embarassed.

He studied the tiny face, trying to recognise himself. Wyn and Hannala withdrew.

Kesh was smiling down in wonder, hardly daring to meet Maina's gaze. This woman who had produced this miracle of new life with him ... he could not speak. In that moment all his feelings of doubt and guilt subsided.

'Such a wonderful creation! This perfect little child in my arms must truly be the work of Harg,' he thought.

Maina must have been right. Harg had used his body to create this child and he should not question why. He closed his eyes and silently thanked Him for His glorious gift.

Maina watched the father and the son as Kesh pushed back the folds of the blanket with one finger. The tiny digits of a tiny hand closed around the finger and father met son flesh to flesh. Kesh glanced at Maina, smiling, utterly enchanted. Rounds later, Maina would cling to this image as to a moment of perfect happiness in a trying life. She would use it to assure herself that the father would care for the son, would protect him and supply all his needs, through all the years when she could not.

Maina eventually broke the silence with the concern that was uppermost in her mind.

"Have you found a suitable nurse-family, yet?"

"Um … no," Kesh said. "I was not sure … I did not expect him to be born so soon."

"No," agreed Maina. "Eager to discover a new world, like his father."

"Maina, I was hoping that I could persuade you to come to Khoulan, to live with your child and look after him yourself."

"Kesh, you know I can not. I am betrothed."

The dispensation document allowing Khoulan monks to marry sat heavy in Kesh's pocket. He had spent all the last month negotiating with the clerics to win their signatures but now he could not bring himself to tell Maina that he had it. He wanted to beg her to break her betrothal bond and marry him instead but the words would not come out.

"Have you a name in mind?" Maina asked.

"Name?"

"For your son. I thought you might want to call him Tarleck, after your cousin, or Emish perhaps."

"I had not thought."

"I would like Bradmutt for a second name, if that would be agreeable to you."

"Of course," said Kesh. "I can not choose between my cousins. My uncle Mattouk Calim was the man I admired most of all. I think I would like him to be named Calim."

"Calim Bradmutt of Khoulan," said Maina. "It is a very fine name."

Kesh looked anew at the baby in his arms.

Maina broke the silence again.

"The new temple maidens will be here in less than half a moon. Seven days later, we graduands will be sailing back to Zoradetra. There is not much time left."

"Must you go so soon?" asked Kesh.

"I must. It is expected," Maina said. "With Bradmutt dead, I am very worried about how my father will face the future. Bradmutt supported him when my mother died. The emperor depended on him entirely for the first few moons, I understand. Now Bradmutt has also gone, I should be there to support my father. I don't know if he will withdraw into himself, as I am told he did after my mother's death, or whether he will be angry and all the more belligerent. If vengeance prevails many more Xouthans will be sent to their deaths and they will, no doubt, take many Mortherners with them."

Kesh did not answer. His dream of living with Maina and his son seemed to be slipping through his fingers like dry sand. The harder he tried to hold on to it, the faster it slipped away.

"Maina is supposed to rest today." Wyn had come back into the room and thought that Maina was starting to look distressed. She held her arms out to take the baby from Kesh and placed the child back into his mother's arms.

"Will you be here tomorrow?" Maina asked quickly, not wanting Kesh to leave.

"Yes," said Kesh. "That is if Wyn can hide me somewhere overnight."

Wyn nodded.

"Apparently I am going to be allowed to dress in the morning," Maina said. "Hannala is keeping me prisoner in my room until then."

Kesh smiled wanly at her joke. Wyn was standing by the door as if eager to take him away. "I will see you tomorrow, then," Kesh said. "Goodnight."

"Goodnight."

Maina sat nursing the child by the light of the candle, thinking. So many things she wanted to say to Kesh the next day and so many more she must not say. Their journey together was in the past. Now the few moments they could spend together were more precious than all the gold in her father's coffers and as transient as a mountain flower. How could she convey her regard for him and yet not waiver from her purpose regarding the war? After seeing so many dead on the battlefield and seeing so much mourning on both sides, she was determined she would do everything in her power to stop the killing. And she held in her arms a child who was both Morthern and Xouthan. It was more important than ever that the two nations should cease fighting one another.

CHAPTER THIRTY TWO

The next day Maina bathed and dressed. She fed her baby and laid him down in the large drawer that Wyn had made into a crib, the community of the Sacred Mountain not being equipped for infants. Once Calim had settled into slumber, she left him in Wyn's care and went in search of Kesh. She found him on the balcony outside the Great Hall, looking out to sea. The cowl of the temple maiden's robe was pulled up over his head but she recognised him by the familiar shape of the shoulders from which the soft cloth hung in graceful folds. A seacrow was walking up and down the coping of the balustrade next to him, like a man pacing deep in thought, except that every now and then it sidestepped or hopped and broke the rhythm.

Maina stepped silently on to the balcony and looked out for a while from a little way behind him.

"Strange, isn't it," she observed, "How gazing at a horizontal line between two shades of blue can be so comforting?"

Kesh turned abruptly towards her, as if woken from a dream.

"Maina."

"Good morning, Kesh."

"Good morning."

"Kesh," Maina drew in a long breath. "I have something

important to ask of you."

"Go on," he said.

"I will need your help if I am going to stop the fighting. All this slaughter that has been going on while we were away – I think it must be stopped and I need to know that you want to stop it too."

Kesh did not reply.

"You do, don't you?" she asked.

When he still did not reply she said, "Kesh, Xouthans and Mortherners have hated one another for a long time now, but I do not hate you and I do not think that you hate me. We should use our friendship to do some good. I will use all my power to influence my father to sue for peace, and I was hoping that you might be able to do the same in Morth. Would that be possible? Do you have any influence with the king?"

"Apparently, I do," said Kesh fingering the dispensation document that still sat in the pocket of the robe. Muttering bitterly under his breath he added, "For all the good it did me."

He would not dare to suggest that Maina should marry him now. It was obvious that she was set on returning to Xoutha.

"So much death, Kesh. So many people mourning for those lost. What is it all for? What can be so important that those people had to give their lives, that mothers had to lose their sons, wives their husbands and us daughters lose their fathers?"

"I believe the Xouthans started this with the raid on Khoulan," said Kesh and then wished he hadn't.

"And I promise that the Xouthans will be the ones to end it, if I have any influence at all," said Maina. "But Morth must agree to end it too. Like war, peace takes the agreement of both parties. I must be sure that, if I can persuade my father to stop fighting, that Morth will also stop."

"How will you persuade your father to stop? He has lost his closest friend. He is going to want revenge."

"I ..." Maina began, and then started more slowly, choosing her words with care. "Kesh, I am going to threaten to renege on my betrothal pledge. I am going to threaten not to marry Thrull. It is the one thing which my father wants most of all from me." Maina paused. "The only problem is that ... if I am successful, if I persuade my father to stop attacking Morth, then I will have to keep my pledge." She looked away. She could not meet Kesh's eyes as she said. "I will have to marry the Lord Benethan."

After a moment of silence Maina stole a glance at Kesh and saw a depth of pain in his eyes that she had not anticipated.

"Kesh, we have been through so much together. My regard for you is very great. My heart will be yours forever," she said.

Kesh turned away and let out a scornful "Ha!"

Maina went on regardless, "But we can not run away to Khoulan and enjoy a carefree life while our countrymen go on killing one another on the fields of Xoutha. How could we do that? If we knew that we had not tried everything we could to stop it, we would never be comfortable with our consciences. Think how we would feel, seeing the dead carried back battle after battle, knowing we had done nothing. How could we bear it? It would poison our hearts. It would rot in our souls. It would destroy our friendship. Your dream of me going with you to Khoulan to look after Calim Bradmutt is a fantasy."

"All my dreams are fantasies," Kesh spat out bitterly. "Maina, we have been so badly cheated. We have all the responsibilities of parenthood but had none of the pleasures of arriving there. We have lived our relationship backwards. Instead of meeting, falling in love and creating children, we created a child, then I fell in love with you and now we are to part. Do you not feel that, in some way, we might be owed a little happiness back from life?"

"Kesh!" Maina said, wondering at how he had changed recently.

Kesh went on, ignoring her interruption, "I dreamt about living out our lives in that shepherd's cottage on the hill. When you decided that we must continue with the Task, I went along with that but since then I have made it possible for us to live at Khoulan instead. Maina, I spent the whole of this last moon obtaining dispensation for Khoulan monks to marry. Now all you want to do is hurry back to Xoutha."

"Marry?" repeated Maina. "Khoulan monks can marry?"

"Yes," said Kesh, finally fetching out the rolled document and holding it up in the air. "I had to do a lot of persuading. I had to visit many clerics and consult ecclesiastical lawyers. I had to get help from the king himself. And I did it, but," and here his voice fell, "I was too late for the child."

"I'm so sorry, Kesh. But you knew I had to return to Xoutha. I explained it to you long ago. I have always said so," said Maina. Then she added, "I must tell Wyn."

"Wyn?"

"Yes," said Maina. "She and Ahbrem are in love."

"Ahbrem?"

"Yes, but I should not have told you. Say nothing about it, Kesh. Say you promise, please."

"So you think it would be right for Wyn to marry Ahbrem? Why would it be right for them and not for us?"

"Because Wyn and Ahbrem do not have the power that you and I will have. Kesh, we have a war to stop. We will not achieve anything by railing against the unfairness in our own insignificant lives. We have to try to make everyone's lives better, our own included."

She looked at his severely shaven head, revealed slowly by the maiden's cowl gradually slipping backwards at each movement of his head. His life had been full of sacrifice and self-denial. Why was that suddenly changing now? She went on more gently.

"I remember you telling me about your great-uncle while we were travelling. You said Mattouk Calim believed that war was evil, that he preached peace constantly. How would he feel if he knew that this war had been started by his death? Kesh, think. Would he have wanted his own death to be avenged?"

Kesh turned away from her. "Both my cousins, Maina, slain by Xouthan weaponry. Both my cousins and my dear great uncle."

"But would he want this war to carry on?"

Kesh was silent, looking out to sea.

"Kesh?"

"No," he said eventually. "No, he would not."

"Well, I do not want my nurse-father's death to be avenged. If I learned anything from our journey, I think it is that the fourth law, slaughter not except for meat, should be for everyone, not just for temple maidens and priestesses. It is the ideal to which we all should aspire, even if we cannot all achieve it. I think that you and I, in our future positions, should take the lead. I think I should embrace the fourth law in its literal sense and I had hoped you might consider adopting your great-uncle's love of peace."

Kesh looked down for a while, contemplating the craftsmanship of the stonework of the balcony floor. Then he gave Maina a look, an expression she had never seen in his face before, with his eyes narrowed as if he was considering whether or not she was speaking from her heart.

He may not have always taken her counsel in the past but he had never before questioned her sincerity. He had always accepted that genuinely held beliefs had lain behind her words. She did not have a defence. How could she prove that she was putting forward an argument from the heart and not just trying to manipulate him? Obviously she wanted to influence his judgement but not without him making his own decisions. She was lost. Whatever she did or said, Kesh was going to question her motives. So she said nothing.

Kesh turned, rested his elbows on the balustrade and leaned heavily against it, stretching his back as if it ached. Maina waited. The sea was dark but empty. Neither boat nor beast broke the monotony of the view all the way to the horizon. Eventually, Kesh sighed and stood upright.

"Very well," he said.

Maina waited for him to go on.

"I will inform the king that you intend to influence your father. I will ask him not to attack Xoutha unless Morthern positions are attacked first. In time, if there are no further attacks, I will ask him to sue for peace."

Maina allowed herself to take a breath. "Thank you," she said with feeling then added quickly, "Only remember I will not be able to influence Xouthan actions until I am back with my father. There's no knowing what he might do in the meantime, so we have to start from whatever the position is at that time. I will leave it to you to decide whether you speak to your king now or leave it until I am there in Xoutha."

"How can I know which will be best? If I explain your

intentions to the king now, I may be speaking too soon. A Xouthan attack would make a liar out of me. If I wait, I could be leaving it too late. The machinery of war might be turning inexorably towards the next deadly battle."

"You will know when the time is right. I have faith in you."

"I will pray for guidance. I trust that Harg will guide me if the path is a virtuous one."

"There is still the question of the nurse-family for Calim Bradmutt," said Maina, returning to the other worry that was plaguing her. "I feel he will be better hidden, and therefore my secret will be safer, if he is in Morth. You will be able to visit him, whereas I wouldn't dare."

"I understand," said Kesh. "I will go tomorrow. I will search the whole of Morth if I have to. I will find somewhere suitable for him, I promise."

"Thank you," she said again, and was suddenly moved to embrace him. She slipped her arms under his and clasped him around his narrow chest, smelling the herbs the maidens used to keep the moths out of the priestess's gown, smelling also the scent of him which had been so familiar in the little house in Hittan, feeling his cheek against her hair, the accepting touch of his arms on her back, clinging a moment longer than she should. A cough sounded behind her and Ship and Kevin came out onto the balcony. She stepped back quickly.

"Wyn wants to know if you are going to take lunch in the dining room, or in the kitchen with Kesh," Ship said. "I think I will suggest the kitchen."

His face broadened into a knowing but kindly smile.

"Who is with Calim?" Maina asked.

"I think Krista went up," Ship told her.

"Excuse me. I will go and check on him," she said and bowed her head to the two humans.

Kesh also bowed to them both and followed Maina indoors. Kevin followed Kesh with his eyes.

"So, do you believe their little story then?" he asked Ship. "The fertility potion working while they were asleep?"

Ship laughed quietly. "I don't know. I've heard of sexsomnia, of course, but I didn't realise it was possible for both partners to stay asleep. Still, who knows, the Penethellans aren't made the same way as us. All I know is there is a new baby and it's my fault. I've just got to do all I can to help."

"Your fault?" repeated Ted. "How can it be your fault?"

"I was the one who sent them away together. I was hoping they would become friends and I guess they did."

"Ha!" Kevin took a breath. "You know, you will be getting a visit from Nathan before too long, I think. He was very shocked when he heard those two calling you a prophet. It offended his religious principles."

"Religious principles?"

"Yes. You have allowed these beings to think you are

something you are not."

"Believe me, I am not pleased that they insist on calling me a prophet and I have tried many times to explain that I am not. But they each seem to have their reasons for thinking that I have foretold events that actually came to pass. It was pure fluke, of course, or rather it was common sense but it makes no difference. To them, I have special powers. It was better than being a god, anyway. Surely the Penethellans must have thought that you four were gods at first."

"Once they stopped trying to kill us, yes. I suppose it was when we managed to start communicating with them that we began calling ourselves kings. Nathan thought it was okay to be thought of as powerful beings, as long as our power was not in a religious context. I remember, as time began to pass and it became obvious that there was no prospect of ever getting back to Earth, he went into a very deep depression."

"Didn't you all suffer depression, then? I know I did."

"It was worse for him. He became very concerned about missing the Second Coming because he wasn't on the right planet." Kevin's voice carried a hint that he did not share this concern himself. "It was Ted who suggested to him that, actually, he might have been put on this planet for a reason. He seemed to like that idea and promptly went off and set up his own religious community. He started converting the Penethellans to Christianity and preparing them for Judgment Day. He was actually only visiting the palace when your envoys arrived. He doesn't live with us anymore."

"So you don't all feel like him?"

"I wasn't brought up with all that Second Coming stuff, just the 'be good and you'll get to Heaven' bit. How about you?"

"I am afraid I have no faith," said Ship.

Kevin drew the air in sharply between his teeth. "Nathan will say you're going straight to Hell, then."

"I try to be good, same as the rest of you," Ship said. "In fact, I think the moral code I tried to live by on Earth was tougher than that followed by some of my believer friends. I believe that my religious colleagues in the forces, for example, had easier consciences than I did."

"I don't see how that can be possible, given that you have no concern for the welfare of your immortal soul."

"Well I saw it like this: to them, if they took a life it was just hurrying things up a bit. Let God decide, or St. Peter or whoever, and then the guy goes off into the next life. With me, it was final, no second chances. If I took a life, I would have been destroying that guy's entire existence."

"So did you?"

"What?"

"Kill anyone?"

"Nearly," said Ship. "I was never put on combat duty, but our surveillance post came under scrutiny, once. I was behind a door with a cocked spit-gun in my hand and this guy came close enough for me to hear him breathing. If he'd seen me,

I guess I would have tried to kill him. I still dream about it, sometimes. Scared the Hell out of me. I got the job with Brannon Industries shortly after. But I've often thought about that guy, just doing his job, his mother's son, probably had a girl somewhere, brothers, sisters, perhaps even children. I could have become responsible for taking away a big part of all their lives. And who's to say he deserved to die any more than me? After that, I didn't want to work with the military anymore." Ship gave a bitter laugh and added, "Then I end up being responsible for the death of half my crew on a failing spaceship."

He looked out over the same empty sea that Kesh had been staring across a short while before.

"That wasn't your fault. None of it was," said Kevin. "That ship had been in space so long, no one could be sure that anything would function properly."

"Humph. Perhaps you're right." Ship drew in a long breath. "So what about you? You ever killed anyone?"

"Not to my knowledge," Kevin answered. "Not a human, anyway. We defended ourselves pretty vigorously against Penethellan attacks in the first few moons, though, and I'm not really comfortable with what Doug is doing in the north right now."

"What's that?"

"Well, there's a Penethellan chieftain on our northern border who is adamant that he doesn't want coal mining on his tribe's land. His son, on the other hand, says he would be quite happy to trade their coal with us. We're running out fast, so the situation is getting a bit tense. Doug suggested we take the old power unit from the escape pod and send one of our Penethellan messengers to hide it in the old guy's mattress, just to hurry things up a bit."

"But it will still be radioactive, won't it?"

"Exactly. Doug loosened the shielding casing and told our guy to take it off only when he was just about to hide it so it wouldn't do him too much harm. Now we just sit back and wait."

"But that's murder." said Ship.

"Is it? They're not human and they die so quickly anyway," said Kevin. "Like I say, I wasn't comfortable with it myself, but Doug said that hurrying one Penethellan off the planet a bit sooner might save a lot of fighting later. He said we'd actually be saving Penethellan lives in the long run. We all came round to the idea, in the end, except …"

A hand bell rang in the bowels of the building.

"Lunch is ready. Except Nathan?" Ship suggested.

"No. It was Ted who objected, the one who was married to a Penethellan for a while."

"I seem to remember the whole point of looking for a planet without intelligent life was so that we wouldn't have to start killing them," said Ship. "Any intelligent beings we found were supposed to be given human status, morally."

"Well, we all start out with good intentions," said Kevin.

"It's always different when it comes to the real thing, isn't it? Anyway, most of the crew joined up because they were hoping we *would* find intelligent beings."

They moved off the balcony to make their way to the dining room.

CHAPTER THIRTY THREE

Kesh left the community early the next morning and Maina was left in the peace and quiet of the Sacred Mountain with her women friends and her new child.

On the third day of motherhood something happened to her that she had not expected and which made her plans much harder to carry out. She fell in love with Calim Bradmutt. She was looking down at him lying quietly in her arms when a great surge of emotion washed over her. His face, his little body, his little hands and arms, his all-seeing, unfathomable eyes which looked deep into her soul. He became, in that instant, the dearest person in the world to her. She thought she had fallen in love with Kesh. It was as nothing compared to the depth of emotion which swept over her in that moment.

Twelve days of blissful motherhood followed, together with the sleepless nights and the constant effort required to see to the needs of the child. On the thirteenth day, the new temple maidens arrived for their round on the Sacred Mountain. That afternoon the whole community attended a ceremony to welcome the new trainees and to award the graduands their certificates and their amulets representing the Four Laws of Living. Maina remembered her first ceremony in that hall and how she had been annoyed at the presence of the Morthern monks. Now she was sad that there were no monks.

On the evening of that day, Maina took her mother's amulet from round her neck where it had long hung, hidden next to her skin. She tied it round the neck of her son, to go with him wherever he would go. It dwarfed his chest but it was the only reminder of his Xouthan origins that she could give him. She wrapped the shawl around him, hiding the amulet once more, praying that his Morthern carers would respect this token and leave it in place.

The next day a messenger from Khoulan arrived at the Morthern gate. He was not admitted but he brought a letter from Kesh, telling Maina that he had found a suitable nurse-family for Calim and that he would come to collect the child the day before the graduates were to leave for Zoradetra.

Maina was filled with relief and dread at the same time. She waited without waiting, wanting to make every moment last a lifetime. She did not leave Calim for a moment but bathed and prayed and ate all in the same room with him and when she went out for fresh air on to the balcony, she wrapped him tightly in his shawl and took him with her.

She even took him into Ship's study when she went for her final meeting with him. Ship admired Calim, telling Maina how he could see that he had already grown. Then he asked her how she felt about her final round of training. Maina answered him with a question.

"We are wrong, aren't we, we Xouthans? You and the four kings, you are unique. There are so few of you in the world. I think perhaps you didn't come to us from across the sea. I think perhaps the Mortherners are right, afterall, and you came to our world from somewhere in the heavens."

Ship's only reply was to drop his gaze from her face to the floor.

"So why did you let us go on believing in a falsehood?"

"I promised myself that I would not interfere with your beliefs," Ship said defensively.

"You make this distinction between belief and truth but, in fact, we want to believe only what is true. Why do you not just tell us what is true? What about the rest of our beliefs? Are you going to tell me that Xouthan gods are false, also? Should I start praying to Harg instead? Or should Kesh be praying to the Xouthan gods? Tell me the truth Ship Prophet. We can't both be right."

"I can't tell you," said Ship.

"But you insult us by letting us go on believing falsehoods. We Xouthans have already been made fools of over the burning ship. We need to know. Why won't you tell us?"

"I won't tell you because I can't. I admit that I should have corrected you on the matter of the burning ship. That was just a confusion of the facts and I should have tried to explain it to you. It was simple cowardice, I suppose, that prevented me from trying to explain just where I had come from. But on the bigger questions, I can't supply any answers. I don't know if your gods are true or not. Perhaps they are, or perhaps Kesh's god is true, or perhaps neither is true. Perhaps both are true and it's just a matter of giving different names to the same thing. I don't know the answer. I am just a human, a flawed mortal being. I don't have the key to truth. You have to look inside yourself, Maina, to decide what you believe."

"I have no answers inside myself."

"But what made you believe? Something made you believe in Tarn and Gorlan before you came here."

Maina thought for a moment. "Well, when we escaped the storm after I prayed to Gorlan, Wyn was sure he had answered my prayers."

"That sounds like it might be Wyn's reason to believe, rather than yours." Ship said.

"Then," Maina began, "I suppose I would have to say it was the time when I was wondering whether or not to go into training for the role of priestess. I prayed late into the night for guidance and the very next morning my nurse-mother brought me the priestess's amulet that had belonged to my real mother. I knew that it was a sign that I should follow her and believe what she believed."

"That's it, then," said Ship. "If it feels real to you, then that is what you have to believe, isn't it? It's the same with your Fourth Law of Living, as far as I can see," and he quoted the first line, "Slaughter not except for meat ... I remember you were telling me it was interpreted differently at first and you wondered if you should learn the ancient language so that you could re-translate the original laws."

"I have found out since," Maina interjected, "that there can be many dangers in translating from one language to another." She was thinking about Kesh's mistake in introducing her to Bim Toegrath as his 'woman'. She went on, "Understanding the exact meaning can depend on so many things – pronunciation, intonation and so on. With an ancient language only available in written form there is a considerable possibility that the original meaning will be lost. I am not sure that further study would help me to understand."

"My thoughts exactly!" Ship said with relief, casting a guilty glance at the original handwritten translation of the Xouthan book of Sacred Texts that sat on his own bookshelf. He went on, "You can translate according to your knowledge of the language but the interpretation of the texts, such as the Laws of Living, surely has to come from within. The original meaning of the texts is hidden in another layer, I think. You have to peel off the layer made up of the words and look underneath. Ultimately, we must each decide between right and wrong for ourselves, must we not, as we go along? We just have to close our eyes and decide."

"I'm not sure I really understand what you are saying but I have already decided on the Fourth Law," Maina said. "I had never seen a battlefield before coming across the aftermath of the battle on the plain of Anthrakat. Seeing so many dead made it obvious to me that killing is evil. It was being with Kesh that really made me understand. Alone, I would have wept for Bradmutt and his death would have justified the revenge I thirsted for in that first moment. But seeing a friend, seeing Kesh, grieving for a loss on the other side made me look at it differently. Fighting more battles is not going to put anything right for either of us. The wars and the battles would just go on and on forever. Kesh and I have since agreed to work together towards ending the war."

"Ah, Maina," Ship breathed. "That is such good news. I do hope you are successful." He got to his feet, bringing the conversation to a close. "I wish you all good fortune for your life, Maina. It has been an honour to know you and I hope you will come back and see me often."

"I will," Maina promised.

As she stepped out of Ship's study into the dimly lit corridor she felt as if she was stepping out into the dark unknown of the rest of her life.

***

The day for parting with Calim came all too soon. Kesh arrived at the Morthern gate, was admitted and given a white trainee priestess's gown to slip over his new deep blue mattouk's robe. He was shown out onto the balcony, where Maina was holding Calim tenderly. She reluctantly handed him to Wyn so that she could have her last moments with Kesh uninterrupted.

At first there were no words. Priestess and mattouk regarded one another, trying to commit to memory the hollows and curves of a face to be remembered through an age of parting. Each felt their sorrow reflected in the other and neither now denied belief in their regard for the other also being reflected.

Maina was first to speak.

"I can not marry you, Kesh, but I want you to know my love for you will endure all that is yet to come. And I have something else to ask of you. Xouthan children make pledges to their friends. It may be a childish thing to do but I want to pledge my friendship to you."

She caught hold of his right hand with her left. Kesh said nothing. He heard her speak of childishness but saw none of the frivolity of childhood in her eyes. With her face set painfully, Maina gently took hold of his long, narrow middle finger with the finger and thumb of her left hand.

She said "We have to touch the middle fingers of our right hands, here, the middle part, between the joints and we have to say, 'ven sellish', which is 'soul friend' in Xouthan. Wyn and I did it when we were children. We have long been ven selli. I would be very honoured if you would become my ven sellish also."

She solemnly lifted his finger up into the space between their faces and placed her own middle finger against it.

"Ven sellish?" she asked.

"Ven sellish," Kesh replied with a brave attempt at pronouncing the Xouthan words. "For ever, come what may."

"Together we are going to stop the war?"

"We will stop the war," Kesh said.

She slipped her arms around his slender body for a second and possibly final time. She clasped him to herself, trying to fix in her memory everything about him that she wanted to remember. This time it was the scents of the Khoulan monastery that came to her from the folds of the hidden dark blue robe. It made her think of candlelit libraries stacked high with ancient parchments. She felt the warmth of him and held the bones that seemed to carry no flesh, but were just as dear to her as the strong, broad frame of her nurse-father had once been. She held him away from her and looked at the face she had come to love. The hair on his head might have gone but the eyes were still framed by a warm profusion of lashes and brows. She wanted to touch his lips but knew that there lay the line she must not cross, there the limits had been set. She knew she would only make it harder for herself if she gave in to the temptation to step over.

"It is time," Wyn said behind them suddenly. Calim was getting tetchy with hunger.

Maina nursed him for the final time, not attempting to dry the tears that streamed down her face as she watched him suckle. Then they all went down to the Morthern gate. Kesh's horse was tethered and waiting. Wyn skillfully bound Calim in a sling to keep him safe against his father's chest while Kesh rode. He set off carefully down the path to Morth. As soon as he was out of sight, Maina ran back through the buildings and up the stairs to the North Tower. It was the old lookout tower that had been staffed with military guards in the old days but was now only used occasionally to watch for expected visitors. After a while, Maina could see a horse and rider moving out into the lower hills that surrounded the Sacred Mountain. Every now and then, she lost sight of him behind a hill or promontory but she watched him for a long time, until he was a black speck smaller than a gnat and indistinguishable from the green of the landscape in the failing light.

A knock came at the door and Wyn's voice told her it was time for the evening meal.

"I am not hungry," Maina said.

"Can I not bring you something?"

"Just my book of sacred texts, please. It is on the table next to my bed."

Wyn duly returned with the book that her own father had given Maina long ago. She knocked and handed it over. Maina thanked her, closed the door and slid the bolt across.

Wyn went to eat with the others but then returned with a lighted candle, some bread and cheese in a cloth and a flagon of water. Maina took the candle and the flagon but not the food and bolted the door once more. Wyn sat on the cold stone steps outside the room and waited.

After a while, she heard mutterings like an incantation. Maina was reading aloud from the book of texts. Wyn dozed, with her head resting on her arms folded on the top step. She heard her friend praying aloud to Veyer to protect her son, then to Tarn to protect the heathen Kesh and guide him in the care of her son. Then more muttering of texts. Wyn fell into a deeper slumber for a while. She was woken by shouts and banging. Maina seemed to be hammering on the walls with her fists.

Wyn called but her friend did not pay her any heed. She tried the door but the bolt was still in place.

"Kesh of Khoulan, bring my baby back to me!" Maina was shouting. "Bring me back my child, you heathen, or by the tides of Gorlan, I will crush and you and your house forever. By Tarn's heaven, I will search you out, I will find my child, I will bring him home where he belongs. Curse your festering nation. Your people will become toads slithering in the slime of hell! Their bodies will burst forth with the puss of lethal pestilence. You are cursed, all cursed till you bring me back my child."

The raving went on into the night and Wyn could sleep no more. Later Maina screamed out against their own gods for failing her. The blasphemy was harder for Wyn to hear than the cursing of the Mortherners. Amid this railing there was a thump and a fluttering sound and a catching of the breath.

Maina sank to her knees as she saw what she had done. Her precious book, gift of the beloved Bradmutt and all she had for a memory of her kindly nurse-father, lay in pieces on the floor. She reached to collect the scattered leaves and the ravings turned to sobs.

When the light of dawn blanched night from the room, she drew herself upright and drew back the bolt on the door. She saw Wyn sitting on the steps, pale and with hollow eyes and she realised she had not been as alone as she had thought. She felt shame at having given voice to the awful curses that Wyn must have heard but she also felt touched by her devoted friendship. She stumbled towards her and they embraced for a moment.

"We must prepare ourselves," said Maina as she straightened and smoothed down her gown, pretending that the ravings of the night were all forgotten.

"Zoradetra awaits," said Wyn.

CHAPTER THIRTY FOUR

Maina no longer feared the sea after her round away. If Gorlan deemed it fit to take her, so be it. As it was, the journey back to Zoradetra passed without incident. The boat slipped through the harbour entrance and as the priestesses started rowing towards the quayside, Maina saw that there was a welcoming party already assembled. The lookouts had posted news of their imminent arrival and, as they drew closer, she could see a procession coming down to the harbour which she guessed would be her father with his entourage. She wished Bradmutt could be with him. Instead, she saw at his right hand Thrull, Prince of Benethan.

She stepped across the gangplank ahead of the other maidens and bowed low to her father before embracing him. She bowed formally to the Lord Benethan.

"Only one moon to wait until your wedding day!" her father said in Xouthan, with a wink directed at Benethan.

Maina did not need reminding. She quickly caught hold of her father's arm, lest Thrull might offer his, and they led the procession through the town to the palace, while the other maidens were reunited with their families.

"So how are you?" she asked the emperor.

"Well. Very well but I have some bad news, I am afraid."

He told her about Bradmutt's death and she listened gravely, not revealing her own knowledge of the matter.

"I'm so sorry," she said. "Is he buried here? I would like to visit his grave."

"We will go together tomorrow. But tonight, we celebrate your safe return. I have commanded a feast fit for a queen and entertainers have travelled from the far corners of the empire to entertain you."

"Oh, father," she said, feeling that she could hardly face any feasting. "That really isn't necessary."

"Nonsense! This is the first happy event in many a moon and no expense shall be spared in our celebration of it."

Back at her father's palace, Maina went to her old room. It was just as she remembered it, only a little smaller. Wyn came in to her with two pitchers of water, one steaming hot and the other cold, and a pile of towels.

"Wyn, why are you not with your mother?" Maina asked. "Surely she needs your company with her husband gone."

"She is worried about you. I have told her about your problem and she says that this might help."

Wyn helped Maina to wrap a steaming towel around her body where Calim's milk was burning fit to burst inside her. After the hot towel, a cold towel to soothe the scalded skin. It did not help much but it was good to have Wyn's support. She helped Maina dress for the feast and pinned her hair up into an exuberant pile on the top of her head, which did not match her mood at all.

There was feasting and dancing. Maina was obliged to dance

with Benethan. He had a strong grip and tried to pull her towards him for a kiss. She noticed a gap in his grinning mouth and guessed the missing tooth had been lost in some brawl. She managed to turn her face aside at the last moment. Her body was sore and her head ached. Finally, the feasting was over and she could go to her bed. Despite her discomfort she soon sank into an exhausted sleep.

Wyn came to her early the next morning.

"There is a rumour flying around the palace about the messenger Imgrin," she said. "He's the one who has been sent to the islands with messages from the emperor to Thrull of Benethan. You remember I told you that there were rumours that Benethan has a woman and children on one of the islands? Apparently Imgrin plans to tell your father that he has seen Benethan with a woman whose children carry his features and he plans to do it before your wedding. Maina, this could be the answer. Your father will be so angry he may demand that you be released from your betrothal vows."

Maina did, indeed, see hope of release but she also saw her chance to stop the war slipping from her grasp.

"I must speak to Imgrin and soon," Maina said. "Is he in the palace now? Can he be found? I could speak to him in secret if he could be sent to the walled garden. Can you get him to meet me there at noon?"

"I will do my best," said Wyn, puzzled. "Don't forget you are going with the emperor to my father's grave this afternoon."

"Are you coming, too?"

"No. Mother and I went there last night."

"Oh, Wyn," Maina sighed. "Tell your mother how very sorry I am for your loss."

"She knows," said Wyn.

Maina went in good time to the walled garden behind the palace and waited. After a while, the latch on the side gate lifted and Wyn stepped through, followed by the stooping figure of Imgrin. Wyn nodded to Maina and waited by the gate. Imgrin came towards Maina and bowed low. His face was twisted into a grin of delicious anticipation. What subterfuge might cause an emperor's daughter to want to see his messenger in secret?

Maina knew she had to take control of the meeting before Imgrin could take advantage of her situation.

"I understand your wife is not too well, Imgrin," she said in Xouthan. "I think she should go to the hospital at Spintaina in Anthrakat. Doctors there are finding ways to help people with your wife's condition, I hear."

"I have heard that too, lady. I can't afford to send her," said Imgrin, although he knew Maina would have guessed as much.

"I will pay," said Maina.

"And how would I repay you?"

"By not telling my father any news you might have about the Lord Benethan for at least another two days."

"You already knew what news it was that I was going to give him?" Imgrin asked.

"I think so, yes."

Imgrin shrugged and pulled a face that showed that he could not understand why Maina would not want her father to know what she already knew.

"And if I don't agree, my wife is left to fester until her death in Xoutha."

"If you don't agree I will still pay for your wife to go," said Maina. "I have decided she needs to go. She will not suffer on your account. This is not a bribe. But if you choose to repay in the way I have suggested, I will be very grateful."

Imgrin raised his eyebrows and thought for a moment.

"Very well, lady. I will wait the two days."

"Thank you. Here is forty dipnats. That should pay for the journey and half a moon's treatment. I will give you forty more in two days time."

"I thought you said you would pay whether or not."

"I am afraid, Imgrin, that I only had fifty dipnats in my purse to start with," she said ruefully. "I regret that you will have to wait for the rest."

After Imgrin had left the garden Maina gave a jewelled brooch to Wyn.

"Please could you ask your brother to take this to the jeweller in Castlegate and ask how much he would give him for it. If it is thirty dipnats or more, ask him to sell it for me, please."

"But it is your betrothal gift from Thrull!" said Wyn.

"Let us be glad I am finding a use for it," Maina replied. "Once my father hears Imgrin's news, I hope he will find a way for me to be released from my betrothal vows."

"I don't understand. If you want your father to hear Imgrin's news, why are you bribing him not to tell?"

"Wyn, can I trust you?" Maina looked into her friend's eyes and immediately felt ashamed. "Sorry. Of course I know I can. It is like this. I want my father to stop the war. I intend to threaten not to go through with the marriage to Thrull unless he does. I am hoping that, in order to save his friendship with Thrull and to save his dreams of a grandson to rule the empire, he will consent to my demands and send a message of peace to the king of Morth. Once the message is despatched, so long as he has not sent Imgrin as his emissary to Morth, Imgrin can give the emperor his news."

Wyn was silent for a long while.

"Maina, you are a priestess now. Do you think it is right," she asked, "to attempt to deceive your own father?"

"It is not right, no, and Tarn may punish me for it. If it was your father, I would not try to deceive him, but then your father would not have tried to force me into a loveless marriage in order to serve his own ambitions. I see an opportunity to stop the war and I must choose between committing this small sin and the alternative which is letting the slaughter continue, bringing more death and mourning to both Xouthans and Mortherners. I will pray for forgiveness afterwards."

CHAPTER THIRTY FIVE

That afternoon, Maina walked with her father and a small entourage to the cemetery next to the Temple of Tarn in Zoradetra. On the way she asked him about the war.

"Tell me what happened. How did it start?"

"Quite unexpectedly the Mortherners attacked the fort at Ghaba Head. They came at dawn. The guards on duty were so taken by surprise that half of them were dead, it is said, before ever one of them was able to raise the alarm." He breathed a heavy sigh. "They are savages, those Mortherners. They think they will get the Sacred Mountain from us, I suppose. Then where will your precious Community be?" The emperor answered his own question. "In Morth, that's where it will be. We must redouble our efforts and most of all, we must avenge our dead."

"Father, I heard that the Morthern monastery at Khoulan was attacked before the attack on Ghaba head."

"There was no attack on any monastery. Not by us. I can promise you that."

"You did not ask Thrull to attack them for you?"

"Most certainly not. Why would I want to attack a monastery? There would be nothing of value there."

"You see, the king's uncle was there and he died in the resulting fire. The king assumed that the attack was linked to you, perhaps through Thrull."

"Absolute rubbish. Thrull may have been involved but it had nothing to do with me, I can promise you."

They arrived at the freshly mounded grave of Bradmutt and Maina laid some flowers handed to her by one of the servants.

"Well, daughter," the emperor said. "Are you going to lead us in a prayer? You're a graduate priestess now."

Maina recited the prayer for the dead and the emperor and his servants supplied the responses. Then she knelt at the graveside and took her leave of Bradmutt for the final time.

On their way back to the palace, Maina asked her father if she could see him in private. He led her into his suite of rooms and sent his servants away.

"What is it, child?" he asked.

"Father, I want you to end the war."

"Of course I will end it, when we have victory."

"No, father," she said. "I want you to end it now. I want you to stop the slaughter before any more of our beloved ones are lost."

He remained silent for a time, studying his daughter for a clue as to why she should have said such a strange thing.

"My dear, I cannot end the war by myself. If the Motherners

attack us, we have to respond or they will simply overrun us and the whole empire will become part of Morth."

"Father, I must tell you that while I have been away I have met several Mortherners. One of my contacts has influence with the king. I think I can arrange for the attacks from Morth to stop."

"Contacts with Morth? My daughter, what have you been doing? I should never have let you go away! You are a child. You do not understand the world of men. You can't trust Mortherners. They talk sweetly then stab deeply. You must stay away from them."

"Father, don't you see? It was all a misunderstanding. Someone attacked the monastery. The grieving king assumed that it was you and attacked the fort at Ghaba. The whole war is based on his mistake. We must stop it now. So many families are already grieving, on both sides. Is that not enough?"

"Maina, we must all be prepared to make sacrifices for the higher good. Those families you speak of all understand that need. The only way the lives of their sons will not have been lost in vain is to press ahead to victory. We must maintain the integrity of the empire and we must take back the Sacred Mountain for ourselves. Then no more honoured maidens of Xoutha will have to come into contact with Morthern filth."

"But Xoutha could be stronger by making peace and setting those young soldiers free to work for the good of Xoutha."

"We are fighting for peace. When we have victory there will be peace, my daughter."

"Father, I am sorry, but you leave me no choice. I must make you listen to me, so I must say that which I have held back from saying until now. Father, if you will not stop the war, then I will not marry the Lord Benethan."

"I am sorry, my daughter. You have made a promise in front of witnesses. You can not go back on that promise."

"I can and I will."

"You think you can stop the marriage from going ahead? It is all arranged. All we need is your word and your signature and that I can forge in a moment."

"But you will never get my word. Do you want to have me dragged kicking and screaming to the temple gate in front of all your guests? I think not. I will never give my word willingly to marry Thrull unless …"

"Unless?"

"Unless you send a message of peace to the king of Morth and pledge to stop the war. If you do that I will marry Thrull and I will smile in front of all your guests. I will even submit to Thrull's advances and give you a grandchild but only if we are at peace with Morth."

"Maina …" the emperor was lost for words. His daughter had never crossed him before but now she was close to getting the better of him. He must be getting old, he thought, if he could not even control his own daughter. She was giving him a choice between the twin ambitions of his reign. To choose between victory over Morth and an heir to the empire was not easy.

He turned away to consider. His need of a strong man to replace Bradmutt was his immediate concern. He had already accepted Thrull into his court to act in Bradmutt's place and the last thing he wanted was to offend him at this crucial time. Victory over Morth could wait. In fact, making peace with Morth might make their northern neighbour more vulnerable when Xoutha was ready to attack again.

"Very well," said the emperor. "I agree to your terms. I will send a message of peace to Morth."

"You will understand that I will want to read the message before it is sealed and it must be sent by tomorrow. I will also want to see any reply that the king of Morth might send and to witness his seal on the document before you break it."

The emperor was taken aback by the lack of trust his daughter was exhibiting. What had happened to the unquestioning affectionate child he had once known? He shrugged.

"Very well," he said. "And for this I will get a loyal son-in-law and a grandson?"

"I can not promise it will be a son," said Maina and smiled thinly. "Thank you, father."

The emperor drew in a breath but did not acknowledge her thanks. In the past he might have embraced her but the innocence of their relationship as father and daughter was forever gone.

CHAPTER THIRTY SIX

The next morning Maina was summoned to the stateroom. Her father was standing by his desk. He held out a sheet of parchment to her.

"Here is that which you requested. A letter to the King of Morth proposing peace."

Maina read it through.

"But there is nothing here to encourage him to accept. We need to offer him something to make it worth his while."

"Worth his while?" the emperor repeated angrily. "He is getting peace. What more can he want?"

"We must offer a concession of some sort or he will not believe in our need to sue for peace. I think the least we should offer is a return to the state of affairs that existed before the war. We should offer to allow Morthern monks access to the Sacred Mountain Community once more."

"You want me to concede the one success we have snatched out of this?"

"Absolutely. We are losing nothing. We are simply offering to return to the pre-war situation."

"Very well," the emperor said tetchily. "But if we never win back the Sacred Mountain, it will be because of your waywardness."

"I am willing to accept that responsibility."

"Humph!"

The emperor sat down at the desk and wrote another letter.

"Here," he handed the parchment to Maina. "Is this more to your liking?"

"I think that might do it," she said as she laid it back on the desk. "Sign it, seal it and send it, father, and I will be a dutiful daughter."

The emperor signed and sealed the letter and then signalled to a messenger waiting nearby. Maina spoke to the messenger as he made his way out of the room.

"Go by sea. It is faster. Do not fly the imperial flag and do not show your imperial livery. Take a servant with you to bring word back to me once you have landed safely on Morthern soil. Ask to be taken to Khoulan and there ask for Kesh of Khoulan, the mattouk. Give him this letter from me."

Maina handed the messenger a second rolled up parchment.

"Tell him your mission and request that he chooses a Mortherner he can trust to escort you to the capital to meet the king."

***

The next day Maina was waiting for Imgrin in the walled garden. Wyn came through the gate ahead of him.

"The emissary's servant is back from Morth," she told Maina. "They reached Morth safely. They were not attacked. The emissary has set off from the coast on his way to Khoulan. I have brought Imgrin. He is eager to speak to you."

"Thank you, Wyn," Maina said. She turned to the man waiting behind her friend. "Good afternoon, Imgrin. How is your wife?"

"Not well," he answered shortly. "She is on her way to Anthrakat with her sister."

"I hope her journey will be fruitful. Here is the other forty dipnats. You must send it on to her. Thank you for withholding your news from my father. You may now tell the emperor what you saw."

"Thank you, lady. I will."

The messenger turned towards the gate.

"Imgrin?" Maina called to him.

"Yes, lady?"

"You know my father will not welcome this news?"

"I expect not, lady."

"Be careful, then."

"I will, lady," he said, turning to go.

"Imgrin," Maina stopped him once again. "If you know my

281

father is going to be angry with you for giving him this news, why are you so set on telling him?"

"I made a promise, lady, to Bradmutt before he left for Larkat. I had told him what I had seen of Benethan's domestic arrangements on the islands and he advised me not to tell the emperor until he returned. He thought the emperor would take it better coming from him. But he said that, if he should not return," Imgrin bowed his head and paused, "...if he should not return, then it would be up to me to make sure that your marriage to Benethan did not go ahead. I was to tell the emperor myself before the wedding day."

"Oh," said Maina, moved by Bradmutt's concern for her well-being and by Imgrin's loyalty to Bradmutt. "Thank you, Imgrin. If you should need anything afterwards, you must send word to me. You understand me?"

"I understand. Thank you, lady."

Imgrin went straight to the stateroom to request an audience with the emperor. His news was not well received and he was thrown out angrily. Wyn was sent to find Maina immediately.

"Imgrin has been dismissed and banished from the palace," she told her.

"Is he hurt?" Maina asked.

"The guards were not gentle but I think he has sustained nothing worse than bruising."

Maina nodded sadly. "I am sorry that he has suffered at all.

It was always going to be dangerous delivering such news to my father."

"Perhaps that is why he has waited so long before doing so."

"Perhaps."

"I have been sent to summon you to the stateroom. The emperor wishes to speak to you."

"Indeed." Maina stood infront of her mirror. She straightened her dress and patted her hair. "I had best go and see what my father wants."

She found the emperor brooding thunderously on his dais seat. He looked at her darkly but did not speak for several long moments. Then he said in a terrifyingly restrained tone:

"You knew about this, didn't you?"

"I did," Maina confessed.

"What am I to do? I can't accept a man who already has a family as my future son-in-law. I suppose it's all around the palace by now."

"It is."

"You cheated me, Maina." He said shaking his head. "I can never forgive you. And you know that I will never trust you again."

"I understand. I am sorry for disappointing you," she said. "I wanted to stop the war. I saw all the dead on the plain of Anthrakat and I could not let it go on without trying to … do something."

"You saw the dead?" repeated the emperor. "How?"

"The Ship Prophet sent us on a task to visit four kings across a mighty ocean on the other side of Anthrakat. On the way back from Anthrakat we came across the battlefield near Larkat. There were no soldiers fighting but hundreds of the dead from both sides lay on the ground. Their wounds gaped and their blood was not yet dry."

"Oh, my daughter! That must have been horrific. Your eyes were never meant to see such things." The emperor shook his head slowly from side to side. "So it was the sight of them that put this poison in your heart?"

"It made me see things differently, but I would not say …"

"But the girl became a woman?"

"I suppose she did."

"My poor child," he said, and stared gloomily at the floor for a while. Then his shoulders began to shake, and he broke into chuckles, "And now," he said. "You have become your father's daughter. You've become a lying, cheating, ruthless she-dog!"

Maina thought for a moment and then asked, "Was that a compliment?"

"I rather think it was." He laughed and held out his arms. "Come here to me."

He hugged his daughter but Maina felt little joy at her father's display of affection when it was given as a reward for cheating him.

"Father," she said after a while. "We don't really need another Thrull, do we? Why don't you introduce a new law that would allow me to take over when you are gone? You have the power to do that, surely?"

The emperor looked at her anew. "Is that what you want?"

"Not really. But if it would stop you trying to marry me off to thuggish suitors …"

"And what about the next generation? Who would there be to take over when you are gone?"

"That would be a problem for me to decide on when the time comes. Perhaps there will be someone more suitable for me in time."

The emperor turned his head and gave her that sideways look that people had been giving her lately.

Maina went up to her room afterwards and opened the window for a breath of air. Her father's approval had made her feel all the more ashamed at what she had become. Her thoughts went back to Calim Bradmutt, as they constantly did. Like a goat tied to a tree, her mind was forever tethered to the fact of his existence and their separation. She had deceived her father partly for his sake, in the hope that he would be able to grow up in a peaceful world, but she could not hope that he would ever come to respect her for it. He would at that very moment likely be looking up at some other woman's face and it was his nurse-mother he would come to love and listen to, not her. If she went to visit him, he would not know her and she would have no power to influence how he was brought up. She had relinquished all control and put her trust in Kesh to choose the right path for Calim to follow.

She leaned on the window frame wearily. Her sleep had been disturbed by dreams since she had been back. She dreamed every night that she had forgotten Calim and that she must go back to the Sacred Mountain to collect him. Sometimes she saw Kesh in her dreams, with his shaven skull and stained eye sockets, looking down at her in the candlelight and it filled her with foreboding. In other dreams she saw Kesh in happier circumstances but her dreaming mind told her that there was something she needed to say to him and she never remembered what it was before it was time for him to go and she then would wake up with a aching in her heart.

Even if she and Kesh could stop the war, she knew her soul would still not be at peace. She took the lock of Kesh's hair tied up with a fragment of ribbon from an envelope that she kept in her pocket. She felt the softness of it and lifted it to her face. It still bore the scent of the soap that Wyn had used on him when she had shaved his head. On the one hand, Maina wished that she had been there in time to do the deed for him. On the other hand, she was glad not to have been the one to dispose of that symbol of their time together.

"The connection has been broken," she said to herself. "Only the wind now travels between us. If only my love could travel to Kesh on the wind. If only my love could travel to Calim on the wind so that he could know how much his mother loves him!"

She gazed northwards out of her window towards Morth and a seacrow flapped down to stand on the ledge beside her.

"Sakki!" she said with surprise. "Is that you?"

Maina reached out her hand and the bird allowed itself to be touched.

"It must be you. Wait there a moment."

Maina went to fetch a piece of sweetmeat for him. He pecked at it and, while he was thus distracted, she drew a gold thread from the trimming on her dress and tied it around one of his legs.

"There," she said. "Take my love to Kesh. Show him I am well. Take my love to Calim."

The bird took off and flew directly northwards, as if obeying her command.

***

The next day Thrull was summoned into the emperor's presence and was formally announced by the court official, as a stranger would have been. The emperor was sitting on his dais and drew himself up in his chair as Thrull appeared.

"I have heard some strange news, Lord Benethan. I have been told that you have a concubine on one of the islands. A concubine with children.

"I will admit that I do have a concubine," Thrull said. "You will understand a man has certain needs. Of course, I will give her up the minute I am married. But the children are not mine."

"That is strange, Thrull," said the emperor, now using the more familiar name for his daughter's once betrothed. "I am told those children look just like you. It is a sad man, indeed, who denies the very existence of his children."

Thrull shifted his weight from one foot to the other like a naughty child but could not come up with an answer before the emperor went on.

"I can not allow my daughter to marry a man who already has a family. It is unlikely that you will give up your concubine upon marriage, as our law demands, if she has already borne your children. I think the betrothal must be annulled. But my daughter is a very generous woman and suggests that we offer some recompense for the annulment. She has suggested the empire could transfer the rule of one of our own islands into your charge. I hope this will be acceptable to you."

"But …" Thrull began.

"I have had documents drawn up ready," the emperor went on. "One for the annulment and one for the transfer of the island. I would be grateful if you would sign the annulment immediately. I have already signed the deed of gift. I think the sooner we get things organised, the quieter this business will be. I assume you would like to keep this business as quiet as possible?" He stood up and stepped towards his desk. "Here are the documents and here is a pen."

Thrull scowled angrily and muttered, "This is so unnecessary."

"Thank you," said the emperor as Thrull put his signature to the annulment document. "And I hope you will understand that I now feel obliged to ask you and your retinue to leave the palace as soon as possible - by tomorrow at the latest. I am sure you will be keen to visit your new subjects. That is the explanation I shall give the court, anyhow. Don't forget to take the deed of gift with you."

He picked up the other document from the desk and held it out towards Thrull. Thrull scowled angrily again and swung his arm around to swipe the deed of gift from the emperor's hand. He turned on his heel and strode out of the stateroom still muttering to himself.

Several days later, a messenger arrived with the reply from Morth. He was shown in to the stateroom and announced.

"You are welcome, messenger," the emperor told him. "What word do you bring?"

The messenger bowed low and held out a rolled parchment that carried the seal of the Morthern king.

"I bring greetings from the king of Morth and this reply to your proposal."

The emperor broke the seal and read.

"This is preposterous!" he said to his daughter. "He demands the Sacred Mountain and Mount Sangbem in return for peace."

"Give him Sangbem in addition to reinstating a right of access to the Sacred Mountain as we originally proposed."

"But Sangbem has never been part of Morth. It is utterly absurd to think that we would ever surrender it."

"Father, consider its position on the map," Maina began. "Sangbem is a barren mountain of little worth. It is situated adjacent to Sankat. Sankat is on the Xouthan corner of the plain of Anthrakat. There may come a time when we could offer Sankat back to Anthrakat in return for their support in other matters. If we did, then who has control of Mount Sangbem would cease to be a problem. It would no longer be of any strategic advantage to the Mortherners."

"Daughter, if we continue to cut corners off the empire in the way that you suggest, there will soon be no empire left. First, an island for Benethan, now a mountain for Morth and possibly a corner for Anthrakat. Where will it end?"

"Father, the worth of Xoutha does not lie in the area of land that she controls. Her worth is in the hearts of her people and that worth will not be reduced by our generosity. If it has any effect at all, it will be to raise her esteem in the eyes of her neighbours."

"I am not convinced, daughter. Imagine, for me, an alternative path. Imagine that that we reject these demands and put our efforts instead into preparing our troops for combat. It is perfectly possible that we could have an easy victory over Morth in the very next battle. We could have the Sacred

Mountain to ourselves and lose no more of Xoutha."

"And more of our soldiers would die and more of our families would suffer mourning. This is not what you promised me, father, when you agreed to my terms."

"And what will you threaten to do to get your own way this time?"

"I am not threatening. I am asking. Father, I don't want more war for Xoutha. How can you want war? Let us have peace. Let us have friendship with our neighbours. Let us take the lead, let us make the most of this chance for a peaceful future."

The emperor sighed heavily.

"I wish Bradmutt were here. I miss his wisdom. He would give me the strength to take the next necessary step. He would always know what was best for Xoutha. He would know what our chances were of gaining military advantage. Without him, it is too easy to give in."

"I wish Bradmutt were here, too, father. But even Bradmutt would surely see that Xoutha might flourish better at peace than it would in a constant state of war."

"I feel uneasy today, but my weakness of heart inclines me to give in to your suggestions, whether they are best or not."

"Does that mean you are agreeing to offer Sangbem to Morth?"

"I," the emperor shrugged dramatically, "no longer care. You write the reply to Morth. I will sign it. The future of Xoutha is in your hands and you must live with the consequences, as must the rest of us."

"Very well," said Maina. "Thank you, father."

"No, don't thank me. You will find that the poison of power tastes less sweet once it has been drunk."

"Yes, father," Maina said, her brows wrinkling a little. "I will try to remember that."

She went to her father's desk and began writing. "May I suggest that we sign the peace treaty at Mount Sangbem? Mortherners will regard it as neutral territory by then, I hope. I will suggest we sign at full moon. That should give both parties ample time to get there."

Maina had achieved more than she could have hoped for - an end to the war and an end to her betrothal, but she knew that her father's feelings about Morth would not allow her to reveal her friendship with Kesh for quite some time. She must remain separated from Kesh and her son until the emperor and her country had the time to come to terms with the fact of the peace and could learn to accept Morth as a friendly nation. She knew there was still much work to do.

CHAPTER THIRTY SEVEN

The Sacred Mountain was in a state of peace once more. Morthern monks were to be allowed access again and Hannala and the other Xouthan priestess trainers were busy guiding the next group of honoured maidens through their final round of education.

The seacrow was back from Khoulan, where Kesh had gently untied the gold thread and now he came in to land on the balustrade of the balcony outside the Great Hall. Ship and Kevin were both leaning on the coping, looking out to sea.

"There's Kesh's pet seacrow," Ship said.

"Seacrow?" Kevin repeated. "Why do you call them that? They're too big for crows, aren't they?"

"They're black and they fly, therefore they are crows."

"We've been calling them banner beaks. Their beaks are such a bright red colour. But how can you tell this one is Kesh's?"

"I can't, but it seems very tame, so I'm just guessing."

"There seem to be suspicions of the supernatural in every culture here regarding banner ... I mean, seacrows."

"Yes," Ship agreed. "The Xouthans regard them as bad omens, to the Enahets they are sacred, carrying the soul to heaven, to the island folk they are a kind of demon, carrying evil doers off to hell. The only culture that seems to be immune is the Morthern one but even Ahbrem seems to believe there's more to Sakki than meets the eye. He thinks the bird understood when Ahbrem asked him to fetch Kesh back. In fact, he seems convinced that Harg sent Sakki in Ahbrem's stead to guide Kesh on his journey and watch over him. He reckons he saved Kesh's life on more than one occasion."

"Why do you think they prompt all those supernatural beifliefs? Is it just their deep, dark colour, or is it, perhaps, the size?"

"I think it's their intelligence. You know, the first creature I ever spoke to on this planet was a seacrow on the beach." Ship chuckled. "It seemed to understand me well enough."

"I got the fright of my life when one tried landing on my head on that battlefield," said Kevin. "When his claws first touched my face, I thought it was one of the dead reaching out for me. Ugh! It was horrible. Makes me shudder just to think about it."

Ship laughed outright.

"I'm so sorry you have to go," he told Kevin. "It has been so wonderful having you here. Having a human to talk to again has changed my whole outlook on life."

"Why don't you come to see us? Come and see where we live and what we've managed to achieve."

"I'm afraid I'm too old to travel now. My joints ache and I get tired too easily. Age is finally catching up with me, even if you don't look a day older than when we first arrived."

"I think you're exaggerating but it's true that time has been very kind to all of us. We've all been wondering why we seem to lead such charmed lives here. No illnesses, ageing so slowly and so on."

"I think it must be something about this place, you know. No chemical pollution in the air or water and the germs here aren't designed for humans. Or perhaps it's the lower oxygen levels. I think there might be less UV from the sun or less cosmic radiation. Also, the ship that was our home for all those years was heavily shielded to protect … to protect us." After all this time Ship still stopped short of revealing more than was necessary to his crewman.

"Doug thinks it's all to do with time dilation, because of all the years we spent getting here. At one time we were beginning to think of it as a curse, you know. You're trapped on a planet far from home, where time seems to pass more quickly than ever but you're immortal. It's a kind of hell."

"I was feeling like that before you came. But now I've seen you ... now I've spoken again to someone from Earth it feels like I've been wasting all my time here yearning for home when, if I open my eyes, I find I'm already in paradise."

"Oh, I don't think I'd go quite that far."

Ship beamed and patted his crewman on the back but said no more.

At Kevin's suggestion, a seat and a table had recently been put out on the balcony and now Hannala came out to it with a tray of tea and three porcelain cups.

"Perhaps it's just the gift of age," said Ship. "The ability to be happy with what you've got."

"Humph! The older I get, the more my ability to be happy diminishes," Hannala said, joining in their conversation. "My dreams are less and less likely to become reality and my fears of ageing become more and more real."

"That's because you're not yet quite old enough," Ship told her. Then he teased her by winking and saying to Kevin, "She still dreams of experiencing romance, you know. And I'm about as much use to her as a talking dog."

"I always wanted a talking dog, when I was a child," said Kevin.

"Most honoured Prophet of the Sunken Ship, you cannot compare yourself to a kirra-dog," said Hannala. "Even if there were such a thing as a talking one. You know that you are the best of company and that you provided invaluable support while Maina was away. I was so worried about her and about the future of all Xoutha. Whatever would I have done without your reassurances?"

Ship gave an embarrassed cough. "I have to confess that I was very worried about her too, especially as I was the one responsible for her being away."

He turned to Kevin and went back to the previous topic. "But you can see what I mean about this planet, can't you? They may have just fought a war here but it was nothing like the neverending wars that we struggled through on Earth.

296

For one thing, most of their weaponry is lethal only to the soldier standing directly in front of them. There doesn't seem to be much hunger, either, or extreme poverty. There is no big business here to corrupt the workings of the state, no stockpiles of nuclear weapons, no sea-level refugees. *It is* a paradise. Why did I ever want to leave? We are so lucky to be here."

"It's alright for you, old man. The rest of us are still alive and hot-blooded and we haven't seen a female human for … I don't know for how long. It's what we all dream about the most, I think. I know our families will all have died of old age by now and the Earth will be in a complete mess but if there's one female human left alive, I still want to meet her."

"You'll get over it," Ship comforted him. "One thing I must mention before you go, though. Tell Doug, if he's got any decency left, he'll retrieve that unshielded power supply he took from the pod. It could cause a lot of illness and not just to that tribal chief. Tell him Captain Shipham commands him to make it safe."

"Okay, I'll tell him," Kevin promised.

One of the trainee preistesses came on to the balcony and announced, "Mattouk Kesh has come from Khoulan to bid farewell to the king."

Kesh came out on to the balcony with his deep blue robe now in full view. Fastened to the robe was a gold filigree pin in the shape of the Morthern royal insignia and round it was tied a piece of golden thread. Ahbrem followed close behind dressed in the pale blue robe of a Morthern monk. Hannala asked the maiden to fetch more tea.

"Ah, Kesh, welcome," said Ship. "And how is the little one?"

"Very well, thank you, and bigger every time I see him," said Kesh. He turned to Kevin. "So you are leaving us this afternoon? I am concerned that you intend to travel on your own."

"I am promised a Xouthan escort as far as the border with Anthrakat. I should be able to find my way across to the coast from there."

"I could spare Ahbrem to travel with you, if you like."

"It would be a great honour," said Ahbrem.

"No, no," said Kevin. "Not necessary, I can assure you. I speak a few words of Anthrakat and they seem to be a pretty amiable people. I am sure I will pass through without any problems."

They chatted and drank tea and Ahbrem fed crumbs to the seacrow. Eventually, a message came up that the horses were ready. It was time for King Kevin to leave. They all went down to the Xouthan gate for their final farewells.

"And tell the others to come and visit me, won't you?" said Ship as Kevin mounted his horse.

"Of course," Kevin promised. "I'm sure they will want to come, now that we know where you are. They'll be curious to see you and your little community. And I'll tell them that, as soon as you saw me, you realised you were in paradise. I think they'll find that very amusing."